Praise for

Insatiable

"The story line is fast paced and loaded with action as the irresistible force meets the unmovable object when two enemies from different life stations fall into heated love . . . This is quite a sizzler."
—*Genre Go Round Reviews*

"Dane has created a fully realized, intricate world with thoughtful, sympathetic characters, which makes it easy to lose oneself in the romance . . . The cliffhanger ending will leave readers panting for the next installment."
—*Romantic Times Book Reviews*

"Lauren Dane is one of the best authors out there writing exciting, on-the-edge-of-your-seat science fiction romance . . . *Insatiable* is also a great suspenseful thriller where the chase will leave some readers breathless."
—*Babbling About Books, and More*

"Another awesome entry in Dane's Federation Chronicles."
—*Book Binge*

Laid Bare

"It's impossible not to love this story. The sex is sizzling, the emotions are raw. Lauren Dane has done it again. *Laid Bare*, quite simply, *rocks*!"
—Megan Hart, national bestselling author of *Switch*

continued . . .

"From the get-go, three elements worked as one: vibrant, drawn-from-life characters, profound emotions and an erotic passion that often set the pages ablaze." —*Leontine's Book Realm*

"This book is amazing! I was so engrossed in the book I couldn't do anything but read . . . This is the best book I have read this year." —*The Book Girl*

"In a word, this book is amazing. All three characters are magnetic and thoroughly realistic. They're expertly woven into a roller-coaster story that will have you crying one moment, aroused the next and laughing with glee at each triumphant step along the way . . . This is Dane's best story yet!" —*Romantic Times*, 4½ stars

Relentless

"*Relentless* will sweep you away." —Anya Bast, *New York Times* bestselling author of *Jeweled*

"Exceptional . . . an intriguing alternative world." —Joey W. Hill, author of *Vampire Trinity*

"Hot romance, detailed world-building and a plot focusing on righting injustice make *Relentless* a page-turner. With passion and politics, Dane delivers again!" —Megan Hart

"Ms. Dane takes readers on a roller-coaster ride of emotions . . . This is a fabulous read for fans of sci-fi with a generous helping of erotic romance. I hope that we'll be seeing more installments in this futuristic world."   —*Darque Reviews*

"Spectacular . . . absolutely brilliantly written."
—*Manic Readers*, 4½ stars

"Pulled in from page one, readers will enjoy the delicious sensuality."
—*Romantic Times*, 4½ stars

"Emotionally charged, passionate and at times volatile, *Relentless* once again proves that Ms. Dane is a first-class author who is fully capable of delivering exactly the sorts of story lines that readers crave."
—*Romance Junkies*, 5 Blue Ribbons

"Filled with heat and erotic passion . . . *Relentless* is a do-not-miss."
—*Joyfully Reviewed*

"This terrific science fiction erotic romance is fast-paced and filled with action in and out of the bedroom."   —*Midwest Book Review*

"Fiery, erotic and rich with plot, this book is definitely a keeper on my shelf."   —*Night Owl Romance*

continued . . .

Undercover

"Delicious eroticism . . . a toe-curling erotic romance sure to keep you reading late into the night."
—Anya Bast

"Sexy, pulse-pounding adventure . . . that'll leave you weak in the knees."   —Jaci Burton, national bestselling author of *The Perfect Play*

"Exciting, emotional and arousing . . . a ride well worth taking."
—Sasha White, author of *One Weekend*

"A roller coaster of emotion, intrigue and sensual delights."
—Vivi Anna, author of *The Vampire's Kiss*

"Hot, sexy and action-packed . . . A fabulous read!"   —*Fresh Fiction*

"Wow! This book rocks!"   —*Romance Junkies*

"It's one of those rare books that will stay with you for a long time."
—*Love Romances & More*

"*Undercover* is a compelling and wild read."   —*Manic Readers*

"Dane has written a sizzling, delicious tale of love lost, found and expanded . . . As endearing as it is molten hot. The friction between Sera and Ash as they resolve their past is intense, and with Brandt added to the mix, it's nothing short of explosive."
—*Romantic Times*, 4½ stars

Mesmerized

lauren dane

heat | new york

THE BERKLEY PUBLISHING GROUP
Published by the Penguin Group
Penguin Group (USA) Inc.
375 Hudson Street, New York, New York 10014, USA
Penguin Group (Canada), 90 Eglinton Avenue East, Suite 700, Toronto, Ontario M4P 2Y3, Canada
 (a division of Pearson Penguin Canada Inc.)
Penguin Books Ltd., 80 Strand, London WC2R 0RL, England
Penguin Group Ireland, 25 St. Stephen's Green, Dublin 2, Ireland (a division of Penguin Books Ltd.)
Penguin Group (Australia), 250 Camberwell Road, Camberwell, Victoria 3124, Australia
(a division of Pearson Australia Group Pty. Ltd.)
Penguin Books India Pvt. Ltd., 11 Community Centre, Panchsheel Park, New Delhi—110 017, India
Penguin Group (NZ), 67 Apollo Drive, Rosedale, North Shore 0632, New Zealand
(a division of Pearson New Zealand Ltd.)
Penguin Books (South Africa) (Pty.) Ltd., 24 Sturdee Avenue, Rosebank, Johannesburg 2196,
South Africa

Penguin Books Ltd., Registered Offices: 80 Strand, London WC2R 0RL, England

This book is an original publication of The Berkley Publishing Group.

PRINTING HISTORY
Heat trade paperback edition / April 2011

Library of Congress Cataloging-in-Publication Data

Dane, Lauren.
 Mesmerized / Lauren Dane.— Heat trade paperback ed.
    p.   cm.
 ISBN 978-0-425-23908-7
 1. Mercenary troops — Fiction.   I. Title.
 PS3604.A5M47 2011
 813'.6 — dc22
                      2010036296

PRINTED IN THE UNITED STATES OF AMERICA

10 9 8 7 6 5 4 3 2 1

Acknowledgments

Thank you to Leis Pederson, who loves futuristics and took a chance on my very first one back in 2007 when she bought *Undercover*. Having an editor who loves the genre you write makes this all the more sweet.

Ray—forever.

Laura Bradford—though I thank you in every book, it's a small measure of just how much I appreciate you.

Joss Whedon—thank you for creating *Firefly*.

Liz Phair—thank you for creating the song that inspired the title for this book.

Readers—where would I be without you? Thank you for all your myriad kindnesses.

This one is for Mary

Chapter 1

Eleven Standard Years Ago
Asphodel Portal City Lockup

"Sir, you can't go in there!"

Andrei Solace didn't bother looking up. Not that he'd have been able to see much with one eye swollen shut from the butt of the rifle he'd taken to the face. The pain had subsided to a dull, all-consuming ache, but the anger burned, low and steady, in his gut. Enough to get through another day.

The outsider spoke again, his tone nearly amused, partly chiding. "I'm afraid you're incorrect about that."

Andrei did risk a glance, curious about who spoke to a jailer that way.

He expected another social worker. Gods knew he'd seen enough of them over his lifetime. Instead, what he got was the biggest man he'd ever seen. It was enough to have Andrei ignoring the pain from his injuries to swing his legs from the narrow cot to stand and edge closer.

"Look, sir, I'm sure you think you're entitled to all sorts of things with your shiny shoes and soft hands. But this is *my* lockup, and I'm telling you there's no entry to the cells without the proper paperwork."

The big man looked down his nose, not a difficulty. Andrei committed the expression to memory as the man looked as if he'd smelled something awful. So much was communicated without a single word. Smart.

The jailer flinched, just a tiny bit, when the big man reached into his pocket and pulled a sheaf of papers from it. "Will these do?" He opened a portfolio to show the jailer.

The jailer read, his lips moving, until he paled and stumbled back. "I had no idea, sir. I . . ."

"Now that we've taken care of the formalities, I'd like to see the prisoner."

With a new target for his anger, the jailer sent Andrei a glare over his shoulder as he led the big man through the hall, unlocking as he went. Andrei didn't want to appear weak, but he really had to sit down again, so he made his best attempt at nonchalance and strolled back to his cot to sit.

Wilhelm Ellis, newly minted Comandante of the Federation Military Corps, came to a halt just outside the boy's cell. Andrei was a mess of bruises and bandaged wounds, one eye swollen shut. His eye, the good one, held a quiet, burning anger.

Barely eighteen standard years, and he was hard. Harder than most adults, even those Ellis dealt with in the corps. Hard wasn't a bad thing. Especially out here. It could be a very good thing indeed, especially in a soldier.

Sighing with annoyance and no small amount of disgusted anger, he rounded on the jailer, pinning him with a glare. "Has he

been seen by medics? I was under the impression he'd been here
for two weeks."

"Two weeks and four days. Not that I'm counting." The jailer
sent a sneer toward the boy that had Wilhelm clenching his fists
momentarily.

Instead, he kept his voice very, very calm. "Care to explain the
state of his face?"

Finally, the jailer understood. He stumbled back, his gaze on the
ground. "He has anger problems. Always attacking. Seven hells, sir,
he was brought in here after nearly killing a man. He's been picked
up on assault and theft charges multiple times in the last years."

"Did. You. Give. This. *Boy*. Those. Bruises?" Wil wanted to
punch this petty little bully for the damage he'd done. Instead, *he*
bullied with his size and position. He rarely did, but sometimes it
was necessary to scare the spit out of a man before he got the picture fully.

"With all due respect, *sir*, the *boy* attacked one of my men. He's
the reason why we have to chain him like a horse in a pasture. The
boy is garbage. A dirt rat just like his mother was. If he'd had a
father around to instill some discipline, he wouldn't be here. I don't
think you can come in here and second-guess when you're not
up to sp— . . ." The jailer's words died away when the boy jumped
toward the bars, held back by the shackle on his ankle.

"Fuck you. You don't talk about her," he snarled, yanking on
the chain so hard Wil wondered if he'd break his ankle. This was
some will. A good sign if it could be channeled correctly.

"Unlock the cell and the chains and get out of my sight before
I show you some discipline myself." Wil kept his eyes on the boy as
he spoke to the jailer.

"He's dangerous. Didn't you hear what I just said? He attacked an armed man. Why don't we get you a chair and you can interview him on the other side of the bars? Safer that way."

Wilhelm touched the personal comm on his wrist. "Operative Haws, inside with me, if you will." He didn't look at the jailer as he spoke. "I'm quite capable of handling myself. Do as you were ordered, or you can join him in the cell next to this one."

The jailer appeared to begin to mumble, but Wilhelm sent him a look so severe, he clamped his lips together, unlocked the cell and shackles and got out.

"Get out of my sight." Wil walked past and into the cell, towering over the boy who shook with his desire to lash out. At Wilhelm, at the jailer, at anyone. Wil knew that expression, having seen it in the mirror enough as he grew up.

He sat on the rickety chair they'd provided, stretching his legs before him, purposely taking up as much space as possible. Daniel would have his back. And most likely he'd learn something from a boy he'd been not too long before that. It'd be good for Daniel to see how far he'd come. How much discipline had straightened his life out.

This one. He shook his head as he took in the wild-eyed Andrei Solace. "Why are you so angry, Mister Solace?" Slowly, taking the boy's measure, he pulled a pouch from his pocket and rolled a smoke.

The boy tried to hide behind an uncaring facade. Keeping his mouth closed, choosing a shrug.

Wil inhaled the rich heat and exhaled, enjoying that moment very much. "This place is a dump, Andrei Solace. This 'Verse, this cell, your life, all a fucking dump."

He enjoyed the flare of anger in Andrei's eyes, the tension of his muscles as he trembled with the effort not to punch Wilhem right in the nose.

Wilhelm nodded, satisfied when the fists unclenched and the spine relaxed slightly. "Good. See? You *can* control yourself. When you want to. I'd wager you were simply never taught any discipline."

With a dismissive wave, he went back to the smoke, wondering how long it would take to get Solace to speak. The boy now had about a 30 percent chance of making it back to Ravena with him.

Each interview he'd done over the last four years as he'd built his special teams had been different. Some he knew before he even saw the person if they'd be a yes. Other times, he'd been convinced one way or another and had his mind drastically change at the last minute.

Andrei Solace was, at first glance, another in a long line of kids from rough backgrounds who fell into violence and criminal activity from a young age. Not unusual at all. This one, though, had scored off the charts on his testing.

The way he'd reacted when his family had been insulted indicated a sense of loyalty. Loyalty when given by a boy like this one would create a bond for life.

"Your silence is interesting. I'm going to take it as you wanting to hear more about why I'm here, shall I?" He narrowed his eyes at Solace, who stared back stonily without speaking or moving.

Inquisitiveness was something he wanted to see in one of his people. He had no room for people without intellectual curiosity. He'd always found candidates who thought critically operated at far higher level of functionality, especially in the field.

Wilhelm stood, straightening and brushing the front of his uniform. The percentages were dwindling.

"Yes." Andrei said it, and the word sounded as if it were dragged from him.

"Progress." Wilhelm sat again. "My name is Wilhelm Ellis. I'm the Comandante of the Federation Military Corps. I might be in a situation to ease you from this place and set you on a new path. One that won't end with you in permanent hold."

Andrei watched him with careful eyes. He wasn't an idiot; he knew the giant blocking his escape was more than capable of felling him in one swipe if Andrei made to run. He also noted the man's power.

Something underlined when he introduced himself. Gods above and below! This guy was the top guy of everything. What the fuck was he doing on Asphodel in a lockup cell with a delinquent?

He had some suspicions. "I don't like men like that."

Ellis paused and then snorted a laugh without much humor. "You all say that. Each time I hear it I'm torn between rage that you all have been so preyed upon your first assumption is that I'm out to bugger you, and amusement. I'm not after your bum, boy."

"Then what? What do you want from me?" He loathed the small spark of hope this man had lit in his belly. Hope was weakness.

"Operative Haws." Ellis spoke and a man—no, Andrei looked again at the male who'd stepped into the corridor—he'd *be* a man in a year or two, but he wasn't much older than Andrei was.

Ellis, despite being as massive as he was, still managed to appear graceful as he rolled another smoke. Andrei didn't know what their game was, but he was smart enough to listen. Just in case.

"Have you ever considered military service?" Ellis asked, lighting the hand-rolled smoke.

"How about I answer you when you've shared those with me?" Andrei tipped his chin toward the pouch.

Ellis's face darkened a brief moment. "No. You're too young. How about you answer me, or we can finish this right now?"

Andrei clicked his teeth, clenching his jaw. His mother had told him he had good intuition, and that intuition told him Ellis would simply walk out if Andrei kept silent. His gut also told him this could be something important.

So he gave up his words. "No."

"Why not? Is the idea of a real bed, a job and some credits in your pocket so terribly unappealing to you?" Ellis waved a hand at the surroundings. "This is better?"

"It's the same thing. I'm a prisoner either way." He shrugged, nearly believing his reply.

"Is it, boy?" Gone was his name, and Andrei felt . . . bereft. Anger surged that he'd care. He preferred it to the sadness.

"What do you know about it? Sitting there with your soft hands and your medals. What do you know about struggling?"

Ellis's mouth tightened and then curved into a rueful smile. "Ah, the hubris of the young to imagine they're the only ones who understand. I suppose the answer is, it doesn't matter. It doesn't matter if I know what it's like to be chained in a cell, beaten for trying to retain my humanity."

It was the way he said it that broke through the anger. He snuck a look to the other one, standing, seemingly at ease on the other side of the bars. Deceiving. There was no ease in the coil of muscles and the quick sweep of his gaze around the area.

"Why is he here?"

Ellis didn't bother looking back to the other soldier. "He's got my back. It's always good to have that. Do you?"

When Andrei didn't answer, Ellis simply went on. "The question—the real question—is are you satisfied with this? Are you so lazy and without vision that you'd allow yourself to be guided toward a lifetime of stints in lockup and an early, probably violent death? If you are, just say so and I'll be on my way. I have work to do."

Andrei took a look at the man outside the bars.

He made eye contact and grew very still as the soldier took him in but remained silent. Andrei was off balance and feeling cornered. Anger and frustration, his diet it had seemed, filled his veins, making him feel trapped.

Which, he supposed, he was.

But he sure as seven hells had no plans to willingly enslave himself to the Federation.

"I can see by your face that you're arguing with yourself."

"Look, Comandante, I don't know you. I don't know why you're here. I'm no soldier. I'm just—"

"Another kid in lockup for the fifth, seventh, thirteenth time." The soldier outside the bars spoke quietly, intensely. "You planning to make a career out of that? That all you ever want to be?"

"What do you know about it?"

"Enough that I'm going to do you a favor you probably won't believe you deserve. This is a dead end. There is nothing for you here. *Nothing*. Stop making excuses not to leave."

"Tell me more," Andrei said with a sigh, hope still a tiny ember in his belly.

Chapter 2

"We've got company," Kenner all but snarled as he stared off across the yard.

Piper looked up from the fuel coupling that had nearly fried just the day before. They'd limped back, and she'd managed to land without any more damage. Storm season was upon them, they'd be grounded far more often, and she hated to go into it without a fat pile of credits to cushion any problems that might arise. Being down a bird would cause delays she would rather not have to afford. Thank the heavens her brother was such an amazing mechanic and could most likely fix it.

Four men had just come through the main gate. She recognized them easily enough as the Imperial people who'd been attempting to entice her into running goods over the line, into the Imperium.

"Imperial dogs," he added.

Unease slithered through her.

She kept working. "Tell them I'll be with them shortly. Let Eiriq know as well. I want some backup."

Her twin hesitated, she knew, wanting to deal with this on his own. He was the one with more military training, he'd always been fond of reminding her. And then she could remind him that the last time she let him handle things it had ended in a seven-person fist-fight and two days in lockup.

Instead, he exhaled slowly, wiping his hands. "Watch your step, Piper."

He stalked off, leaving her to clean up and steady her nerves. She began to scent ozone and knew a storm would be coming. The sky above darkened, deepened, and she hurried along.

The heat rose from the ground in waves that battered her, stole her breath. All the recent storms so close together had left the air unsettled.

Soon, hot, blast-furnace air would send dust hurtling through the sky with so much force that it'd flay the flesh from bone in less than three minutes in some of the worst storms out in the Wastelands. Visibility would be next to nothing, and the electrical fields would rub against each other, bringing a terrible need to grind teeth along with the stench of an Asphodel windstorm.

Asphodel wasn't for amateurs; that much was for certain. Just existing here meant a constant dance with the 'Verse itself.

For some reason, this appealed to Piper. The very act of living there and making a life in the dust and canyons had been one of defiance for as long as she could remember. Though, she could admit it became tiring just treading water year after year.

Certainly the increase in the thugs the Imperialists sent to the Edge over the last year or so disquieted their little family compound. They were not part of her life, nor did she want them to be. She may exist on the edge of the law, but she wasn't a traitor.

She paused, looking over the group waiting for her near the front gates. There were four of them. Each looked exactly like an Imperialist spy sent here to smuggle something very bad back and forth across Imperialist/Federation lines. She did not need this. In fact, it offended her sensibilities, a truly rare occurrence.

"What the seven hells do they want anyway? I've said no three times now," she said to Eiriq, who'd just joined her.

In the distance the winds kicked up, sending the seeds of the storm upward, giving birth to the beginnings of it. The static in the air rose, bringing the hair at the back of her neck to stand.

"Don't know, but if we don't get rid of them soon, we'll be stuck with them until after the wind dies." Eiriq motioned skyward.

She quickened her steps until she came to a halt before them. Giving them what they expected, a dirt farmer with no formal education, she put her hands in her pockets and rocked back and forth on her heels. It would also save her the potentially troubling refusal of their hand clasp.

"Storm brewing down in the caldera. Time to get under some cover. What brings you around these parts?"

One of them eyed her, attempting to make her look away first. And if he'd been a predator instead of a bully it might have worked. Instead, *she* was a predator and he was the kind of man who routinely got killed because he stayed too long out in the canyons. A stupid, soft off-worlder who sneered at everyone he saw because he thought he was better than they were.

The scent, that burning, dry stench, began to build as the body of the storm took form in the distance, its fingers digging into the ground and the sky above. This one might be a big one, so she was doubly invested on getting rid of them. "I'm going to have to get my aircraft under cover and our camp locked down, so if we could get to the point, I'd appreciate it."

"You're speaking to a high minister on behalf of Supreme Commander Fardelle himself!" The pug-faced off-worlder squealed, offended to his toes.

"Asphodel is a Federation 'Verse. Fardelle isn't *anyone* here." Kenner stood with his arms crossed, anger clear on his face. She knew he'd been pushed far enough already. He didn't wave a flag, but he was patriotic enough to be offended by the mere sight of these people. He'd done his two standard years in the military corps, plus one extension. Piper did her standard two years. He learned how to fix things, and she learned how to fly them. Oh, and he learned how to get into fights. At least he'd been strong enough to come out of it harder and more fierce than he'd been before.

Kenner had a wild streak. That's why he and Andrei had been so close. She sighed inwardly. No time for fantasies in her head that would never come true. At that moment she needed to be sure her brother's wild streak didn't activate his big mouth and get himself in up to his neck with the Imperialists.

She stepped forward to get their focus off him.

"Time's up, Minister. We're on a timeline, and I have things to do. So what is it you're here for?"

Minister Cheney, clearly the one in charge of his little entourage, cleared his throat, laying a hand on pug-face's arm to quiet him.

"We'd like for you to think about our last offer again. We have to move this cargo, and we'd like it to be you doing the moving."

Piper turned to Eiriq. "Get the birds under canopy and sealed."

She focused on the Imperium lackeys again. "I've said no several times. I don't run that kind of cargo."

"You're a mercenary. You're not supposed to want to know what the cargo is." There was no mistaking his distaste in the sneer he tried to cover up.

"*Exactly*. And because I know whatever it is would not only be illegal but treasonous, I'm going to pass. There are others on Asphodel who have less compunction about such things. I suggest you seek them out. Now, if you'll excuse me, the storm is airborne, and you have a ways to go before you can get back to town."

She turned, stalking away. Trusting her people to cut anyone down who moved against her.

The highest ranking minister called out to her, "Ms. Roundtree, your cooperation in this matter would be looked on very kindly by my superiors."

"We don't have the same bosses. Now, get your ass off my land and back to town where you'll be safe," she called back over her shoulder.

He ran toward her, taking her arm. Even over the static-laced hum of the gathering storm she heard the click of weapon safeties being thumbed off. She was at least a foot shorter, but if he thought he could take her with a dozen weapons trained on him and overcome her righteous anger, he was dead wrong. And she'd show him in person and up close.

She kept her muscles easy as she showed him her teeth. "I advise you to remove your hand from my arm. Now. Before my people feel like you're threatening me."

He must have heard the promise of retribution well enough; he let go and stepped back. "Be reasonable. You've run goods across the line before. I know this for a fact. If it's a matter of credits, we can arrange for that. Or to get rid of your competition as a way of saying thank you."

"Yes. *Medicine*. Food and other goods that at best helped people and at worst were morally neutral. I'm not dim, you know. Four Imperial higher-ups show up multiple times and ask me to run through a back channel private portal? That's not food. Or medicine or shoes. You want me to run something *not* morally neutral into Imperialist territory, and I'm not going to do that. I've said no, and I've said it nicely. You're wearing out your welcome, Minister. Next time I won't have any patience left."

"This coy act isn't serving you. I don't want to be here any more than you want me to be. But I can't leave until we agree to terms, and your sudden attack of morality is tedious and wearing very thin."

She lowered her goggles as the dust began to kick up. "Since neither of us wants you here, take that as a message and go. You're standing here in my yard attempting to induce me to betray my own government. I don't like that much, and I especially don't like it after I've said no so many times."

"You'll come around to my way of thinking soon enough. And you'll be sorry you waited."

"It's time for you to go now. We're locking down, and anyone not authorized to be here would be shot on sight."

She turned her back again and stalked away, almost wanting him to do something that would free her to punch him in the face a time or two.

Jumping into the storm preparations, Piper let the anger burn through her muscles as she covered the copter and the zipper, taking extra care to seal them tight against the grit that could kill the engines.

The sky had deepened to the color of the inside of a ripe melon. Electricity sparkled across the atmosphere as the storm began to move. The fine hairs on her arms stood. The desolate background of pale gray cliffs only made it more eerily beautiful. In a short while, visibility would be so poor the cliffs would be gone.

"He's not going to take no for an answer," Kenner said from the doorway, tearing her from the view. "Not without a hard physical lesson."

"Maybe not even then. They're up to something. More than their usual weapon-running."

They locked the ties down, rechecking the seals on the shelters holding the vehicles and gear before heading back toward the houses scattered around the compound. Even a small bit of dust messed with the gears and moving parts, shortening the lifetime of her gear, and she didn't like that at all.

She took one last look, satisfied that all her people had taken cover, before heading into her own house.

Her older brother, Taryn, looked up as they entered. "I think whatever's going on out there could bear some investigation. If we had some knowledge about what they were doing, we'd have something to use as leverage to keep them off our backs."

She moved to join the others, pulling shutters down, sealing the windows and doors.

Dim coolness settled in around them. Piper did a mental count, making sure her household was all accounted for.

"Or, we could turn them in to the authorities and get them out of here." Whereas she and Kenner handled all operations, Eiriq was in charge there at the compound. Responsible for all their security. Sort of the mayor and the polis at the same time.

"Just got confirmation from Bird. Says the Imperialists got into the main portal lodging just as the city gates were closing." Taryn dropped into a chair at the table.

Kenner looked up from his place in front of the data screen. "Given the speed of the wind out there and the readings, I'd say the storm will be here in less than a quarter of this hour."

Piper hoped it passed quickly so she could move some merchandise.

"May as well prepare a meal while we're inside. I went on a water run early this morning. Can you grab some?" She looked to Eiriq's wife, Lune, who nodded, turning in a shimmer of beads, sparkles and the clink of her bracelets.

After washing up again, Piper went into the kitchen and began to cut the fruit, placing it on a tray as she spoke. "I don't like this at all. They're hanging around, and only trouble will come from the situation. After the drama from Parron, all those people dead, the Imperium is behind it, and I don't want any part."

"What I'm hearing from people on the other side is there's a total lockdown. Restrictions on travel. Information is at a premium. People tossed in lockup, or worse, just disappearing. Things are getting worse by the moment." Kenner spoke from his place on the other side of the room.

They were. All her life she'd generally ignored the government, and as long as her crimes remained petty, they left her alone right back. But the tensions of the last two standard years, all the drama and the treason, had changed that. She'd had to confront all the wrongdoing of her government and come to respect the way it had, in turn, dealt with the traitors.

She preferred to do business and not engage in any hostility with others, but she would always be on the right side of any fight against her people. She was smart enough to know that even the backwaters of the Federation 'Verses were better than the Imperium.

The time was quickly ending when she could simply run her cargo and collect her credits. "The scent of blood is already in the air."

Lune put the water on to boil while Kenner set the table.

"What do you mean?" Taryn asked.

"They've drawn blood. The Imperium's attacks on its own people are bad enough, but they've killed Federation citizens here on Federation soil. Lyons won't stand for that. We're in a bad spot, and I'm not sure there's going to be a way out of it without a war."

The memories of that were fresh enough. Varhana, the famous battle where the Federation had pushed back an assault by the Imperium and won the war, was only a generation old.

She didn't want that for her people. She'd reached the end of any time when she could pretend to ignore the situation. It was time to act.

"I think it might be wise to be sure to speak within the right hearing, about these Imperium types sniffing around. We don't need to tattle, but a little whisper on the wind ought to get word where it needs to be." Piper wasn't fond of the law. They had never done much for her and hers. But some things were simply wrong. Unacceptable. And treason was one of them.

"I'll be at the public house in town later. I'll make it happen." Kenner lit a candle. "May as well be prepared in case we lose power."

"How do the supplies look?" Piper asked Taryn quietly.

He sat back in his chair as the noise went on all around them. "There's plenty of food and ale. I was thinking of going out tomorrow to set the moisture traps. The one out back needs fixing."

"There's always the tunnels." Some of the other groups out their way—okay mercenary groups—were building a series of tunnels to connect with town and also to the water station just on the other side of Bristina Canyon. Since they'd begun to raise some livestock and the greenhouses were finally pumping out fruit and vegetables to feed everyone, having enough water was imperative.

But it was a sore spot, because Taryn and Kenner both opposed opening up a back door into the compound by strangers.

"I trust you. I trust Kenner and our people. I don't know who these other mercs are involved with, and I don't like them having access to us via that tunnel." Taryn glowered.

"Well, given the general desperation of our *friends*, I take it the others aren't going near this deal of theirs either. That puts my mind to rest a little." They weren't all bad. Most of the merc groups were like her own.

But not all.

"I remain opposed. If we increased our cistern capacity and got working water traps, we wouldn't need a tunnel. Just because they're not working with them now, doesn't mean they won't. And anyway, there are plenty of bad people to worry about other than the Imperialists." Taryn narrowed his gaze, uncomfortable as always with the way she straddled the lines between lawful and not so very much.

"I think that's a very good idea." If she let him have his way, he'd feel better. And he was right that total trust of the others would be stupid.

He sighed heavily. "You know things are very bad, right? I really think we all need to watch our backs very carefully. War is coming, Piper; I can feel it."

He'd seen the wars on Earth, had felt the results so severely he brought them all to Asphodel as refugees, hoping for a better life.

And he was right. War was coming.

Chapter 3

The tug in his belly, followed by the arrival chimes, signaled the transport's arrival at the Portal. Andrei stood and stretched. Thank the Gods he'd be stopping off in Mirage with Julian for a time. Too much portal travel didn't sit well with him. He hated the confinement of it.

He nudged his traveling companion, who started awake and nodded up at him sleepily. Julian had been down, adrift after the loss of their friend and an old flame of Andrei's, Marame, not too very long ago in an attack at the Portal Station on Ravena. Andrei had agreed with Daniel, his boss of sorts and the leader of the Phantom Corps teams, that Julian needed the work to keep his mind off the loss. To give him something to do.

After Marame's murder, they'd ordered Julian on leave, but he'd only wallowed, drinking too much, and he'd ended up in lockup, so Daniel hauled him from the cell and handed him to Andrei as he'd come back from a trip to Borran to check the munitions depot.

As it happened, they all had plenty to do, so it wasn't difficult. Julian most likely knew it was about getting him away from Ravena to get his mind elsewhere, but he went where he was told because it was his job, and grieving or not, he believed in it. Just as Andrei did.

Julian was good at his job. A good man to have at your back. Agile. Intelligent. The best hand-to-hand fighter he'd ever seen. And he had a fire inside to avenge the death of his friend. Truth be told, they needed people like him out in the field just then.

That didn't mean Andrei was taking him along to Asphodel, though.

Asphodel was full of ghosts, and Andrei didn't want to share that with anyone else. Aside from assignments with Daniel, he preferred to work alone anyway.

"Let's go. We're meeting Vincenz shortly." He grabbed his bag, tossed Julian's at him and unlatched the door.

The hallways of the transport were already a hive of activity. Porters wheeling carts around, passengers leaving their rooms, some heading back to them. Safety crews were on the high walks checking the seams. Others stood near the exits with their bright yellow vests, holding signs written in standard, telling each group where to disembark.

The noise and chaos of it rose as Andrei and Julian moved toward the disembarkation ramps. The white noise of it allowed Andrei to focus on important details. Allowed him to flick his gaze around the area, at the hidden spots, the elevated places where an attack could be launched. Allowed him to be sure everything was in the place it should be. Even chaos had its rules, and a crowd always worked in a few, certain ways.

This one seemed to be fine. Worry was in the air, which was normal, given the way things had been going lately between the Federation and the Imperialists. And it was close to the Edge, where tensions had been heightened for far longer than those deeper in the Federation had experienced it.

Julian stood at his side, Andrei knew, calculating everything. Julian's brain was like a machine. He was always making computations, always extrapolating data, working best- and worst-case scenarios.

"Documents," the bored ticket taker barked as they approached.

Phantom Corps operatives always traveled with civilian documents, though they could, and did, pull in clout when it was necessary. Andrei preferred to slip unnoticed through the public berths.

Most people hated crowds, but as they were waved through, Andrei again thanked all the reasons crowds were so annoying. All the noise and bustle tended to interfere with people's ability to really concentrate. Not so him, but most others. And while they stumbled around, he could get his job done.

Julian tipped his chin toward the line of public conveyances for hire. "Let's catch one to Vincent's." Vincent was Vincenz Fardelle, son of the leader of the Imperialist Universes. He'd left some standard years before, seeking asylum in the Federated Universes, and had been integral to their information gathering here on the Edge.

Andrei followed him toward the conveyances. Shadows lived in Julian's gaze. Andrei knew them well enough; he supposed he had some of his own. It did no good to give in to the gulf of grief simply waiting patiently to swallow a man alive.

Julian *was* alive. Andrei had known Marame. Intimately for nearly a standard year. He knew she'd agree that being alive was a good, solid thing. It was all a man had at the end of the day when the lights were off and there was no one around to lie to him.

In the meantime, there was work to be done and Marame wouldn't have been offended one bit to know they were going to avenge her murder.

The conveyance driver nodded as Julian gave him the address. Andrei approved of the surly, quiet man who drove expertly through the madness of the crowds.

Settling back against the cracked, stiff material of the seat, Andrei looked through the window at the passing scene outside. The streets of the portal city teemed with travelers. With vendors and polis. Hustle and bustle, Daniel had called it. But beneath the frenzied stream of people and the hum of their activity there was also tension.

People were stirred up, scared and feeling adrift. Andrei understood it. He had far more details than they did, and he'd thought himself beyond being stirred up. Not so, as it happens when one discovers one's enemy capable of biological warfare and collapsing portals, cutting off millions of people.

Vincenz's house wasn't very much farther, but they didn't want to get out too close, so Julian had the driver pull over, and they walked the rest of the way, each man in his own thoughts, not speaking, but keeping an eye on their surroundings.

People they passed moved just slightly farther out of the way than was necessary, kept their gazes down. Their insides knew these two men were far more than two guys out for a stroll.

Vincenz opened his door, his blond hair—nearly as pale as his sister, Carina's—standing on end. "Come in. The connection just established, so head back." With that, he turned and hurried back into the house, clearly on a mission. Andrei figured the connection would be Daniel Haws, the leader of Phantom Corps, right hand to Wilhelm Ellis. And their boss.

Julian locked up, setting the alarms again before trailing Andrei back to the communications center at the heart of Vincenz's home.

Vincenz indicated the table with the vid screen at the head. Daniel was there, looking back, his features drawn.

"Glad to see you've made it safely. I want you all on high alert. One of the special teams had two losses last week. Keep your communications to the phoenix level only. Even our contractors are under scrutiny to find these leaks. This new interface is as locked down as we can possibly make it. Please be sure to use this in the future when you communicate back with anyone on these issues unless it is absolutely necessary. The new code has been loaded into your personal comms."

Andrei paused, mulling over the way Daniel had just told them they had leaks at high levels within either the Federation Government or within the military corps. Gods, or both. He shivered, uncomfortable with the rising tide of distrust spreading through their world.

"Andrei, I received your data about the munitions issue. Lyons agrees this is a priority. Julian, you're the liaison between us and the special teams. Ash Walker will be contacting you soon about their plans."

Julian nodded, and Andrei noted the brief flare in his eyes. It was the most interested he'd looked in a week. He knew Daniel would have noted that as well.

Daniel spoke again. "We know this is all about Parron, Mirage and Asphodel. So let's find out what we don't know, like what exactly it is each 'Verse holds for the Imperium. We can't stop it if we're going in blind. Vincenz, keep on the data and your analysis. Julian, I want you on the issue of just what it is we're looking for."

"Yes, sir." Julian nodded his head toward Daniel's image on the screen.

"Andrei, I need to speak with you privately. Julian, Vincenz, contact me with any problems or questions."

Andrei had realized where this was going, had for some time as each clue kept pointing to the Edge. Anger flashed through his senses, a small flick of the rage he had learned to channel. The slice of it was sweet after so long. Even so, by the time the others had left the room, he'd put it away, focused on what he knew needed to happen.

Daniel hesitated, looking him over carefully. "Maybe I should send Vincenz."

"This is my job, Daniel." Andrei knew Daniel meant to send him to Asphodel. Though it had been some time, Andrei's contacts on Asphodel were substantial. He was the best candidate for the job.

He sipped the mug of kava Vincenz had left near his right hand. Despite that momentary flash of rage earlier, his control had slid back into place. Easily enough that Andrei knew the time when it had been a struggle to exert control was long past. There was no small amount of peace in that feeling.

Daniel exhaled hard and nodded once. "You're to go on to Asphodel and make contact with the mercs there. If anyone is going to get us solid intel on the Imperialists operating on the Edge, it'll be them."

Andrei nodded.

"Keep me updated as necessary. You're my second-in-command, Andrei. Do what you need to, to get this situation dealt with."

Andrei allowed himself a small smile. "Is that a battlefield commission of sorts?"

"I put in for it when we got back from Caelinus with Carina. I managed to push to process it, hoping it would be before you left again, but you know how it goes."

"I'm honored. Thank you, sir." Warmth suffused him. Not the burst of heat from anger, but pride.

"The pay raise is modest at best. The hours are even longer. I'm not doing you much of a favor. But there's no one I trust more." Daniel turned his head a moment, speaking to someone out of screen range. "Get me that intel, Andrei."

Piper eased the zipper up, banking right to avoid an outcropping of deadly, jagged rock in the narrow canyon. Asphodel rarely felt as good as it did the first minutes she returned after making a merchandise run.

This one had brought with it a very healthy pile of credits and no small amount of work to evade the increased Federation military presence at all portal cities. The rogue portals the mercs favored would only remain secret a while longer.

And then prices would go even higher as the job got far more difficult.

But for the time being, the sun was going down, the horizon looked calm and they'd be home shortly.

It wasn't until she'd come around the final edge of Bristina Canyon's west edge that she took in the sight of a trail of vehicles approaching the compound. Her radar wasn't tracking them at all, so she uttered a curse and commed in to her command center at the compound. The Imperialists were using radar dampeners, not a sign of people out for a friendly visit. If she hadn't been flying over right then, they would have gotten closer to the compound before they'd have alerted her people.

"Company coming. I want it all locked down. Weapons hot. I'll be there shortly."

Behind her, Kenner strapped in as she got lower and headed to the landing pads.

"I don't like this, Piper," he muttered, checking his weapons.

"Like I do? Look, follow my lead, all right? Hold on to your ass." Opting for speed over finesse, she touched down and jumped from the cockpit as soon as the engines quit.

Eiriq met them, tossing her a las-rifle. As weapons went it wasn't sophisticated. But it could put a hole through anyone who got in her way, which was just the sort of message she wanted to send.

"Everyone is in place. We've got the kids down in the shelter with the pregnant women and the elderly."

Taryn ran up. "There are more than you first thought, Piper. This is going to be a possible problem."

She sighed at the sight of the dust plume rising from the convoy of vehicles approaching the compound. "You can tell none of the ones in front are soldiers. They may as well have voice projectors announcing their arrival." She glanced at Taryn. "We may have to call in some help. Be ready."

The high, solid fencing surrounding the compound halted the vehicles' movement.

"Cover me," she called out, keeping to the edges of the buildings as she moved closer.

The lead conveyance opened, and Minister Cheney got out, sneer firmly in place.

"I believe I did tell you we'd be back and you'd regret not taking our offer earlier," he called out. "Why don't you let us in so we can discuss this privately."

"I have no intention of inviting you into my home. I said no. I mean no. I'm not interested in what you're peddling."

One of the others, this one clearly a soldier of some sort, identifiable by the way he carried himself, approached the gate, pulling a weapon free.

Kenner stepped up, swinging the barrel of his blaster straight up, making his intentions unmistakable.

"Supreme Leader Fardelle does not favor these sorts of games. He is busy. Far too busy for this. Now open these gates so we can broker this contract and I can quit this place."

Driven to anger, she spoke her mind. "I don't give a care for your offers or your murderous boss. What your Fardelle does or doesn't want is nothing to me and mine." She said it loud and very clear. Her people snapped to attention all around where they stood.

"Is that what you need? To be assured this is about goods or services that won't hurt your precious Federation? Fine, fine, that's what it is. A humanitarian mission, if you wish." He bowed, mocking.

"She told you to leave. Take your people and go. You're trespassing, and trespassers get shot." Kenner gestured with the weapon to underline that.

"You're playing a dangerous game, girl. The kind of game that gets people hurt. Take your profit, keep your mouth shut and deliver the goods."

"Profit is one thing. Betraying my government is another entirely." She shot at the ground near his toes, satisfied when he emitted a high-pitched squeal as he jumped back. "Get the fuck outta here."

She turned, and if she hadn't lost her footing when she tripped over her kit bag, she'd have taken a blast to the back.

People scattered, shouting orders as the whoosh of auto-loading las-guns zinged through the air. Bullets cracked. The stench of black powder and laser off-gas from the blasters was enough to make her eyes water as she managed to get behind some shelter.

"Don't waste ammo. Shoot to kill," Kenner ordered into his wrist mic. Shots rained down on the Imperial soldiers from the sniper posts in the courtyard towers.

"Gas!"

She managed to grab a mask from the kit Kenner had tossed to her, her tears already flowing.

"There are two dozen heavily armed soldiers. I don't know how I feel about these odds," Taryn said, mouth set in a grim line.

Kenner hissed. "Eleven. Yeah that's right, Imperialist scum! I will kill each and every one of you!" he called out.

"Gods above and below," Taryn grumbled. "I don't suppose I could convince you"—he paused to fire his weapon, grinning savagely as the body hit the ground—"to get down in the shelter, could I?"

"Me? This is my fault. I'm the last person who should be running right now." They'd managed to get to one of the outbuildings. She quickly booted the compound's vid system. "By the west fence. It's Stahl. They've got him pinned down."

Eiriq called out that he was on the way, and Taryn took off after him for backup.

"We are fucked, Piper. We gotta call in for some help. We've got four men down. You and I are pinned here. They're inside now. It's only a matter of time." Kenner continued to pepper the advancing Imperialists with fire.

The ground at their feet took fire, sending dust skyward. "If we bring in the polis, we expose everything! We invite them into a compound they've wanted to search for ages." They'd all likely end up in lockup.

"What if they think we're working with the Imperialists? Have you thought of that, Piper? Because I have. *Fuck!*"

"Give yourselves up, and we can discuss this," Cheney called out via loudspeaker.

"How can you think we'd work with you now? Bastards, get the fuck off my land or end up dead," Taryn responded, and it came through, loud and clear, via her wrist mic. He was still unhurt, which eased the knot in her belly slightly.

The heat of a blast from a las-rifle stirred the hair at his temples as Piper grabbed the back of Kenner's shirt and yanked him back.

"Guess they don't care. Stay down!" She growled at him. "Don't you fucking die, or I will bring you back and kick your butt."

He sent her a crooked smile. "You'd have to do all the laundry yourself."

"We're stuck. On our way back to you as soon as we can break free," Taryn spoke over the wrist mic.

Shit, shit, shit.

The sound of the Imperial soldiers swarming their compound rose, though she was gratified each time they set off a trap or one of them got taken out by her people.

Inescapably, they were gaining the upper hand, and Kenner was right, she'd have to call for help, even if it meant lockup.

One of them came around the corner, training his weapon on her. Kenner brought his own up, but the soldier fell before either of them could get a shot off.

Kenner looked up, confused, but thank seven heavens he didn't move from their little corner. They watched, shooting as they could, as, one by one, soldiers began to fall.

"Who is up there?" Kenner scrambled for his field glasses.

"Eiriq maybe?"

"No, he's bringing Stahl back toward the clinic."

One by one, as Piper watched the monitors, soldiers fell as they were sniped from above.

She spoke into her wrist mic. "I want that tower, the east corner, protected. Move!" She stood, Kenner next to her. "Cover me. I'm headed across the courtyard." Before he could argue, she darted out, keeping low. Whoever was up there needed to be protected.

The next moments passed as if she were watching it all via vid screen. One by one, the soldiers would attempt an approach. And one by one, the sniper took them out.

"They're leaving!" Taryn called out via his wrist mic.

"Make sure of that. Have them monitored," Kenner instructed.

It was then, through the dust, their savior emerged, long, dark hair lifting on the breeze as he walked casually toward her.

Her heart stuttered, even as she mopped her forehead and pretended to be casual.

His eyes were still serious. Still the palest of blues and still fringed with long, dark lashes. He was still so intensely beautiful it made her stomach clench.

"Dear gods, Andrei?" Kenner sounded just as surprised as Piper was.

His gaze locked on hers, not giving anything away. Eleven years, and he hadn't changed that much. Eleven years, and the sight of him still thrilled her senses, even as anger and hurt won out.

She took one step, and then two. The last one and she'd already cocked her fist so that by the time the movement was finished, her fist had connected with his mouth. That part had been satisfying. Not so much when she said his name, meaning it to sound angry, but it was almost a plea.

Andrei wiped his lip, tasting dirt and blood. That combination took him right back to his youth. Much like seeing Piper had. "That was your one free shot."

Taryn jogged up, and seeing it was Andrei, he shouted his greeting, grinning and clapping Andrei's back. "Andrei! You came back at just the right time."

Andrei looked around the yard, at the bodies and the blood soaking into the earth. "Guess so." His heart still thundered in his chest at the thought of losing her. At the thought that she could just simply cease to exist. Thank the gods he'd arrived when he had.

When it came to her, his emotions were not so easily brought under control. He'd been a fool to think otherwise.

"What are you doing here?" Piper demanded. Hurt danced in her eyes, lancing into him.

"I would like to speak to you," he looked to each Roundtree sibling, "to all of you. In private."

Taryn nodded, making the choice for them. Good to see he was still in charge. He had a strong, steady hand, which was responsible for the fact that Kenner and Piper were still alive. Andrei had envied that sort of devotion, had never had anything like it.

"We need to deal with the wounded and the dead first." Piper looked out over the carnage, blinking back tears.

"I'll help."

Kenner's gaze flicked to his sister, just briefly. He grinned then, coaxing a near smile from Piper. He clapped Andrei's shoulder. "Just like old times, huh? Andrei and Kenner cleaning up after a fight."

Andrei snorted, tossing his jacket on a nearby fence. Body disposal was hot, hard work, but he'd done it enough that he was efficient at it. There was no need for Piper to be touched by it any more than she already was.

"Pile the bodies on that cart." He indicated the nearby transpo. He'd take them out to the caldera where the storms would take care of the evidence. It would also get him away from the group so he could relay more intel to Daniel.

"Why are you here, Andrei?" Kenner asked, thankfully not in the way his sister had. "Don't get me wrong, I'm grateful to you for saving our asses today. And I'm glad to see you. But—"

"I'll explain it when we talk."

"All right. I want to know about your life, but it can wait until these grim deeds are behind us." He indicated the bodies with a tip of his head. "This is insanity, Andrei. This many Imperialists here at once? Attacking us."

Andrei said nothing, but he nodded his head briefly. Understanding lit Kenner's eyes, and he exhaled sharply, getting back to his work, which they finished quickly enough.

"You help with the rest of the clean-up. See to the wounded. I'll take care of this."

Kenner thanked him and jogged off, leaving Andrei to it.

The trip out to the caldera would give him enough time to work on a plan.

And to contact Daniel.

"What?" Daniel exploded from his seat at the news of the battle Andrei had happened upon on his way to check out the Roundtree compound before he reached out to meet with them.

"Two dozen men. Four of them were Skorpios." The Skorpios were Ciro Fardelle's private shock troops. His special ops forces.

Very well-trained and deadly. That some of the soldiers at that compound today were Skorpios meant the Federation had been correct that something integral to the Imperium's portal collapsing device was on Asphodel.

"I'll bring it to the proper people, Andrei. There will be a push to send more troops and I'm not sure I'd oppose that at this point. We still need answers. So get them for me."

Andrei agreed and ended the communication.

Chapter 4

He'd approached the compound in the same trajectory he had earlier. The light was lower now, having been several hours later, but the memory of that time when he'd had to force himself to patiently wait for the right opportunity to get up into that tower brought a cold sweat.

And then, as shots rang out all around her, he had to force the quiet so he could take out each and every threat to her. Knowing she was down there. Knowing that a movement to the left or right could have gotten her head blown off.

It was over. She was fine, and there was no reason to let his boyhood love for Piper Roundtree get in the way of getting his job done. And if it put him in a position to keep her a little safer, even for a short while, then that was all right, too.

Piper stood in a doorway, leaning casually there as she watched Andrei approach. "I imagine you'd like to clean up." She handed him a drying cloth and some soap. "Through here." Pointing, she pushed herself upright and led him back through the cool, dim house.

He nodded his thanks, needing the time to get himself together. He'd been surprised by the place, he had to admit. The bathing area he used was spacious, the water warm and copious. A lot of houses, including the one he'd grown up in, didn't have indoor plumbing at all. He hoped he'd helped, even a small amount, to give them a better quality of life, and here he was faced with evidence that he had.

It had been a stupid thing, sending the packets of credits. He should have disappeared totally, though it wasn't mandatory to do that and be a member of Phantom Corps. He knew they needed the credits. They would have simply because it was Asphodel and want was a common way of life there.

He'd had them, and he'd given them freely. Still would. They had built something here, and he'd support that when he could. And yes, he supposed he could admit to himself it kept a link with her. Even though he shouldn't. He couldn't let go all the way.

Piper tried to remain casual about his being there. She shouldn't be upset. After all, he'd been her friend. Had been a friend to her family. He couldn't have left the way he had without some measure of pressure. Asphodel had been a dead end for him anyway. She understood that. Her head got the logic of it quite well. Her heart wasn't as logical.

Kenner tossed himself into a chair at the table, across from where she sat. "Don't pretend you're not off balance."

She shoved a mug of kava at him, regretting how nice she'd been to make it for him to start with.

"Of course I'm off balance. It's not every day a horde of Imperialist troops breaks into my compound and tries to kill me and my
people."

He looked at her over the rim of the mug. "This is how you're
going to play it? With me?" He shook his head. "I was there. I remember what it was like when he left."

They'd thought he had been taken to a work camp. Or worse.
He'd been arrested, both he and Kenner had been, for a bloody
fight at the tavern in the portal city. The man who'd tried to rob
them and the man's two friends had ended up in a medi-clinic.
Kenner had been sent home because Taryn had signed off for him.
But Andrei had no one who'd claim him.

She'd railed then. Had cried and screamed at the unfairness
of Andrei being there when Taryn had been willing to sign off
for Andrei, too. But they hadn't let him, and Andrei's mother had
been murdered only two seasons before, so there was no one to
help him.

They hadn't let anyone in to see him, which had made matters
even worse.

Then he'd been gone, and no one would say where. The guilt
of that, of him being alone when he needed her had lay in her heart
every day since.

"Aren't you glad to know he's alive?" Kenner asked softly.

"I knew it when we got the credits." Never in the years since he'd
disappeared did they hear anything. But a year after he'd gone, the
first packet arrived. A little bit. Signed with an *A* at the bottom.

Over the years there'd been more courier packets. The amount
of credits had grown. Always signed with an *A* at the bottom. Each
packet had arrived, and each time she'd hoped there would be

more than that scrawled *A*. And each time she'd been disappointed by that lack.

"That put food on the table in the hard times. Kept us warm in the cold months." Kenner's mouth flattened briefly.

"I'm not denying that." In a way, she was sure it was why he still affected her the way he had. That was the only explanation for the way he still made her weak in the knees.

He came out of the bathing room, his hair bound at the base of his neck, exposing the beauty of his face. The facial hair had been a surprise. The scruff of it suited him. The pale sand colored clothing he wore was good for extended periods in the Wastelands or out in the open away from encampments, water and shade. It also suited his skin tone.

He was tall. That much she'd remembered. Only her memories had rendered him smaller. *This man*, this hard muscle and sinew was a machine. He moved with far more grace than he'd had as a boy. Most definitely with more control. He *prowled* through their living room, setting out little pieces of equipment. Dampeners to block eavesdropping. But when he reached the shelves where Taryn's stone carvings sat, he paused, the ghost of a smile on his face. He simply looked at them, picking each one up, examining it closely before putting it back.

All she could do was sit there and stare at him.

If he'd asked for her forgiveness on his knees, it wouldn't have touched her more than that smile.

The three of them watched him as he turned and noticed them with a small start.

"Sit down," Piper said, deciding to be less vexed with him. "Kava is fresh and warm."

He did, with that nod of his head for a thank-you.

This Andrei made her nervous on some level. Not frightened, but wary. This quiet man wasn't much like the fiery, sometimes stoic person he'd been as a boy and young man. Wherever he'd been, whatever he'd done, *this* Andrei was a man who didn't make rash mistakes.

What had happened to him?

"I need your help." He sipped the dark, sweet liquid and perked up a little in response. He hadn't realized how dry he'd been until he nearly drained the mug in three swallows. But Piper must have known; she pushed a bowl of sliced fruit his way.

"How? What?" Kenner spoke, Andrei knew, on everyone's behalf.

"I'm going to tell you something most people don't know. It's a dangerous something. You need to understand that before I go any further. Helping me will expose you to danger. I'll do my best to protect you all." He paused when his fingertips brushed Piper's when she pushed the refilled mug back toward him.

"And though I know it's not necessary to even ask, I will anyway. I'm asking for your word that what I say won't be repeated."

Piper swallowed hard. While they processed what he'd said, Andrei took the opportunity to study her while pretending not to. He'd never forgotten the color of her skin, milky kava. Or her eyes. Deepest of dark brown with a hint of amber at the iris. They'd been the first thing he'd noticed about her. So innocent-looking, but she'd been the best pickpocket of their group. Fearless, especially in the defense of her family.

He'd been family at one time, which is why he was there about to tell these three a Federation secret. He didn't want to involve them, but things were getting worse by the moment. He had no choice; they were his best hope.

It was Piper who spoke then. "You know you only have to ask. Tell us what this is about, and we can plan to make it right."

Warmth banked in his belly.

"Make sure no one can get in. The dampeners will thwart eavesdropping."

"No one will enter."

"The Imperium is close to developing a device designed to collapse portals. We have evidence to suggest at least one important element of this device comes from Asphodel, or through Asphodel."

They gaped at him, and he shrugged.

"How do you know this?" Taryn managed to ask.

"They've managed a few tests. We believe the incident in the Imperialist 'Verse, Krater, was a fatal error. The 'Verse has been closed off to all outside traffic." Even if the Imperialists had sent traditional spacecraft it would take months to reach them from the closest outpost.

"That's . . . that's monstrous even for them." Piper's voice caught, and he wished he hadn't had to bring this to her.

He nodded. He couldn't tell them about the biological agents, the bombings and experimentation camps they'd recently gotten word about.

"What do you need from us, Andrei?" Kenner leaned forward, intent.

"I need an in."

"I think we might have just fucked that one up for you, mate." Taryn snorted a laugh.

"No. There will be more come to check back after the ones gone missing. They'll know you had a part in it, and when they come to you, you'll tell them you want a rise in your credits or they'll end up like the last. Can you do that?" He looked between them. "They are craven. Greedy. They would believe you killed their men for money. The situation will be level for them because they'll believe you as criminal as they."

Piper sighed, kicking her boots off. His fingers spasmed a moment with the urge to help.

"All right then. I'll need to speak with Eiriq. You can trust him, Andrei." Piper locked her gaze with his. "I'll do my best to only tell him the barest of details."

"The less he knows, the less danger he'll be in." From the Imperialists and from Andrei. If he proved other than trustworthy, Andrei would make sure the situation was contained.

"We'll bring you on as one of our people. There are some here who'll recognize you. Will that be a problem?" Kenner asked.

"No. It'll be a good thing, actually. My less than wholesome past will lend me credibility with the right people. I came because I heard in town that the Imperialists were on their way out here to attack the compound, so I followed and helped take them down."

"Helped? Andrei, you pretty much single-handedly took out a good portion of those Imperialists today." Taryn stood, moving to the cabinets at the other end of the room.

"No one but you saw it, Taryn." Andrei shrugged.

"You'll stay here. Do you remember how to move cargo?" Piper's question was more of a challenge.

She had no idea just how much illicit movement of goods and information he took part in on a regular basis. "I can manage it, yes."

"Where were you?" Kenner asked it, but Andrei knew it was for Piper.

"Gone. It's best you don't know all the details."

Piper snorted but held her tongue.

"Piper, go talk to Eiriq. I'll get a meal started. Kenner, check on the people at the clinic. Make sure they're well and that they don't need anything. Andrei, you can help me." Taryn moved to the closet at the end of the kitchen and began to pull out food items, placing them on the nearby counter.

Piper looked at her brother for a long time without speaking. She finally sighed and stood. "Andrei can have the spare room next to mine. There's bedding in the linen closet. I'll be back shortly."

Once they were alone, Taryn looked to him. "You're like one of my siblings. You've been gone a long time, but you paid your dues, and I trust you to sleep under the same roof as my family. Is there any reason this should be a problem? Other than the ones you've been up front about?"

"I'm not here to hurt anyone."

"Doesn't answer my question."

"I know. I'd put myself in the path of a las-blast for any of you." This was true.

"That's enough. For now."

Taryn's trust meant a lot. More than Andrei could even begin to express. Instead, he cleaned the root vegetables, dicing and dropping them into the salted water on the cooktop.

"I'm glad you're alive," Taryn said as he walked past.

"Me, too," Andrei muttered.

"Don't know how you fooled those people in the Federation into giving you a job." Taryn's mouth split into a grin as he handed an ale Andrei's way. "But I wanted to thank you."

"Nothing to thank me for." Andrei shrugged.

"Incorrect." He clinked the glass against Andrei's. "You saved us today. You didn't *help* fight the Imperial soldiers off. You did it pretty much on your own."

"You were in trouble. I helped." Uncomfortable with praise, Andrei stirred the vegetables, testing for doneness.

"Years and years of credits. Andrei, there were times that without your help I don't know if we could have survived the storm season. And when the next packet arrived, at least we knew you were alive somewhere."

Andrei didn't know what to say. Emotion thickened his tongue.

"You've always protected my family. That's something deserving of thanks." Taryn turned back to the table, finishing laying out the plates.

After the meal, after they'd cleaned up and the sweetness of that old connection had fallen over her, Piper stood beneath the spigot, hoping the water would wash away not only the dirt, sweat and blood, but the feelings for Andrei she'd thought were long dead.

Her muscles ached from having to be so heavy on the stick when she flew back so fast through the canyons. They hurt from the concussive echoes of the las-rifle. Her eyes hurt from the bright and from trying not to cry.

He'd come out of that cloud of dust like an angel from a story she'd heard as a child. And like a children's story, she'd nearly fallen into a relieved heap at the sight.

His hair had been so long. It had jarred her, still did, mainly because she wanted to touch it. It would be stupid to want to touch it.

It had been short before. Short and soft. Soft against her hands as she massaged his scalp and neck, trying to bring him calm. She smiled, not entirely willingly, at the memory of how she'd been the only girl allowed to touch him the way she had. Especially after he'd returned from a stint in lockup to find his mother had been murdered. To find the polis had done very little to find out who'd killed her or even why.

His anger at the world had been worse after that. Worse after the authorities came to take his younger brother away.

Despite the fights with others, despite his anger, Andrei had been gentle with her. Always. Everyone else, he'd had a point to prove to. A point he probably wasn't aware of.

With Piper, the wild-eyed, hard boy fell away. Only with her had he been soft. He'd been the first boy she'd ever given herself to. And, she thought with some regret, the only one she'd felt like she mattered to.

Heaving a sigh, she turned the water off and reached for a towel. She'd trusted him, and he'd left.

Shimmying into underpants and a worn but comfortable sleep shirt, she headed back into her room, passing his door as she did. Right there, within her reach. He was just beyond, and she ached to go to him and have him give her enough reasons to make his absence okay.

In her bed she shivered a moment, caught between warmth that he was back and horror at what had happened that day. It wasn't that she was a stranger to violence. She'd been in more skirmishes than she could count since they'd begun running cargo.

Violence had been common enough in her life. Asphodel was hardscrabble. Hostile. People got old early. Using your fists kept a certain kind of order, showed people you weren't an easy mark.

Piper had a big brother with even bigger fists. Strangers wouldn't know how sweet he was in reality. They only saw his size and the easy way he had with weapons and, when necessary, his bare hands. He'd kept them safe.

Kenner and Andrei had run in a pack of kids from their sector. Bright, quick boys whose talents were wasted by the way things were for them. At first it was fun and silly, but the older they'd all gotten, the more some of them began to resent the way their future was so narrow. That resentment had sent more than one of them to lockup.

Kenner had learned his lesson after Andrei had disappeared, thank the gods. With a sigh, she flopped onto her side, trying to get comfortable. Andrei had been part of her life, part of every single day, and then he hadn't. Kenner had been thoroughly dissuaded from that potential violent life by that absence. Until that afternoon, anyway.

But what happened that afternoon was not common. Not anything she wanted in her life. Thieving was one thing; *killing* was another thing entirely. Her sum total of experience with authority was hiding what she did from them. But these men, these *soldiers* sent from the Imperium were out to kill everyone in her compound. People she and her brothers felt responsible for.

Andrei had protected them. All of them. He didn't seem comfortable with the praise Taryn and Kenner had sent his way, but they all knew what he'd done. What would have happened had he not come along when he did?

All about Andrei, connected to him on some level. His return had only underlined just how empty her life was outside work. She couldn't remember the last time she had been excited by a man's presence.

And agitated. Enraged. Begrudgingly charmed by the nearly wild boy transformed into a quiet, watchful man who carried death in his hands like it was common. He was dangerous. It came off him in waves.

Gods help her, she liked it. She should run the other way, but she knew she wouldn't.

*A*ndrei sat at a table near the door, one leg on the surface, the chair tipped, an ale at his left hand. A book in his right. For all outward appearance, a man with not a care in the world. Some might take him for an easy mark here in this bar full of criminals. But most would wonder just what he had to make him so confident in his stance. So utterly unconcerned with danger.

The smart ones would realize that for the threat it was and give him a wide berth. The rest were dealt with easily enough that he didn't need to give them much thought.

What he was thinking about, however, was just how woefully inadequate the security and basic infrastructure at the compound the Roundtrees lived in was. He made a mental note to look around that next sunrise. The guard towers weren't even manned when he'd come through the gates. They needed more than one cistern, that was for sure. He hadn't failed to miss Taryn's blush of guilt when he'd told Andrei they only had the one.

They sure as seven hells needed to be training two or three of their residents to be medtechs. Being so far from a clinic and medical help, it was a necessity to have personnel capable of triage in case of an emergency. Storms didn't care if a body broke a leg or received a bad burn. Moreover, the compound had several women of childbearing age and several children. Basic surgical skills would be a welcome thing to have.

Andrei had been adding to his mental list when he caught

movement near the door. Andrei lit a smoke as he waited for Benni to see him there.

The young man's gaze casually took in the space as he swaggered in. He caught sight of Andrei far quicker than he had the last time they had worked together. Andrei smiled, satisfied, as he leaned forward and grabbed his ale.

Benni tossed his bulk into a rickety chair across from him within a few minutes, a fresh ale in his hand.

"Seems there's some hiring going on out in the Wastelands."

Interest sharpened his wits. The Wastelands were a day's long drive wide. A vast expanse of the harshest environs Asphodel served. Dust storms skittered all over the basin with winds so high they'd strip flesh from bone in seconds. The heat was extraordinary during half the year and frigid the other half, with blizzards and their perilous mix of razor-sharp dust mixed with snow.

There was nothing out there but death, some mining communities that had been abandoned when Andrei had been very young and a few encampments of people generally regarded as insane.

"That so? What for then, and is the pay any good?"

"Queerest thing is no one's of any mind to share details on the whats and whyfors of the situation. I'm of a mind to believe it has to be mining of some sort. All's out there anyhow."

That would be Andrei's opinion as well.

"Who's running this show?"

"Don't know those details either. Did see some fellas who didn't look so native to these parts. One stayed in the back of the conveyance all fancy-like. Had a big scar on his face from here," Benni pointed to the middle of his forehead, "to here." He ended up on the opposite cheek.

Andrei knew that scar.

"I was thinking 'bout signing on. A man can always use some extra credits in his account."

Benni had been one of his first local informants. A native of Borran, Benni had an illustrious future as a prisoner all lined up when he'd shadowed Andrei for days and had broken into his room to steal his belongings.

Unfortunately for Benni, Andrei had been a better thief and had been lying in wait for him. But Andrei had seen in the boy a great deal of himself. He'd given Benni a chance to work off his debt. He'd been with Andrei ever since. The year before, his wife had joined them, becoming another one of what Benni called *Andrei's people*.

Everyone deserved a few extra chances in life. Especially people like Benni and Aya, who'd never been given much by way of example. Ellis had given that to Andrei, and in turn, Andrei tried to return that favor with others when he could.

"I don't know. Body's got a right to know what he's to be hired on for. All the way out there and all." This was dangerous work. The kind it was up to Andrei to do. He wouldn't risk Benni for a job like this.

"What I figured you'd say." Benni pushed a small data chip across the table, and Andrei palmed it.

"I'll be off then. I've got a lovely lady awaiting my attentions." Benni looked back over his shoulder at a young woman standing near the entrance, Aya, Benni's partner in life and in the game.

"Have a care, then." He meant it. There had been enough death to last Andrei a lifetime.

Some time later, after another ale, he brought himself back to the compound, not being stopped, or even noticed by a single person.

He needed to speak with Kenner about posting guards or at the very least training the ones they had to keep a better watch.

He paused, passing by her door, but forced his feet to keep moving. He needed to look at that data and if necessary, report back his findings.

Chapter 5

"Try it this way," Andrei murmured, adjusting Shilo's hold on the hand ax. "Hold it like that and when you"—he drew her hand back—"strike, you're using your strength more efficiently."

Shilo gazed up at him, adoringly and, annoyingly enough, lustfully. Piper wanted to step in and shake the girl. Instead, she managed to swallow her satisfied hmpf when Andrei ignored it, returning to repairing the dust screen.

"You're a lot of help, Andrei." Shilo fluttered her lashes at him. Wasted, because his attention was on his hands. "I'm sure you could help me with other things, too."

It was a minor miracle that Piper's snort didn't break free.

Then again, he didn't respond, not even to look up.

Shilo stared at him for a while longer until Piper took pity on them both and cleared her throat, moving toward them.

"Shilo, your father was looking for you," Piper said as she tossed her knapsack on a nearby bench and pulled the tool belt on.

The girl skittered off with a backward look toward Andrei, who studied the tools in his hands very intently.

"Did I ruin your moment?" She couldn't resist the jab. And she wasn't sorry when he looked up, one brow raised imperiously, a smile on his face.

"She's a little young."

"And her father is a lot big."

He snorted. "That, too. This is in bad shape, Piper." He indicated the valve.

"It's been struggling. Eiriq put in an order for a new one, but you know how long that takes."

He sighed, looking it over. He drew a soft cloth over it, noting the pockmarks. "Don't know if this can survive another big storm. Do you have a shop here? I can fashion a replacement if you've got the tools and raw materials."

"You can?"

"I have a few skills that come in handy at times like these."

"So you say." She stood, brushing her hands off. "Come on. We've got a shop of sorts. Let's see if it's what you need."

He stood and followed. A fierce need to know about him had burned her gut; now it flushed over her skin. What had he been doing that he was so proficient at mechanics as well as killing men?

What she did know, as they moved through the compound, was that he didn't miss anything. His careful, wary eyes took in everything and everyone.

"This is good." He looked around, placing the valve on the tabletop in the makeshift shop. "What you've built here."

"Things need fixing. It makes sense to have a place to repair our gear."

He bent to look through some scrap metal, pulling out pieces, rejecting most. "I meant the compound."

She hopped up onto a nearby stool and gave over to the simple pleasure at watching him work. "Thank you. We try. You know Taryn. He saw a need and wanted to fill it. Most of the families here are his doing."

"I've taken a look around. I'd like to speak to the three of you later about some ways to improve on what you have."

"Talk to me now about it. I'm here."

"Yes, you are. But I'm sure your brothers have a few things to say about how things run around here as well."

She wanted to know more but would force herself to be patient until later. "They do, yes. But they'd be the first to tell you I make all the big decisions. The final choice, I mean. We do try to run things by consensus."

"You need a better water collection system. Given the rate of population here, you're vastly underequipped. One cistern is not enough."

"I know. It's on the list of projects. But the list is long."

"There are thirty-one adults living here. Most of them are able-bodied. Why are they not all working on it now?"

They'd asked for volunteers, but it was slow going. Not everyone had the expertise, and she told him so.

"Does everyone here drink and use the water for home and cooking? Yes. Everyone here eats the produce from Taryn's greenhouses. There's no volunteering when it comes to using the water, so why not assign people a task? You can't make this work if everyone isn't invested."

Kenner had made a similar comment, but coming from Andrei, it was easier to hear for some reason.

"They look to you for direction, Piper. It's why they stay. They could live in town if they wanted. But they choose to be here, and you provide them with something. Let them be invested in this place, too. Starting with giving them some shovels and getting some pits for the cisterns started. I can draw out some rough plans for the cisterns themselves."

Eleven years later, he walks back into her life and begins taking care of her again. "I'll discuss it with the others. Thank you. Where'd you learn all this?" She indicated the tabletop strewn with bits of metal.

"I was stuck on Parron once. Eight standard months." He shuddered as he made some quick calculations and began to measure out the piece he needed to replace. "The place I stayed in was little more than a pile of broken shit."

The way he was now might have been different than he'd been before, but there was something very comfortable about being with him. The way he moved was graceful and predatory. His focus as he cut and worked the threading on the new parts to slide together was impressive.

"So you taught yourself all this?"

He shrugged with one shoulder. "Either that or deal with broken crap and time in lockup for assaulting the owner for not taking care of business."

"Wouldn't be the first time you were in lockup for knocking heads."

"No. But I don't do that anymore."

"All right. What do you do then?"

He looked up at her briefly. "Pretty much what I did before, only I don't go to lockup for it. What do *you* do then?"

She snorted at his evasion, waving a hand around. "This is what I do. I run cargo. My crew isn't so big as to attract unwanted attention but big enough that most of the time we're left alone by the others. That took a while. I've got a great right hook, or so I'm told."

"I remember that about you."

That warmed her. Odd as it was.

They fell into long, quiet periods as she cleaned her weapons.

She was conscious of him on a whole different level, in ways she hadn't known to even be at seventeen. She knew it now. There hadn't been a steady man in a long time, but there had been enough of them for her to recognize that purely female fascination with an attractive male. Even through the sharp scent of the lubricant and heated metal, she could pick him up. He smelled good. Like warm earth and a hint of something else. Something wholly male. There was darkness in his eyes. Enough a wise woman would understand and avoid. But she was never very wise.

His hands were nearly delicate as he worked. Hoping he didn't notice how much she stared, she continued to watch him. His shoulders were nice and wide. He'd taken off his sweater so he was in a short-sleeved, snug-fitting shirt. A dusting of dark hair lay against the golden toned skin of his arms.

There was nothing left of the boy he'd been, not physically. The years had done him good. Fleshed him out. Brought a gloss to his hair. Self-conscious, she patted a hand over the ropes of her braids, captured at the base of her neck.

"I like it that way."

Surprised, she drew her fingers back, blinking. She couldn't have stopped her pleased smile to save her life. She'd inherited her mother's hair. They had the photographs to prove it. Jiao Roundtree had been a beautiful woman. Strong, but three children, several miscarriages, famine and violence had done her in.

Piper shook her head to free that memory and send it away.

It was silly to have long hair when her job had her traveling all over the place in storms and intense heat and cold. But she hadn't allowed herself many luxuries, and her hair was one of those few.

It made her feel like a woman. Even if her hands were work-rough and her nails were a mess. "I should cut it," she said, hoping he'd argue.

"That would be a shame. Though your face is certainly beautiful enough that short hair wouldn't harm it."

"Thank you. I hope you won't cut yours either."

"Not unless I absolutely have to."

There was a story that went with the way he worded that, but he didn't add anything. "You're . . . taciturn, yes, that's the word."

His laugh did things to her. Low, dirty things, and she allowed herself to wallow in them a bit.

"Shooting your mouth off can get you in a lot of trouble."

"Thank you." She said it quickly and with finality.

"For what? Not shooting my mouth off?" He looked up from his work, all the focus in those eyes on her.

She wondered what he'd be like in bed as a man. They'd been in a sweet, young, passionate love. A smile she couldn't stop came to her mouth. There was not much evidence of the boy who'd been just as virginal as she had been. This Andrei would most assuredly know his way around a woman's best parts.

"For the courier packets."

He shook his head and went back to work. "Nothing to thank me for."

"I beg to differ. Also, Andrei Solace, I have known you a very long time. Don't you presume to know what I do and don't need to thank a body for." She crossed her arms and gave him her best glare.

He chuckled rather than skittering off like so many did. He put time into her, attention. She narrowed her eyes, waiting.

"Okay then. You're right, and you're welcome."

She played through his words, looking for any sign that he'd patronized her, and found none.

"Last night I noticed you didn't have guards posted, and correct me if I'm wrong, but you don't have anyone here in medtech training?"

"You've been busy." Anyone but him poking around that much, and she'd be suspicious and angry. She respected his opinion, and it helped that he was right.

"Just took a look around. I spoke with Kenner about doing some defense training while I'm here. That can address the lack of posted guards. Really, Piper, with all this upheaval around you, there should be guards posted every moment of the day. Perhaps a little update on munitions would be helpful as well." He shrugged like it wasn't a big deal.

"How long will you be here?"

"Long as it takes."

"You used to be nice to me," she teased with a laugh. If she hadn't, she might have blurted out how glad she was to see him. How much she'd missed him.

He looked up again, amusement clear on his features. Her gut squeezed at how he looked, at the way it felt to simply be with him again. She fisted her hands rather than let them shake.

He went back to work, the smile still on his lips. "You used to say that all the time. Usually when you wanted to be involved in something inherently dangerous, and I said no."

Unwillingly, she snorted, totally guilty. She supposed she might have—at one point in her life when she was very young and had the most beautiful boy around—been a tad spoiled. He'd guarded her. Protected her. Everyone had known she was his, and because of that, no one dared harm her.

"You wound me." She sniffed delicately and looked back to the valve in his hands. She still had the little tributes he'd brought back to her. A bracelet made from the shiniest of baubles he'd boosted from some outlander down at the Portal. A picture in a delicate frame. Someone else taken somewhere else, but the lady in it had been regal and beautifully exotic to Piper's eyes. A scarf, a pin, a hat, gloves. Most precious of all were the books. Two classics from Earth. Because he knew it meant something to her. And a collection of poetry from Ravena's top modern poet, Eleni Portony.

"I read *Little Women* to Eiriq and Lune's children."

He swallowed and licked his lips. Inside, in that place she hadn't wanted to face, the place where the voice in her head had told her he didn't care anymore, that place eased, dissolved like smoke.

She *did* still affect him. To what extent she didn't know. But it hadn't been some memory she'd embellished over the years. That connection, that bright spark that she'd always felt was special and unique, really *was* between them.

Then and now. Perched near him, watching him work and enjoying his presence, it was as if those years hadn't existed. It was so very simple to her. She wanted him now, as she'd wanted him then. No, no, she wanted him more. She was older. More experienced. Harder in many ways. She wanted to know what he felt like, naked, against her back. His lips on hers. Wanted to know what it felt to have his cock inside her when they didn't have to worry about getting caught. When they both knew a few more things about pleasure.

"Do they get any schooling?" he asked, bringing her back from the dirty place in her head where she'd been riding his cock, his hands all over her.

"The children here? The town school sends out teachers a few times each lunar cycle. We supplement with practical life work. Taryn works with them in the greenhouses and nurseries."

Her grin lightened his heart. "He told me you were able to provide eighty percent of the food for the compound with the produce from his greenhouses." Taryn had also let it slip that it originally had been the credits Andrei had sent that had financed the rows of indoor growing areas within the well-guarded fences around the compound.

"Taryn's greenhouses have brought us through many rough patches. Kenner teaches them how to hunt. How to use weapons. How to fix things. I teach some of them how to fly, and I like to read to them, too. I don't want them to only have the rough parts of life." She hopped down from the stool and began to pace.

"Of course they have to know how to fix a generator and how to make effective dust seals. But I want *more* for them. I don't want them just existing. I want them to live their lives with enthusiasm and happiness. I want art and music in their lives."

The soft hope in her voice tore at him. That she still had the book he'd given her so long ago *really* tore at him. That it had meant anything to anyone but Andrei had been something shattering to him.

Books were so fine and beautiful. They were the very symbol of what made humanity special. There hadn't been very many books in Andrei's life until he started with Phantom Corps. But when he came by one, he did all he could do to make it his.

To that day, when he held a book in his hands, it was a sign of how far he'd come in his life. The spine, cracked or supple, was the backbone of whatever journey the pages took him on. There was nothing in the Known Universes like a book.

"I can send books. If you need them, that is." He kept his head down, tried not to think of how desperate he'd been for them as a child. "The wife of one of my friends is a teacher. She would most likely have some good suggestions."

"I . . . I'd like that. Thank you."

He wanted to touch her. Wished he could just let himself want her without feeling guilt or shame.

Instead he continued to rebuild the valve, thankful for that diversion. He'd jerked off twice since he arrived, and it hadn't helped at all. Andrei wasn't a slave to his prick, but damn it if his cock wasn't at attention every second in her presence.

It was stupid of him to be here this way. There were other merc camps on Asphodel. None of them had this . . . baggage. This weight of memory.

He repeated to himself that this was the best option. And it was. He knew enough to understand the Roundtrees were the only mercenary group where he'd get the trust and access he needed.

He needed to keep his dick in check. Needed to keep his focus on the mission. If there had been any time in his life where it had been more important to avoid mistakes, he wasn't aware of it. The cost of failure here was higher than he was willing to pay.

It didn't mean he couldn't help out while he was there. It would be good for his cover if he acted like one of them anyway, so why not combine it with getting a few things repaired and helping with some skill building.

And it would keep her safer. He still needed that. Accepted a long time ago that he would always feel that need and that he would obey it when he could.

She mattered in a way no one else ever had or would.

A flash hit him then, straight in the gut. Piper's braids in his fist as he fucked into her body from behind. Her pussy, hot and creamy around his cock as she writhed against him, pushing back to meet each of his thrusts.

Her skin would be moist and salty from sweat as he licked up the line of her spine. She'd whimper when he sucked hard just below the edge of her shoulder blade, marking her.

"Where do you go?"

Startled, still vibrating with the need to be in her, he risked a glance to her. It was funny how little she'd changed, even after eleven years. She'd been a lovely child. Lively. Pretty and smart. Sullen then as her mid years had hit. And then she'd been perfect and small and all his. At his side always as they marauded through the streets. She'd sewn up their wounds, had been their lookout when they'd nicked food or gear.

He'd laughed with her. Been her shoulder when she cried. And then she'd been his in every way. Had given herself to him shyly, but no less beautiful for her inexperience. She'd been the place he was never angry. The person who gave to him without expecting something in return.

With Piper there'd been acceptance. The quiet place in the noisy storm of his daily life. She'd brought him calm when the rage had pumped through his veins like fire.

He hadn't tasted her in eleven years, but the phantom feel of her skin against his fingertips still tingled from time to time as the ghost of her lived in him for a breath or two.

The velvet of her voice still soothed, even as she teased. Maybe because she felt comfortable enough with him, even after all they'd been through.

"What do you mean?"

"You think so deeply. You just go away. Your eyes show it. Where do you go when you think like that?"

He nearly choked, and she laughed. "*Oh!* You were in *that* place. Tell me about it. Who is she, this mystery woman you were with in your head?"

"A true man does not kiss and tell, Piper." Desperate to change the subject, he held the valve up. "I think we're good. I'm going to go see if that's so."

She put a hand on his arm. "I'll go with you. And then, shall we take a trip to town? See what business we can get our way?"

He nodded, hoping she'd go out first. Of course she didn't, and he had to hold his things in front of his crotch so she couldn't see the raging evidence of just exactly what place he was in.

Work then. He needed to put his mind back to the job.

He'd checked in the night before, after he'd read over the data Benni had passed him. Mining for something. Clearly they were Imperialist troops, there to guard the dangerous open pit mines. No one would notice them so far away from population centers.

Daniel would pass the information to Julian and Vincenz and told him to report in daily, even if it was to say he saw nothing. They had the key, at least one of them anyway. They now needed the lock. In the chip, on the very edge, there had been a sliver. Andrei assumed it was the material being mined.

With the parts he found around the compound, he'd managed to extract enough data to send to Vincenz. He and Julian would figure it out and he'd hear back and they'd know what the next steps were. In the meantime, Andrei wanted to get closer to the Imperialist minister and his lackeys who had shown up there in the Portal town.

Chapter 6

$\mathcal{T}$wo days later, Andrei sat next to her in the truck as they headed toward the ramshackle cluster of buildings on the north end of the portal town often referred to as Thieves' Alley. Though he'd been there a few nights before when he'd met Benni, the place was different in the light. Despite the ominous name, really it was several bars, a few houses of prostitution, boardinghouses and flats and food carts. Those streets had been his second home for years of his childhood.

He pondered a trip down those memories, just to take his mind from the alarming rate of speed they traveled at.

She drove like she did everything else. Fast and bordering on reckless.

In the case of driving and flying, the pleasure of watching her so intent on her job, on the level of skill and competence she had, was nearly too much. Not that it would stop him from watching her. Watching her had become something of a favorite activity since he'd arrived.

When they'd returned from running cargo, Kenner had told them that on his trip to town that morning, he'd seen some Imperialist types around. Imperialist types attempting to hire on a crew.

"More troops around lately." She slowed as they entered the more populated areas heading into the center of town.

"Yes." She had no idea how truly bad things were. He found himself caught between wanting to keep her safe from the truth of it and telling her everything so she'd be better equipped to handle any trouble.

"Listen, I need to make contact with them, but that doesn't mean you have to. Why don't you stay here or go to the mercantile to grab supplies? I'll find you when I'm finished."

"Oh, you mean while you go over there and get hired on because you have a penis and therefore are more qualified than me? Me, who has a reputation here as a cargo runner?"

He nearly growled at her. Until several days before when he'd saved her ass from being murdered by Imperium troops, he'd not been tempted to growl at anyone in years if one didn't count Abbie Lyons and Carina Fardelle. They were other men's problems though. This one—he glared in her direction—was most definitely his problem.

"Don't growl at me. Just look pretty and scary in that way you have. I'll do the talking. I will, however, take any advice you'd like to give me on what it is you want me to say." She said it as she pulled the conveyance to a stop.

Annoyed as he was, he had to admit she was right to take point. They knew her, though some knew him, too. "Fine. But if I start giving orders, you take them." He ignored her snort and continued speaking. "We just need an in with them again. We want to run goods, but *not* whatever it is Cheney wanted you to move." He'd been working with others like him so long, he wasn't sure if he was making the distinction clear.

They needed to earn enough trust to look around, but not to actually do the bidding of the Imperium that would cause harm. He'd be sure to drop the location of the cargo, whatever it was, to the Federation, but there were other parties working on other things, other pieces of the puzzle, and he had to keep his pace even with theirs.

"Good." She sat back a moment, clearly relieved. "I don't want any part of this whatever it is they're trying to do. I want to help stop them. I'll do everything I can, even take orders from you if necessary."

"If I could do this all without you, I would." He hesitated.

"You can't, and no matter what, I'm happy I can help." She pushed from the door she'd opened, hopping to the ground, and he followed.

Her walk was confident. No one would get the drop on her out here, which made him relax marginally.

She headed toward a man Andrei had seen in his briefing materials. Jan Karl, one of Fardelle's top ministers after Hartley Alem had been put to death some months before. There was strong suspicion the man had engineered the recent biological outbreak in the Imperial 'Verse, Faelene. So many had died, even before all outgoing communication had been halted.

And here he was, in Federation territory engineering their own natural resources to aid them in murdering Federation citizens. Anger spiked through him at the sight of this man who shat upon

the Federation with such impunity. He wanted to punch someone over it.

Dust, rage and impotent frustration. The scents and memories
of Asphodel all knotted within him.

"You owe me quite a packet of credits." Piper's snarl at the man
in the chair next to Karl yanked Andrei from his anger.

It also began to revive his cock. At this rate, he'd lose all sensation in the area from overstimulation or something.

The man twisted a smile up at her. "So I do." Drawing out a
pouch, the man counted out the chips, sliding the small pile to the
center of the table, where the magister checked and then handed it
to Piper.

"I assume this makes us square?" He leaned back, and Andrei realized who the man was. Back in their youth, Kenner and Andrei had
done numerous not-even-legal jobs for him. Porter, yes, Rhymen
Porter. Andrei was surprised to find him still drawing breath, but
then, he always had been a canny bastard.

"This a new crew member?" He tipped his chins toward Andrei.

"Only if by new you mean someone who ran *your* cargo back in
the day."

Porter cocked his head, examining Andrei.

"Hair's longer now. Your sister worked at my tavern for many
years before she finally married and hooked up with that husband
of hers and hied off to wherever she did." He grinned, standing and
holding a wrist.

Andrei clasped it, wondering where Hali had gone. Wondering if
he should try to find her. He'd tried to find Carmine, his younger
brother, but there'd been nothing after he'd been taken by the authorities. Chances were his name had been changed and he'd been
fostered somewhere else. Andrei hoped he was well, wherever he was.

"Walk with me." Porter didn't ask as much as he pulled on Andrei to follow, which he did, Piper with him.

"Piper, why don't you two just go back to your compound? Come back in a few turns." Porter lowered his voice as he gestured off toward the town. "These Imperialists, the ones who attacked you. Yes, of course I heard about it." He rolled his eyes at their silly ignorance. "They want that cargo run. You have a good head for business, Piper. Got people to keep alive back at the compound. Don't go messing with this rabble."

Andrei looked to Piper, loving the curve of her cheeks. He wondered if Porter was trustworthy, and she gave him a short shake of her head. "What is it they're moving?"

"Nothing you want any part of, boy."

"But, you see, I do want part of it."

Porter looked at him closely, as if deciding Andrei's intent.

"I had family on Krater." Which was a total lie, but he was a professional liar, so that worked out well. Krater had suffered so much both sides of the line had heard about it, had been affected by it. Most didn't know Fardelle had used a primitive version of the portal collapsing device and it went horribly wrong, sealing Krater off to her own fate. Space travel would take two standard years from the nearest 'Verse. Even the private portal had been cut off.

It had served to turn attention to just what Fardelle wasn't doing to protect his own people. While most didn't know he'd wantonly murdered his own people, they knew he was doing nothing to help.

"These men are not easily played, boy." Porter narrowed his gaze.

Andrei didn't need to tell him he had no intention of playing. He just waited as the gears turned in the old man's head.

"I'll make the introduction. If you want my advice"—he paused to chuckle—"not that you need it. But they'll know about the others. Cheney survived it, limped away, licked his wounds and was called off 'Verse. Own it."

Andrei planned to do just that.

Porter showed Piper the next cargo he wanted her to run. Clever woman gave him a discount for the introduction.

By the time they'd finished their business with Porter, Karl was still there, looking agitated. Good. Andrei would take great pleasure in bringing these fuckers down.

"Do you want me to do the talking on this, or do you want to take it?" she murmured as they walked back toward the table where Karl sat.

He nearly laughed. Instead, he shook his head. "You take it. You're right. You have the reputation here."

"Jump in if I miss anything. I don't want to mess up."

Andrei took her shoulders and turned her to face him. "You're doing just fine. I'm sorry to put you in this position."

She tipped her chin up, locking her gaze with his. "You should kiss me."

Surprise made him a little wide-eyed. "I should? Other than the fact that you're a beautiful woman with delicious lips, why should I?" Not that he was opposed to the idea in any way.

"I like it when you cast aside the taciturn thing and flirt with me, Andrei. You should do it more often. And as we're here having this little conversation in full view of the table of men over there, there should be a reason for it. Don't you think a kiss is a good reason?" Her teasing smile brought out the dimple at the right side of her mouth. "Also, I want you to."

How could he resist?

He bent his head, meaning to deliver a quick kiss, but she grabbed him, holding him tight, and he was lost in the taste of her, lost in the way she felt there against his body after all this time.

Instead, she opened her mouth on the sweetest of sighs. He inhaled that sound, inhaled her breath and then her taste, gods her taste, the sweet, hot tang of her echoed through him.

Images battered him, tearing at his resolve until all that was left were shreds. He wanted her, craved her taste, reveled in it as his tongue found its way between her lips and into her mouth.

Hot and wet, gods. The inside of her welcomed him here, as he'd dreamed her cunt would. The idea of it, the way she'd yield as he slid deep, the way her inner muscles would hug and give way around him. Gods.

He'd take her to the solid warm ground they stood on, shove her pants down and fuck her if he didn't call a halt to this exquisite madness. When he broke the kiss, she tiptoed up and nipped at his bottom lip, sending shards of pleasure through him once again. "Well, I think I was wrong."

Every fiber of his being wanted more. It was only from years of training that he restrained himself from going back for more and then more after that. He vibrated with it, unused to having to work so hard at it anymore.

He managed to say, "About what?"

"That a taste of you would fix this bone-deep craving you've awakened. It hasn't." On that, she turned to stalk back to the table, leaving him embarrassingly hard and uncharacteristically flustered.

"Next time you send thugs to my door, I'm going to come looking for you."

As opening salvos went, Piper's was pretty damned good. Though he was proud, Andrei had trained his face into a mask. No emotions. Standing at attention next to Piper, he continued to sweep the area for trouble.

"You killed nearly twelve of my men, Ms. Roundtree."

"Would have been sixteen if the rest hadn't turned tail and run. *No one* comes to my gates with weapons drawn and walks away unscathed. I don't know how things work on your side, but if you try it again, you'll get the same result. Credits are credits, but don't come here to my 'Verse and insult me like that."

She held the other man's gaze without flinching. He finally shrugged with a sneer on his lips. "As you wish. We still need cargo run."

"As I told Cheney, I don't run treason."

Karl's gaze narrowed, but he said nothing else for long moments. At last he turned to one of his guards and spoke in the man's ear. "Moore will take you to the cargo and arrange for payment."

"Nice doing business with you."

Andrei would be damned sure to be certain what they carried wasn't harmful. He didn't trust any of them, not at all.

The winds were rising, and Andrei hurried her along as best he could. It was a small crate, and Moore handled the details for pickup.

"Winds are picking up. You can run this tomorrow. It'll be in the usual spot." Moore looked off to the south where the storm was building.

Piper nodded, said her good-bye and led the way back to the conveyance.

"We're going to have to push it to get back the compound." Andrei looked at the radar screen and noted the mass of the storm. "This is a big one."

Without saying more, she tore from the area, dust flying in her wake. Others were leaving as well, while those at the camp behind them were battening down the windows and doors, getting out of the open.

"You did great back there." Andrei continued to monitor the storm while she drove.

"I did? I worried about pushing back too hard. I suppose it made me feel better to have you with me. I don't like Karl. He's worse than Cheney, I think."

"Stay away from them as much as you can. I'll handle the load of the cargo tomorrow. I'll collect the credits." He hated the thought of her even being near them.

"Why? I'm around villainous men doing evil deeds daily. I am a villainous woman doing evil deeds." She never took her attention from what she was doing, moving along the floor of the canyons to cut through and get back to the compound faster. The ride was not a comfortable one, and he made a mental note to look at the under-carriage when he next had the opportunity.

"You are not villainous. You run cargo. It's not strictly legal, but it's not what they do. They kill their own people, Piper. They tor-ture them and experiment on them. They are nothing like you."

"You see things so clearly."

He exhaled sharply. "Why do you say that?"

"You're sure of yourself. Of what you're saying. It makes me feel better. I don't like being a tattletale."

He laughed. He'd done more laughing and smiling in the three days he'd been there than he had in a long time. Probably since Marame, and even with her he kept guarded until it drove her away.

"Imagine how I felt. Especially the early years in the corps. I was suddenly the authorities. Made me damnable nervous."

"What changed?"

"I got better at my job. Understood it and my place within it. I wouldn't do it if I didn't believe in the outcome." The small details were not pretty, but the long view of it was right.

He'd never felt particularly useful. Never felt as if he'd been born to do anything in particular except get into trouble. But the job had given him direction.

Ellis had seen something special in Andrei. Something Andrei hadn't been able to see in himself until two years later. He'd forever be grateful to his boss for that. For the training to get his anger in check, for the sense of direction Andrei finally had at long last.

He was good at something. At many somethings. He was making a difference with what he did, and to a kid who'd grown up a "dirt eater" with a dying, invalid mother, never enough food in the cupboards and no future, that had meant everything.

Ellis had given Andrei a future, and he'd be forever grateful for it.

"We're going to make it. Barely, but we'll get inside before the storm finishes rising. Call ahead and let them know to have someone man the gates."

Piper concentrated on keeping the conveyance on the road against the force of the advance gusts. She wasn't so disciplined that she'd been able to put the kiss he'd given her back at Thieves' Alley from her head. It had shaken her. Though she'd tried to be casual and flirty, that kiss had made her tremble inside. He'd tasted better than she remembered, better than she'd imagined since he returned.

She wanted more.

Once they'd arrived back at the compound, he turned to her. "You did a great job today. Thank you."

Never in her life had she craved approval the way she had with him. That he thought she'd done a good job meant something.

She swung down from the cab. "I hate them for putting me in this position."

He followed, helping her tie the windscreen cover down. "You aren't alone."

"At least tell me it helps in some way." She kept pace as they hurried back toward shelter, her shorter strides to his longer.

"I need this in with them. If only to see what they've got in terms of people on this side helping them." He shook his head at the flash of guilt he saw on her features. "No. You never ran anything that could have brought harm to anyone. Food and clothing, luxury goods. Don't take on what isn't yours."

"You're still really good at that."

He paused, hauling the door open for her to get inside. "What?"

"Making me feel better."

The confusion and sweet embarrassment on his features got to her more than anything else he could have done on purpose.

$\mathcal{A}$ndrei left her in the kitchen as he headed to his room to update the team. It would be better that way. If he stayed at her side just then she'd want to talk about the kiss. Or want to do it again.

Gods, he wanted to do it again.

Annoyed, he put out the scramblers, making sure they were all on and working to distort the signals before he began to dial in to the Phantom Corps team comm.

After some time to establish the connection, Julian, Vincenz and Daniel showed up on his comm screen.

"Just set up a run for Jan Karl."

Daniel's eyebrows rose briefly. "Something we suspected. Ellis will want to hear this. Be sure to scan it before you deliver. We'll arrange for pickup on the other side."

"Fine. Piper made it clear she wasn't interested in running treason. Karl's face was beautiful to see. Any answers on our substance?"

Julian shifted forward. "Downloading the data now. It's liberiam."

Andrei looked down at the data streaming on his screen.

"It's a mineral. Rare. Especially so near the Edge. We don't think it's found anywhere in Imperialist territory at all." Julian spoke with Vincenz at his shoulder.

"Obviously an ingredient in this device of theirs."

"That's what our scientists believe. They're working on it, reverse engineering to see what it might provide to a device like the portal collapsing one. Still working pretty much blind here."

If they could do that, at least a little bit, they might be able to figure out what the Imperialists were taking from Mirage and Parron.

"Status on other mercenary camps there?" Daniel appeared to be running three screens at once, and Andrei thanked the gods yet again that he didn't have to worry about any of the details and politics Daniel did. He'd far rather be out in the field than stuck in meeting after meeting all day, every day.

"The Imperium is having trouble getting their cargo moved. Most of the mercs here are refusing to run it. It does make it easier to work with them after I killed so many of their people. Piper warned them it would happen again if they tried a second time."

Julian paused, and on the split screen, Daniel's lips quivered a moment as he tried not to smile.

He would not ask.

"Lots of talk about this Piper lately." Julian's amusement would have been annoying if the mere sight of a smile on his face hadn't made Andrei's heart a little lighter.

"Lots of talk for him anyway. Which is five words, three of them being Piper." Vincenz smirked.

"So what's the news on Parron?"

"Nicely dodged. Next time I'm going to put Carina on. She'll get us answers." Daniel sat back in his chair.

Vincenz shuddered. "My sister united with Abbie would devastate any of Andrei's defenses."

"Moving right along. We're doing a run for them in the morning. I'll advise afterward."

Andrei severed the connection and scrubbed hands over his face.

Chapter 7

*F*ive days he'd been there. Days and nights he'd slept just next door. Right on the other side of the wall lay a man she'd loved for as long as she could remember.

Earlier that day, they'd been on the way back from a cargo run. Just something quick and not exceptionally lucrative. But necessary in any case.

He'd sat next to her in the small cockpit of the zipper and had calmly navigated. Utterly unflappable. Even Kenner got a little grouchy when she flew too fast. She liked that Andrei trusted her.

They'd made the run for the Imperialists. He'd checked the cargo, and it had been body armor. He'd had a grim face as he called in some information back to whoever he reported to. His face had given away nothing until they'd seen exactly what it was. A flash of anger had darkened his cheeks as he'd taken care to catalog every piece, and later he sent that information somewhere. She doubted the cargo would reach its final destination, which did make her feel better for dealing with the Imperialists in any way.

Even in the short time he'd been there he'd made himself indispensable at the compound. Eiriq had begun to gather the raw ingredients for the new cisterns. There would be three more. Digging and reinforcement of the trenches had started, and not a single person had complained about being assigned to the work crews. Andrei had taught Kenner and some of the others a quicker and better way to repair the engines of the conveyances and had, true to his word, begun to work with them on long-distance shooting and hand-to-hand combat.

When he left, they'd be better for him coming. Even if she'd hate having to go on jobs without him.

And, as she was just musing in her head and all, she really liked the way he'd been all manly and protective when they'd gone to negotiate their cargo runs. Earlier that day when they'd gone to collect their pay, one of the others had attempted to crowd her, intimidate her with his size.

Andrei's hand had shot out, grasping the big man's wrist and turning it until the lout was on his knees, red-faced and nearly in tears. He hadn't said a word during the entire incident, but the other man had kept his distance after that.

He'd packed the cargo into the zipper's hold and they'd left.

"I don't need protection." Not that she'd minded, of course. She always protected. It's what she did every moment of the day, and that small span of time when he'd protected her had been, well, like a little present.

"Don't need it, no." He gave her the coordinates, and she got moving. "Deserve it, yes."

Three days and the echo of that last sentence, the knowledge that he thought she deserved protection even while able to provide for herself, rang through her brain.

Five days and she'd begun to get used to having him around. Had begun to get used to the new Andrei, with his intense blue eyes and the quiet way he didn't miss a single detail. She found herself craving interaction with him. He didn't say much unless it needed to be said. Each conversation had been a shiny secret she'd tucked away. Each time she got near him, she found herself trying to engage him. Whenever he did, his focus turned to her totally as he spoke.

It drove her mad. Mad with longing. Mad with ridiculous sexual energy. Eleven years ago he'd been a handsome boy, filled with passion and emotion. He'd called to her as like to like. She couldn't lie to herself now that she'd wanted to fix him, wanted to soothe and calm him. Part of his allure had been that he'd laid aside his darkness when he was with her.

But this Andrei, this man, this breathtakingly handsome and sexy man wasn't alluring. He was mesmerizing. She realized with each passing moment that she'd never lost her craving for him. Andrei Solace wasn't going to leave there again, not without lying with her, not without telling her where the hells he'd been.

He'd given her scraps, and now she wanted more of the story. He'd given her the merest of kisses and a lot of secret, smoldering looks. She wanted more of him. Period.

Determined, she looked herself over in the mirror across the room. She shed one of her shirts, leaving on a semi-threadbare camisole and the soft, worn pants that she thought made her butt look pretty nice, too.

Two glasses and a bottle procured and dangling between her fingers, she headed to him.

* * *

$\mathcal{A}$ndrei stretched out on the now familiar bed and considered the problem. His cock. Since he'd first seen her, he'd constantly been hard. Twice, three times a day when he could find the time alone, he'd jerk off, imagining her cunt surrounding him, imagining her on her knees, looking up at him as she sucked his cock. Always her face, her body. Gods, the filthy things he wanted to do with her. To her. His hands shook with the effort to walk past her bedroom door each night and not stop.

Only to lie in bed, his fist around his cock, thrusting, sweating, dreaming of her and not having her.

It wasn't enough, and for the first time since he'd started Phantom Corps, he doubted his ability to resist temptation during an operation. The kiss two days before had ripped the restraint from him, had weakened his resolve. He knew her taste again, and his body, his mind and his cock wanted more.

He could seek his satisfaction with one of the numerous women he'd come across since he arrived, but it wouldn't have been enough. Worse, it would have disrespected her.

Yes, he'd loved the girl. Fiercely. Enough that he wasn't sure how she could ever forgive him for leaving her behind. For making her less safe than she'd been with him to protect her.

In the years since, he realized now, he'd compared every woman he'd fucked, every woman he'd flirted with or spoken to, to Piper. To the Piper of his memories.

But *this* Piper was a craving. A deep, aching need. This Piper was indelible in a way he hadn't truly understood until earlier that afternoon when she'd had her head tipped back, a laugh bursting from her juicy, luscious lips, her eyes dancing with amusement.

More than the kiss, this glimpse at the woman so few ever saw had humbled him.

It had been a good thing they'd been sitting or he may not have kept his feet. It slammed into him, the raw, bare truth of it. Their attraction was still a heavy, consuming thing. Only now they were older, and the sexual tension had ramped up so the air was thick with it any time the two of them were together.

She was a powerful woman. Independent. Fiery. Intelligent. Absurdly, ridiculously beautiful. Gods, the light on her skin. Kava with a bit of milk, nearly bronze. She mesmerized him. The way she moved with purpose and command. Her lips: seven hells, he looked at them as often as he could, thought about them more often than that. The dark gleam of her hair, the long, thick braids pulled back, exposing the grace of her face. Delicate. Such a contrast to her will, which was hard and implacable. Her breasts were sweet. A mouthwatering handful with pert, beautiful nipples he remembered the taste of still.

He'd been her navigator since he arrived. Had taken several trips a day with her out and about. Her scent lived in his senses. The way she sounded when she was delighted or angered. She was in charge. A wholly tough-assed bitch when she dealt with potential clients. That's what made him so hard when she went soft when she was with her family. The contrast in her—hard to soft, gentle to rough—no one but Piper could be so alluring simply by being exactly who she was.

He drew fingertips over his nipples, idly thinking about her. She never shut the fuck up either, which he thought he'd be annoyed by, but instead seemed to find charming. He sighed heavily and sat up, swinging his feet to the floor.

And a knock sounded on his door.

He knew it was her before he opened it.

Thank the gods he wasn't wrong. She stood there, holding up a bottle and some glasses. "Want some company?"

He should have said no. But there was no way he would have. He stepped back so she could pass.

"So." She placed the glasses on the bedside table and poured them both a few fingers of the amber liquid.

He took his glass and clicked it to hers before swallowing it down. A fiery trail led to his gut, but it also did the trick, easing his energy back a little. Though, as he took in the way she looked, he realized that was only temporary.

His cock thought the sight of her nipples through the thin material was just wonderful. The rest of him knew that his cock had entirely different motivations for wanting her so close.

She took another sip and shrugged when he sent her a raised brow. And then she settled down onto his bed as if he'd asked her to.

He stood for long moments, just looking at her, letting himself paint the portrait of her in his bed so he could draw it up any time he wanted to.

"I won't bite you, Andrei." She patted the bed beside where she sat.

That was too bad. He liked biting.

Attempting to appear cool and collected, he moved to sit beside her, trying not to breathe in too deeply and get a noseful of her, instantly regretting it because he hardened further.

"I'm here now, and you're going to tell me exactly where you've been the last eleven years. No, don't put that expression on. You're too handsome to spoil your face." She paused, looking at him intently, daring him to try skittering around the subject once again. "Eleven years. I worried. I cried. I thanked the gods each time a courier packet arrived, not only for the credits, but that it was a sign you were still out there, alive."

He was weak, damn it. Weak and tired, and she'd always gotten to him in ways no one else had.

"I know it must have been a shock when you got my note. I'm sorry. I had to go."

"Note? What note?"

"When I left with them, I gave a note to the jailer to be delivered to you and my sister."

Her eyes widened and then narrowed. "We never got the note. We assumed you'd been taken to a work camp. Or worse."

Andrei realized he'd simply disappeared without a word and how that must have been for her. "I apologize," he said simply. "I had no idea."

She shrugged. "He didn't die well." She clearly meant the jailer.

"Good."

"You said you're in the military. What happened? How did you end up on that path? You used to sneer at the corps." She turned, half-reclined, reaching to touch him. He had to close his eyes when she drew a strand of his hair between her fingertips and twirled it.

They'd had this level of comfort before. They used to sit on her bed, much like the one they were on right then, and talk for hours and hours. Now, though, now it was raw. And so good he was afraid of it.

"I've been in the military. They took me directly from here into training. I've been with them ever since."

She cocked her head, lying back against the pillow after she'd examined him closely. "Super secret stuff? I can tell you're no ordinary soldier." She closed her eyes a moment, and he wanted so

badly to lean in and brush his lips across hers. So badly he had to
fist his hands, pressing the nails into his palms.

"Something like that."

"Are you happy?"

"Sometimes."

"You used to talk a lot more." She grinned a moment, and before he knew what he was doing, he'd closed the gap and his lips
were on hers. She gasped, but then her arms were around his shoulders and she wasn't letting go.

Not that he was complaining about it as she pressed herself
against him, her mouth opening to what had started out as a brief
kiss. Her taste, the taste of a woman who could fly at full speed
through a narrow canyon without breaking a sweat, swirled through
him. Taking root with deep, indelible digs into his soul.

Her fingers wove through his hair, her breasts pressed against
his chest so hard her nipples burned against his skin.

He rolled on top of her. Her eyes opened but quickly went half-
lidded again. "Not that I'm arguing with this direction, but you
should keep in mind that I still want to hear about what you've
been doing since you left."

"*You* don't talk less than you used to."

Her smile was quick and infectious. "I have to fill the void for
you." She arched her neck to reach his mouth again, capturing his
lips in a quick kiss. Without a thought, he captured her bottom lip
as she began to retreat, holding it between his teeth and sliding his
tongue against the juicy swell in the center.

Her groan was dark and sweet, a puff of her breath against his
mouth. Enough to send the throb at his lap into a full-blown crash-
ing *boom, boom, boom.*

"I've been all over the Known Universes." He rested his fore-head against hers, trying to get his breath back.

"What's it like?"

He rolled to his side before he wasn't able to resist grinding himself into her. "It's beyond anything I ever imagined as a boy. Oceans, rivers, streams, lakes. Beaches. Tall mountains, grassy plains and miles of farmland. So much diversity I still haven't seen it all."

"And do you live on Ravena?"

He nodded.

"Alone?"

"I travel too much to have a pet."

She snorted a laugh and belatedly realized she'd been fishing to see if he was with anyone. He could tell her he was. She'd back off, being an honorable woman. Without the temptation she presented, he could finish the job without any entanglements.

"There's no one else," he found himself saying, instead.

Her smile was his reward, he supposed. "Good." She nipped his chin, and he realized he was setting a bad example to let her get this close.

Though he had no plans to make her stop.

"There's no one for me either. No one else, that is."

He shouldn't care. He should actually be happy that she had someone. But he was selfish, apparently. And petty, because it made him happy to know.

"Why did you leave? I understand your life, our life, was hard. I don't fault you for getting out. I just want to know why."

He swallowed hard. "They made me an offer." He shrugged. "It was a dead end here."

"Don't be flip about it."

Her voice was sharp, the fingers she'd threaded through his hair tightened and then she yanked. He growled, moving forward, his body against hers, pressing her back into the bedding. Instead of anger on her features, that slid away, revealing raw desire that tore at him.

"I'm sorry." He tipped his forehead to hers again. She wrapped her arms around him, holding him tight.

"All right. Andrei?" She looked into his eyes, her face, her mouth so very close to his.

"Yeah?"

"I'm glad you're here. I'm glad you're alive."

Anyone else in the Known Universes, and he'd have been able to bat it away with a cool response. But not her. Not Piper, because Piper got to him. Understood him even without having seen him for years.

He didn't trust words, so he kissed her.

Which, he thought as her lips met his and sent electric arcs through his system, was stupid. Her taste wended through him, owning him, marking him, making it impossible for him to do this with anyone else and not feel as if it were a sad parody.

Her tongue traced the seam of his lips, inciting him. Heat banked in his belly, turning his limbs to lead. There wasn't a single place in all of creation he wanted to be more than right there, right then.

Her mouth was hot, wet and sweet as she teased his tongue, sucking it, stroking the underside with the tip of hers.

It was only because his hands gripped the bedding so hard that he hadn't ripped her clothing from her body. Each time she arched against him it sent shock waves through his brain.

"Are you happy?" she repeated when he managed to drag his lips from hers.

He blinked to clear his head, and Piper couldn't stop her

laughter from bubbling up. "In your life, I mean. I *hope* you're happy right now. Part of you is anyway." She canted her hips forward, grinding herself against his hard-on.

"I'm good at what I do."

This was important to him. She could tell by the way he tipped his chin as he said it.

"What is it you do exactly?"

A hint of a smile flirted at the corner of his mouth, but he didn't give in.

"Come on, Andrei. You know I'll pester you until you tell me. Save us both the effort."

The right corner of his mouth quirked up briefly.

"I'll let you see my tits."

His amusement darkened into something else. Something raw and starkly sexual. Appraising.

That expression unsettled her. Reminded her she wasn't playing flirtation with some silly boy from town. The man she wrapped about like a wanton was dangerous. He was a predator as clearly as the day was long.

The intensity of their chemistry hummed between them. The playfully sexual nature of the moment melded into something headier, thicker. The humming between them became a throb, stealing her breath.

"You should go back to your room, Piper."

She paused, mulling over how to respond. All the while lost in his eyes. That pale blue had darkened with emotion.

"I'm not a universe traveler. I don't have fine clothes. But I know some things. I know what I feel. I know who I am, and I'm proud of that. I know my flaws. My weaknesses as well as my strengths. One thing I'm not is a liar. Least of all to myself.

"This thing between us is long past me leaving the room. I could. And we'd still want each other. A man like you? How often do not get what you want? Hm?"

He licked his lips, and her pussy spasmed. So much control. His muscles coiled as he lay against her. She moved in, her lips just against his. "I want you. You want me. This is going to happen."

She could sense all that power drawing within him, sense his ability to leash it, and his growing resistance to stopping her. "I'm not good for you."

She laughed. "Gods, you're right about that. You were trouble when we were young, and you sure as seven hells are now. But my pussy is wet for you. My nipples ache. I don't want to masturbate. Again. I want you. In me. I don't need you to be good for me. I just need you to be who you are."

He groaned. "This is a bad idea." He tried to pull away, but she stayed, her limbs holding him to her.

"I want your mouth on me."

He froze, and she realized he was as bent as she. "Do you now?" he murmured, the tension falling from him.

She nodded, her bravado slightly diminished as he looked at her with such raw appraisal.

He took her wrists, stretching her arms above her head, holding her in one of his hands. Tight, but shy of pain. She was where he wanted her, and that sent her heart beating wildly in her chest. She swallowed hard on a wave of pleasure at being restrained that way.

He pressed an openmouthed kiss to the side of her neck. A series of sharp nips of teeth and the flat of his tongue laving away the sting followed.

She struggled against his hold, and he pulled back to look into her face. She paused, fascinated by the way so much played over his face. He was usually so implacable, but just at that moment she saw the argument he had with himself.

It was important that he understand her struggles were play. She only knew she wanted him totally unleashed. She'd waited eleven years. Piper didn't want nice sedate four or five fuck sessions and then he would leave. She wanted all Andrei had to give, wanted him to trust her enough to let go.

"Give it to me, Andrei," she urged, rolling her hips. "I don't want you diluted. I won't break. Use me. Let me use you."

His eyes darkened as his lips parted.

"You don't know what you're asking for."

"Don't fucking insult me. I know exactly what I'm asking for. You like holding me like that. You like restraining me, being in charge. So what? I like it when you restrain me like that. I like it when you're in charge. I'm no virgin. You of all people should know that."

He pushed up, hopping from the bed to pace.

"I know you want to fuck me, Andrei. Your cock is hard. You kissed me first."

"I told you, I'm not good for you."

She got to her knees on the bed, peeled her shirt off and then shimmied from her pants and underthings. She waited, naked, unashamed of her body, especially when he looked at her with such raw longing it tugged at her belly.

"You've grown up. And so have I. What good will denying yourself do? I have no intention of you leaving Asphodel without having sex with me. At least once. I didn't survive this fucking place by being nice and taking no for an answer, and you know this better than most. I am offering myself to you, and you try to remain aloof. Am I unpleasant to look upon then?"

He scrubbed his hands over his face. "You're beautiful, Piper. You always have been. It's not that. I'm here on a job. It's an important job. I need to keep my focus."

"Right now?" She sat, back resting against the wall. And slowly drew her knees up, exposing herself to him. She'd never been this bold with anyone before. But he was Andrei. She wanted him, and if she didn't take some drastic action, he'd keep trying to make up reasons to be noble.

His gaze snagged on her hands as they slid over her knees and down her thighs, toward her pussy.

"I'm going to come. You can make it happen, or I will, but you can't expect me to walk out of here without it." She spread her pussy open to his gaze, delighted in the way his attention sharpened. Watched his control weaken. "What's it going to be?" Her breath hitched as she tapped on her clit a few times with the pad of her middle finger.

With a groan he was back, moving her hand out of the way, replacing it with his mouth.

Her taste shocked him. Memories rushed back, memories of the way she'd been, juxtaposed with the Piper of today. Bold. Sexually aggressive. Hot and sweet. Creamy and juicy. Her fingers wove through his hair and tugged, holding him in place.

He groaned again, his mouth open against her, his tongue flicking over her clit. Backing up, he pulled her with him, tugging her hips to bring her to the edge of the bed. On his knees there he could get to her better, brace himself as he pushed his face into her cunt, brushing his lips from side to side until her thighs began to tremble.

She was everything he tasted, smelled, saw, felt. In that moment she was utterly his, and that exploded through him, shaking him, cracking his resolve to keep his distance. Each time he had to make a hard choice, he found himself doing it with her in mind. How could he let himself touch her? See her? How could he let himself kiss her? And here he was, mouth on her cunt, submerged in her as much as he could be.

Knowing this was over the line. Knowing he should stop after he made her come. Knowing he should draw a halt to all this right then without another breath of her. But he wouldn't.

There were no excuses he could make to himself to allow for this with her. None. Nothing more than that he wanted it with a ferocity that caused him pain to resist. She was his greatest weakness and his greatest joy. He could not refuse her.

Wouldn't.

His fingers dug deep into the muscles of her hips. Above him she writhed, keeping as quiet as she could because others slept nearby. Knowing she wanted to scream out instead shook Andrei, sharpened the sensuality of what they shared just then.

And then his nails abraded her skin as he moved down to push her thighs open, exposing her totally to his gaze. So beautiful, he gentled, taking long licks through her, paying homage.

Teasing, he slid his fingertip around her gate over and over, getting a little deeper each time. She couldn't hold back her gasp when he added a second finger, curling his wrist to catch her sweet spot on each stroke.

Her fingers against his skull, urging and cradling all at once, he allowed her to move him upward again where he flicked that sensitive spot just beneath her clit as he sucked it in between his lips.

Her muscles tightened as her hips rocked. She whispered his name hoarsely as she came. And then he gave in and bit. Right on her thigh. High enough no one would have cause to see it unless she was naked.

A cry escaped her as his teeth sank into her skin. He pushed her right to the limit where pleasure had flowed into pain, but she held on through that burn, and it bloomed into a bone-deep near-orgasmic sensation.

She sighed through it, soaking it in as it flowed into her climax, extending it and leaving her a warm heap of satisfied woman.

He laved over the bite and picked her up gently, settling them both in his bed, beneath the blankets. Relief flooded her that he was making no attempt to leave or start making excuses for leaving or not doing this a few thousand times more.

"You still have your clothes on." She frowned once she had full control of her muscles again. Leaning on her elbow, she shook her head. "Rectify that at once, or I shall be very vexed."

The serious look on his face wisped away as his mouth curved up at the corner. Not wanting to resist, Piper dipped her head to draw the tip of her tongue there.

He turned his head then, meeting her lips with his own, and she rolled atop him, taking her time as she explored him. He tasted of her, but mixed with him, which made it alluring and taboo.

His lips called to be licked and nibbled so she did, while he caressed every part of her he could reach. Kneading, scoring lightly with his blunt nails, a tug and pinch of her left nipple.

Piper had been warm and relaxed after that orgasm, and now she began to burn for him again. She rolled off, trying to catch her breath. "Go on then." She winked and laughed when he snorted his response.

But he got up from the bed anyway and pulled his long-sleeved shirt from his body, exposing a torso that made her purr with delight. Lean muscle lay flat across his shoulders and down his arms. His chest was lightly dusted with inky-dark hair. He'd only had a little body hair before. A boy only barely entering manhood.

His belly was magnificent. She moved to sit so she could get a better look at him. Flat. Row after row of ridged muscle. And in the center, at his navel, a dark line of hair trailing down to where she knew his cock was.

"Wow." She looked him up and down, and every part of her sprang to life.

"A fine compliment, milady." He bowed theatrically, and it nearly made her swoon. More than that mind-altering climax he'd given her with his mouth, the way he'd just shown her a moment of whimsy was ridiculously flattering. As if he'd given her a compliment, which, she supposed, he had.

"What else have you got hiding in those trousers?" She looked at him, mock-stern.

His bark of laughter was rusty, as if he rarely did it. "Am I to worry over my virtue then?"

"Oh yes. Most assuredly." She nodded.

He shoved his pants down, along with his underwear, and it was a very close thing that Piper did not clap.

"Andrei Solace, what lovely treats you bring to my party."

Like the rest of him, his legs were long and lean, tightly muscled with thicker thighs, again with a light dusting of hair, and hard calves.

Piper moved from the bed, walking around him as he stood there, allowing it. Unable to resist, she unbound his hair, letting it wash over his shoulders and back and down to what had to be one of the finest asses in all of existence.

"You're the most beautiful man I've ever seen." She trailed around him again, taking his hand and drawing him back to bed.

"Such flattery to draw my pants away." He smiled at her, and she soaked it in.

"It worked." She laughed and scrambled astride his body, rubbing herself over his cock.

"Indeed." He rolled them so that he was on top, teasing her with his cock as he pinned her. And again, she found her hands over her head as he held them tight in a firm but gentle grip. This time there was no hesitation in him when she struggled.

Piper found herself outrageously wet as he teased her with his cock. He nibbled down the line of her neck and across her collarbone, pausing to lick and kiss the hollow of her throat. His free hand moved to her nipple, where he worked some sort of magic with the way he rolled it between his thumb and forefinger, twisting and pulling it just exactly right. Keeping that edge.

"What is it you said you wanted?" he murmured, kissing the underside of her jaw, still teasing her with the head of his cock. Just barely entering her before sliding it up and over her clit and then back to her gate again.

"You know what I want." She managed not to pant, but it was a close thing.

"Yes. Do you know what I want?"

Oh. Gods, she nearly came when he brushed his cock against her again, just from the realization. He wanted her to beg for it, meant to tease her and then make her beg. It shouldn't make her hot. It shouldn't make her whimper.

But it did.

"Please put your cock inside me. Please fuck me."

And he was slowly pushing into her as he let go of her wrists and angled himself to his haunches. He grabbed her ankles and pushed them up and then slid that iron grip up to her knees to spread her wide, her ass resting on his thighs as he began to thrust.

Her position allowed for little movement; he controlled the entire process, and she couldn't seem to get enough. He was overwhelmingly sexy this way. Dominant and aggressive. Taking what he wanted from her. And yet the way he touched her, looked at her, only made her feel beautiful and sensual.

"I want to see your fingers on your clit," he murmured, though it was quite clearly an order.

She walked them down her belly, impressed with the way he'd changed his strokes to add a swivel of his hips. Each time he pressed all the way inside he hit all new bundles of nerves, lighting her up in an entirely different and no less effective way.

All the while he looked at her, looked at her body as if she was something altogether precious and mesmerizing. No one but he had ever looked at her that way. There was a sense, right then as she slid a fingertip around her clit and he watched with hungry eyes, of coming home, of completing some long quest and having this as her reward for all her struggles.

"Not yet." He spoke as she began to grasp hold of the edges of another orgasm. She backed off a little and tightened herself around him, earning herself a raised brow. But he sped a little, thrusting harder so that the frame of the bed began a small groan on every third thrust.

"Please."

He leaned down to kiss her quickly and kept his pace, bent over her a little more so that he restrained her with his body. What should have felt, what *would* have felt claustrophobic with another man, felt only exciting with him.

There was only pleasure and anticipation as he took her closer and closer, as his breathing began to lose its steady rhythm and she knew he was getting close.

"Now."

It only took two circles around her clit before she exploded into orgasm. He snarled a curse, and deep inside her, she felt the jerk of his cock as he came as well. She arched with a too-loud moan when he bit the side of her breast and again, that edge, hurtling toward pain, wading in and the bloom of velvet pleasure when she came out the other side.

He rolled to the side to keep from crushing her.

"There's a lot to be said about whatever you've been up to that has trained you for this."

He snorted again, and she kissed his chin.

"I hope you don't think I'm going back to my room now. I'm sure half the house heard the bed groaning anyway. I'm here for the night."

"As if there was any doubt you'd do what you wanted anyway."

"I'm glad to know you still understand me so well." She snuggled into him.

Chapter 8

"After we finish this run I need to make a quick transmission."

Piper didn't take her gaze from the screen in front of her as she flew low and fast to avoid detection. "Where do I need to take you?"

"I can go alone."

"I'm sure you can. But I'm right here and we'll be out already, so why do triple the work unless you think I'm going to eavesdrop and tattle."

He heaved a heavy sigh. Piper was unmanageable. She did not stay put when he told her to, and she didn't mind him at all.

"I know you're over there thinking about how I never obey you."

He groaned under his breath, and she laughed.

"I would like to take this opportunity to remind you that when it is important, I do obey you. Didn't I let you punch that idiot Targon in the face when he grabbed my ass back there?"

He had, and while he should feel bad for the lapse in his self-control, he did not. The man had no business touching Piper anywhere at any time.

"I think *let* is not exactly the correct term. In any case, the less you know about what I'm up to, the safer you are. Period. You may take me to the transmission spot, but I will make the transmission without an audience, and not because I think you'll tattle."

She hit the reverse thrusters hard, yanking them to a stop and then carefully lifted the zipper from the canyon floor near the mercenary portal they'd used to run the cargo.

"Uh-oh," she mumbled, right as Andrei saw them. A conveyance with far too many men in it. "Are those Imperialist soldiers?" Andrei liked the outrage in her voice.

"Yes. Stay out of range and set down on that plateau to the south. I'd like to keep the upper hand here."

"I think I've kept out of sight a few times. I may be able to manage it."

He nearly grinned at her, instead taking her comm pad and fiddling, finding their channel and inside he went utterly cold at what he heard.

They spoke the language native to Caelinus. Skorpios. There in a Federation 'Verse. They spoke openly on an unsecured channel. A boast that they could do whatever they wanted.

She set the zipper down with ease and utter silence. He barely had the chance to be impressed though, as he picked up bits and pieces.

He took his field glasses and the comm, recording the conversation, which he also transmitted back to his people. Vincenz would decode it quickly enough.

Why out there so far? Nowhere near any portals he knew about, private and the sanctioned one in town. The conveyance easily seated a dozen men, and they carried some sort of cargo. Probably the liberiam they'd mined.

"Do you know what they're saying? I haven't heard this language before."

He didn't startle, not entirely surprised that she'd crept up behind the place in the rocky outcropping where he'd set up a watch on the action below.

They couldn't be allowed to move that cargo.

He went back to the zipper and pulled a panel free to get at the bag just beyond.

"I want you to take the zipper and get back to the compound immediately." He didn't take his attention from the plas-rocket launcher he put together, piece by piece, from the bag.

"Let me call for backup. You can't handle them all on your own."

He simply looked at her until she snorted. "Not even you can do that!"

"I can do all sorts of things. If I'm not back by moonrise, dial this contact." He handed the comm back. "I used it to send the conversation, but I've downloaded the data to my comm now as well."

"You're out of your mind!"

"Piper, those men down there have a substance that could power the machine I told you about. I cannot allow that to happen. They're no ordinary troops, they're Skorpios. Fardelle's private shock troops. And they have no reason to be here."

"I'm not arguing with your response. I'm saying you need me to watch your back, and I'm going to. I know how to load one of these. Don't ask." She grinned when he sent a questioning glance her way. "Let me help you. Do you think I want them here either? This is my home."

By the time he put the plas-rocket launcher together and set it to charge, the answer had come back from Daniel to Andrei's request to neutralize the threat. *You are go.*

He wanted very much for her to leave, but he knew she wouldn't. At least if he kept her close he might be able to shield her pretty ass in case things went upside down.

"If you get hurt, I will let your brothers kick your ass, because they're not blaming me for your inability to know what is best."

"Well, thank the gods for that. Being a silly woman and all, however would I know what to do unless one of you told me?" She clicked the barrel into place after it charged fully. It shouldn't make him want to take her to the dirt and fuck her, but the easy way she had with whatever task was before her really turned him on.

"When I fire, use the confusion to take out as many as you can. They *will* regroup. We need to kill as many of them as we can with the first strike." He examined her features carefully, gauging her response, but she nodded, checking her weapon over and moving into a better position.

He didn't use the finder to lock the target. He had better aim if he followed his gut, which he did. A long breath out, emptying his head of everything but the target and the slow squeeze of the trigger.

Below them, chaos broke out as the plas-burst hit the conveyance, sending shards of glass and metal into the air.

While he waited for it to charge again, he reached for his sniper rifle and began to target those who were left.

Piper tried to remain focused on the scene in the basin, but it was a close thing, given how ridiculously sexy Andrei was just then.

Protective. Fierce as he concentrated on targeting. The burst hit the mark perfectly, and she began to shoot. Squeeze after squeeze, like he'd shown her just the day before.

It only took them a short period of time before the remaining soldiers had taken cover behind the burned-out hulk of the conveyance and had begun to return fire.

"Hold a moment."

She took cover as he messed with his comm pad. "I'm going to hit them again from over there." He indicated another outcropping precariously higher than they were.

She wanted so badly to tell him he was totally out of his mind. But he knew his job, obviously, so she tried not to appear anything less than 100 percent in support of his ridiculous plan.

"I need suppressive fire. Can you do that?"

She nodded, picking her weapon up again. "I'll head over there." She pointed in the opposite direction and scrambled over, careful not to kick up any dust to identify their position.

Below them was bloody, smoking chaos, and she aimed at it and fired over and over, hoping the diversion would help him get into position.

Her question about his situation was answered as another plas-rocket hit the group below. She kept shooting, trying to think of her people as she did. Trying to think of the people who needed her to be strong and steadfast in this war. They were on her turf, her 'Verse, and they wanted to destroy it.

Within minutes, they were all gone. Andrei came down from his perch, very carefully, she happily noted.

"Are you all right?" He looked her over carefully, his face set in that inscrutable mask of his.

"Better than they are. Shall I fly us down there to be sure they're all dead?"

"I'll handle that part. Keep the zipper up here. We don't need the connection between you and them in any way. Go back to the compound. I'll join you when I finish."

"This again? I'm good enough to shoot at them, but not to help you with the rest?"

He took her upper arms, hauling her to his chest. The mask was gone, replaced with so much depth of emotion it rocked her into stunned silence. "Have I ever given you a reason to believe that?"

She shook her head because words wouldn't come.

"You need no part of that down there. I will do it." He pressed a kiss to her forehead and let go as if burned, only to head down into the bloody, smoky mess below.

It hit her then, as she stood watch through the scope on the weapon, protecting him, that he was doing the same. Protecting her.

He counted each one. Made sure they were dead, those who weren't would be within a breath. If they hadn't caught them by surprise, he was sure their victory would have been a far closer thing.

Andrei dispassionately recorded the scene, or what was left of it. Daniel spoke from the mic in Andrei's ear as he relayed the data via his comm. "A dozen Skorpios. On our soil. Bold, isn't it?"

Andrei thought the same. "Shows a certain . . . confidence on their part. Now, why is that, do you think?"

"Dispose of that garbage. Get me some samples and let's see what Vincenz can make of them."

"The run we made earlier had more body armor. I used the slow-acting powder." The powder was a little something Benni had brought him only the day before. When used in a closed container, it would eat away at the contents, leaving nothing behind but dust.

"Andrei," Daniel hesitated a moment, "things are rapidly declining. What else do they have there?"

Andrei managed to dig the comm chip from the melted console. "Chip looks moderately damaged but salvageable."

"Vincenz can crack it in no time. I want you to take care of this mine. Can you do that?"

"Yes. I'll get the chip to Vincenz."

"Take it personally. I don't trust anyone else to do it."

Unexpectedly, he balked at the very idea of leaving again. Not of leaving Asphodel, that was happily at his back once he got on a transport. But of leaving *her*.

"Understood."

He signed off and headed back up to where she actually waited with her weapon trained on the scene below.

"I need to do a few things. I have to borrow the zipper. I'll return it later." He began to disassemble the rocket launcher and stuffed it back into the bag. He'd need to clean it more thoroughly.

He'd deal with the issue of getting off-'Verse later. Right then he needed to get her back to the compound and get back out here to clean up. May as well take the bodies out into the caldera. No one would find anything left out there. Storms danced all day long in the caldera.

She got into the cab and fired the engines up. "No one flies this but me."

He sighed. "Fine. I'll hire one in town."

"Why would you do that when I am right here?" She flew right down to the scene below, and he cringed inwardly. "We need to get rid of the bodies, right?" She laughed. "What, you thought I didn't get that?" She hopped out, tossing him an extra pair of gloves.

"Just stay in the cockpit."

She grabbed a fistful of his hair and yanked. "Hey! Why don't you try listening to me for a change?"

He showed her his teeth, and her eyes widened briefly.

And then, being Piper, she showed her teeth right back. "There he is. I was wondering if that part of you had been sliced out altogether or whether you just hid it well."

Spinning to deal with the dead was easier than having this discussion. "Look around the site to find anything we may have missed. Clothing, shoes, whatever may have been blown off. Leave the body parts to me."

"This might work with the other women you deal with. But I'm not like them." Which was true, of course, but holy matrons of heaven, this was not pretty to look upon.

"No one knows that more than me." He continued to wrap the bodies and drag them into the cargo hold, where he'd begun to stack them like bloody tinder.

"Do you think I'm too fragile to see this? Growing up here?" She found a boot with a foot still inside and tried not to gag.

"Do not think of them as people or you'll get sick. And this is not what we grew up seeing." He motioned at the carnage. "But if we don't stop it, it could be what the next generation does."

"Which is why I care to help you. I can handle it."

He growled, and she realized the only way he'd part with his precious words was if she pushed him so hard he lost control. She wasn't sure why that had escaped her until that moment. After all, she was a master at needling her brothers into a response.

"One really needs to wonder," she tossed another shoe into the hold, "what sort of women you consort with."

He must do this sort of thing on a fairly routine basis. His manner was automatic and efficient. Wrapping, tossing, moving back to do the same. How he managed to keep totally clean while doing it she had no idea. Probably because the blood was too scared to dare land on his body.

"What shall we do about the conveyance? From the air, it'll be visible, and while this isn't a very well-traveled road, it does get flyovers from the polis and some of my compatriots."

"I have no munitions with me, but they did." He jerked his head at a partially melted ammunition box he'd pulled free of the rubble. "I'll improvise a solution."

She noted the crystallized dust on the windscreen. "What is that? What were they carrying?"

He paused and then, as if he'd given himself permission to speak, did so. "An ingredient in the device they're building to destroy portals. They're mining it here."

She froze. "We have to stop that!"

He turned to face her again, stripping his gloves off and tossing them into the cargo hold with the bodies.

"I do. Yes."

"It's past that *I do* bullshit, Andrei. We. We. We. I am here. You're sleeping in my house. After last night you're sleeping in my bed. This is not yours anymore. It involves me and my 'Verse. My family and friends. It involves you, and because of that, it involves me, too. So. What are we planning to do to stop it?"

He heaved a long, long sigh as he got to his knees and wrested the lid of the ammo box open.

"This is my job, Piper. It's what I'm trained to do. I'm good at it. You have been a great deal of help so far, but there's no reason to involve you in every single aspect of my mission. They will not take another load from that mine. I will see to it."

She watched, fascinated, as he began to pull things apart and wire them back together. "Handy." She indicated the mass he held on his lap.

"Yes. Get in the zipper and get the thrusters up."

"Caldera?"

He nodded, his attention elsewhere.

She closed the cargo doors and hopped into the cockpit, firing the thrusters and setting her course for the outer edge of the caldera. Once they arrived she could eyeball it, see where it was safest to fly in.

"Let's go. We won't be safe here in less than a standard minute." He strapped in and leaned back, opening up the nav tray and checking over her course as she picked them up and got the seven hells away.

Her mental countdown was underlined by the sound and shockwave of a very large explosion in their wake.

"Won't there still be debris?"

"They had liquid fire grenades."

"I thought they were banned after Varhana."

"Your shock and surprise that Fardelle and his animals would use such horrible weapons only makes my point that this is not business you should be involved in. It was stupid of me to involve you." He closed his mouth, as if surprised he spoke at all.

"This is tedious. You're determined to see me as incapable of doing things."

"I think you're too good to have to see the . . . outcome of what I do."

Oh. "Well. Thank you. Sort of. You're totally wrong, of course."

He kept his head down, ignoring her, and she allowed it as they were in the middle of something, after all. But she'd revisit this topic very soon.

"The fire will destroy everything then?"

"Yes. They were meant to destroy metal. The Imperialists will send a crew out to find them, and there will be nothing left but a burn mark."

"You want them to know the conveyance was intercepted?"

"Yes. I want them to know someone will kill every last one of them he finds. Head due east. Skirt Mandaball Peaks." He examined the radar. "We should be able to drop these bodies and get gone. Landing will be tricky, though." He tapped his chin as he thought it over.

"I can hold her in place for two or three minutes. Pop open the cargo doors. Strap yourself in with a harness and push them out. There's a mass just north of here. Storm rising, and it'll sweep through this way. Problem solved."

He shrugged as he eased from the seat and headed back into the hold.

Five minutes later and the problem had been solved, and she was heading away from the storm as quickly as she could.

Chapter 9

"You need to head back to the compound. Nightfall will be a better time to seek out the Wastelands."

Piper glanced over his way, watching the way his fingers flew over the keypad, readjusting the map and the coordinates to take into account the weather patterns.

"That's where the mine is? Makes sense no one has said much about it. How can they move all this, what did you call it?"

"Liberiam. I'm told it's a rare mineral and not found anywhere in the Imperium."

"Suppose that's why they're here. How do you know the location?"

He simply looked at her with one eyebrow up, and she snorted. "Sneaky."

"Yes. I'm going to tell you to stay in the zipper, and I mean it this time. I have to travel some ways on foot into territory that is inherently dangerous. This is my operation." He held up a hand to stay her. "I make the decisions here, and if you don't like it, take me back to the compound, and I'll get my own way out here."

"I don't understand why you won't let me help."

"You are helping. Right now you're taking us back to the compound like I asked you. Otherwise, you don't need to. This isn't a debate where you need to prove your side or I need to prove mine. Just let me be in charge for this one thing."

She narrowed her eyes and rode out a gust of wind that sent the monitors and readouts skittering and blinking out until she got them through the other side.

The zipper landed easily enough once they arrived back home and he sprang out. "I'll clean this up."

Kenner strolled out to meet them both. "What have you been up to?" He looked Piper up and down, noting the smudges and dirty spots. Andrei, of course, appeared to not even have gotten a single wrinkle.

"You should tell him." Piper tipped her chin toward her brother.

"I should get this cleaned up is what I should do." He gathered supplies and returned shortly with a bucket of sand, good for cleaning, and some brushes.

Kenner's eyes widened, but he moved to pitch in, scrubbing the dried-up blood and other debris from their earlier cargo. "Someone needs to tell me what the seven hells is happening here."

"Kenner, they're here and running a mineral to use in their machine."

Andrei sent her a look, but didn't interrupt her story.

"And this is the remains of that problem? Good."

"There's more. We're heading out to fix that part later."

"No. *I* am heading out later to fix that part." Andrei straightened. "For now I plan to get cleaned up and see what's in the kitchen."

"He took on an entire squad. He was . . . he was magnificent, and he thinks he's a villain. I hate that." Piper and her brother watched him walk away.

"We'll help him. He says he doesn't need any. And hells, doesn't look much like he does. But he's our family and this is our 'Verse. We can't not help."

She grinned. "I knew there was a reason I loved you."

Kenner paused, putting a hand on her arm, just briefly. "Aren't you worried?"

"About what? Danger? In case you haven't noticed, we're up to our necks in it. This way I can get some of my own back."

Her brother sighed, a familiar, put-upon sound that never failed to make her smile. "No. I mean, well, it looks like you're getting attached to him again. What happens when he leaves? Have you thought about that? I can see it on your face. You can't afford to love him, Piper."

She had thought about it. A great deal. "If and when he does, I'll survive. What can I do other than love him?" It seemed so clear to her. "He needs that. Needs me."

"He's a big boy. He does just fine on his own."

But that wasn't it at all. Sure he did just fine on his own. But it was the "on his own" part that got to her so deeply. As far as she could tell, he let very few people close, and even fewer close enough to watch his back.

"Who does he have, Kenner? He has us. He has me, and I like it that way." She gave herself to him freely and without expectation of whatever he'd do in return. Did she want him to stay or work a way to be with her? Yes. But love wasn't about what you got from the other person. It was about what you gave. And because he never asked anything, it only made her love him more.

Her brother took a deep breath and nodded. "All right. If he breaks your heart, I'll have to beat him. After he is asleep, or we drug him or something." He quirked a grin and kissed her cheek before ducking away.

*A*ndrei allowed himself the luxury of a shower that lasted longer than three minutes. They'd refilled the cistern earlier that day so there was enough for it. The death wouldn't wash away, but he'd gladly take it on to keep her safe. To get rid of this threat to his people.

The door opened, and he sighed. Shilo again, he wagered. "Someone is in here."

"I know."

Not Shilo at all.

"I'll be out in a moment."

She walked into the space, naked and beautiful, and every single resolution he'd made to keep away from her fell right from his head.

"You look even better wet. Turn around so I can get your back."

He obeyed, even as he knew what a horrible idea it was to let her get away with this sort of thing.

Ha! Let. As if he had any choice.

And even if he had, he wouldn't have stopped her hands now kneading his shoulders and back.

"You're not a villain, you know."

He snorted, turning the water tap back on and letting it sluice over his head and body. Warmed by the sun, the water felt good against his muscles.

"I'm flying you out to the Wastelands. Period. Kenner wants to help as well, and I know Taryn will. This is ours. *You're* ours. Mine most especially." She pressed herself to his back, hugging him from behind.

Warmth settled in his belly, and he hadn't the strength to resist.

"Come back to my room. Be with me before meal time." She climbed out and handed him one of the robes hanging nearby.

Why he allowed it, he wished he couldn't say. But it was that he didn't want to refuse her. Even knowing he was not good enough, he still wanted. Wanted her so badly his hands shook from it.

The small room smelled of her, and he took a deep breath, pausing a moment to take the space in. It had its own kind of femininity. Despite the rifle in the corner and the scuffed work boots under a nearby desk, there were bits and bobs strewn here and there. A shiny necklace, a bright scarf, a tie for her hair. Her bed was large and not slept in.

They'd slept in his bed the night before, and he'd laid there when he first woke up, breathing her in where she lived on his sheets.

Here it wasn't a wisp of her scent; her scent lived in the air, wrapped around his senses and squeezed to get his attention.

She dropped the robe. "I think I need some recharging. Can you help me with that?" Her mouth—Gods, her mouth—curved into a half smile. A knowing smile a woman wears when she knows the man she's smiling at will be inside her shortly.

Two steps and he was on her, his mouth descending to meet

hers, taking it in a kiss of possession. He wanted to mark her in every possible way.

When it was really the other way around. She'd marked him for most of his life, and it was still there. Her fingerprints on his very soul. Nothing had changed, but everything had changed in ways he didn't know if there was a way around.

But for that moment, for those stolen moments between them, it didn't matter, because she was his and he hers. Naked to the bone.

He tried to hold back, but it was useless to try. His desire swelled, bursting through him until it was everything and drowned him.

Her back met the wall, her arms around his neck and her legs about his waist. Skin to skin, the heat of her was a fever. He eagerly swallowed her surprised breath as he continued to kiss her. The sounds she made deep in her throat drove him mad for her. Made the blinding, crippling desire for her crawl over his skin, marching onward until he gave in.

His teeth caught her bottom lip as he spread her a little wider. She hooked her ankles at his back and suddenly, her cunt engulfed his cock, welcoming him in a tight, hot embrace so good he had to pause or come right that second.

She writhed, trying to get more, and he pushed her back, his body against hers enough to keep her in place. Instead of being horrified, her wide-eyed gaze went half-mast, glossy with need. "Yes. Take whatever you need from me, Andrei."

Her words settled in his mouth as he licked over the curve of her bottom lip and he groaned, pulling out nice and slow, only to reverse and push back in as deeply as he could. Her nails dug into the muscle of his shoulders. Pinpricks of pleasure/pain like hot sparks.

"Tell me, Andrei. Give me your words." Her voice was laced with pleasure and something else. Whatever it was, it stoked his own response, his own pleasure, and yes, he accepted what they had, what they once were and what she had always been to him.

"So good." He kissed the hollow below her ear. She tasted like tears. In that place where heartache and great joy can sometimes slide against the other. He stroked his chest against hers, her nipples hard points against his skin, bumping over his nipples in the bargain. He gasped, and she tightened around him.

"Your pussy is so fucking hot and wet. Perfect."

Her upper back rested against the wall, rough-hewn enough to scrape just a little. Enough to remind her of the intensity of the moment as his cock filled her and left her empty in turns again and again until she writhed to get more, until she could no longer hold back the words.

"Please. Gods, Andrei, please." She moved her head from side to side, hissing when he scraped his teeth over her collarbone, right at the place where it met the hollow of her throat.

"Please what?"

Oh he was so arrogant! With reason, no doubt about it. He used every part of himself against her. His weight to pin her hips in place, his hands, fingers digging into the muscle of her thighs and ass to hold her up. His cock fucking into her pussy, driving her mad with desire.

"I need to come. I want you to come in me."

"You first." He adjusted his hold, the tips of his fingers brushing against her labia, only adding more friction. He pushed her together, sealing her around his cock, and it was only a breath until the first tendrils of climax had begun to latch on, dragging her hip deep into it.

His openmouthed kisses were hot and sensual, the heat of his mouth a brand against her skin.

"Go on." She panted. "Bite me. You know you want to, and I'm offering myself."

His groan was laced with anguish, threaded with desire and need. And his teeth played against her shoulder, where they met her skin. Anticipation flooded her, sent her reeling headlong into climax. And then he bit, his teeth sinking into the muscle, and still she felt the fine tremble as he kept himself in check.

She rode it, let it take over, sing through her veins as she came around his cock, knowing he felt it. Knowing it only made the experience better for him. "Yes. Gods. Yes."

She didn't care how loud she was. Didn't care about anything but how he felt. How he was, naked to her right then as he lifted his head and locked gazes with her. In that moment he was vulnerable, and it made her feel like she could do anything for that trust. Anything to see him this way again. Unguarded and open. Something she knew he rarely, if ever showed anyone else.

She wanted to writhe. Wanted to swivel, but he held her exactly how he wanted as he fucked into her body. Held her in place as he thrust over and over again. He bent his knees, digging into her body in fierce, deep presses until his head fell forward onto her shoulder and he came with a groan.

A groan of her name.

He slid to the ground, keeping her on top as he lay on the floor. When she sat upright, she looked down on him and sighed happily. He opened his eyes, a smirk on his lips.

"You look awfully satisfied with yourself." She shouldn't let him get away with his outrageous behavior. But, to be honest with herself, she loved it. Loved the way he acted. Perhaps it was those

moments when he eased up and let her in, gave her a few words or
a smile. Whatever it was, she was utterly charmed by it.

"I was about to say it was you who sounded satisfied." He lazily
traced the outline of the bite mark. That sensation shot straight to
her clit. "Did I hurt you?"

The arrogance slid away, worry in his gaze. She couldn't help
but laugh; this tough man worried a love bite had harmed her. A
man who'd taken out an entire squad of Skorpios. She found it
wildly flattering.

She dipped her head, kissing his mouth and then his chin. "Yes,
it hurt a little. At first. Then"—she licked her lips, trying to find the
right words for him—"then the pain melts away and there's this
white-hot wash of pleasure. I loved it." She touched the one on her
inner thigh. "This one, too. I like it that you've marked me." Glad
for the way her skin color hid blushes, she ducked her face, and he
caught it, easing her back to face him.

"I like that, too."

She grinned. "Oh. Well, good." Tipping her chin, she indicated
the other rooms beyond her closed door. "I think, perhaps, our
cover is blown." She was loud enough to have let the entire household know they were fucking. Thank the heavens the children were
all still in school.

When he moved to stand, she watched, as always, awed by his
grace and the strength of his bunched muscles. She took the hand
he held for her and let him haul her to stand next to him. "Are you
concerned? I don't wish to cause you difficulty."

A laugh bubbled through her as she hugged him. "The only
difficulty is that nearly every woman in the compound and a few
men want what I've got. And they can't have it, because I don't
share."

"I guessed that about you. I have to clean up the launcher and get some things in place for my work later this evening."

She cocked her head, narrowing her gaze at him.

"Fine. Our work. But it still has to be done."

"The basin is right behind you. Clean up a little and go on out. The evening meal is cooking. Lune's stew is one of my favorites. Don't be late, or you'll have to eat bread and fruit while everyone else has second helpings."

She made no secret of looking at his backside as he washed his face and hands before skirting next door to get his clothes on, robe clutched around himself.

"Well, then." Taryn looked her up and down when she sidled up to the counter and began to clean the vegetables they'd serve with dinner. Taryn made a delicious sauce to go with them. Pungent and tart with herbs and oils.

"Well then what?" She tried not to smile at Lune, but the other woman's wink did her in.

"Are you all right?"

"Taryn, he didn't break me. He'd never hurt me. It's not like that."

Her brother snorted a laugh. "That falls into the far more information than a brother needs to know category. I meant the outing. Kenner told me there'd been a spot of trouble."

She put her hands over her face momentarily, feeling the heat of her embarrassment against her palms. "Yes, there was. He handled it. Pretty much single-handedly. Everything is fine. Well, not the big picture everything. That is not fine at all. But today, here and now, everything is fine."

Taryn sighed. "Piper . . . don't get attached again. He's got a job to do. He won't be staying. Even if he wanted to, things are dire, and he has big responsibilities."

At least she knew Kenner hadn't run to him to tell Taryn all about their earlier conversation. Quickly, and very briefly, she told him the same thing she'd said to Kenner.

She could fight it and make grand statements about how she knew it was short-lived and she was just having great sex with an old lover. But it was more. She knew it, and it seemed disrespectful of them both to claim otherwise.

He listened, patiently, as he worked and finally hugged her, one-armed, before turning back to what he was doing. "All right. I just want you to be happy."

"I love you, Taryn. Have I told you that lately?" She looked up, and up some more. Her older brother had been her father since their own father had died shortly after their first winter on Asphodel. He favored their father. His skin nearly ebony, his eyes big and brown, hair in the short knots like their father had worn.

"But butt out? Was that the next part?" he teased.

"Not at all. Thank you for taking over after Dai was gone. For struggling to keep us fed and clothed. For being the father of us all here. There's nothing here, no one who hasn't been touched by something you've done for them. I admire you. I'm proud of you. I don't say it enough. I appreciate your concern about my heart. But the truth of it is I love him. Never stopped most likely, and here he is as an adult and I am, too, and he's even more than he was then. If he leaves, I will still love him, because that's who I am, and how can I regret even a week or two with him when before I had nothing but far-off memories?"

He blinked his eyes a few times, bending to haul some more vegetables to the table where she worked. "Thank you for that."

"He doesn't think he's a good man."

"What do you think?"

"I know he is. He's back here and protecting us all. Today, you should have seen him. Fierce. There was no way those Imperial soldiers were going to get away with being here and trying to harm us. He simply was not going to let that happen. I've never seen anything like it."

"I can't lie and tell you it doesn't concern me. That I don't worry for your safety. But he protects you. I've seen it. I can be happy with that."

She needed more than his body between hers and danger. But she could certainly appreciate that nonetheless. It was his mind and his heart she was more interested in. Wanted more.

"I think he's a good man, too." And with that, Taryn left the kitchen, whistling, leaving her alone with her thoughts.

Chapter 10

They hiked from the place where they'd left the zipper. He hadn't wanted to risk being discovered or the zipper being damaged. So she'd left it on the edge of the Wastelands in the shadow of the cliffs, and they were currently moving at a fast clip toward the mine.

Andrei was impressed with the way she easily kept up with him as they took a fairly brutal pace.

They couldn't speak and risk being detected by any possible portable listening stations. The constant wind meant their footfalls would not be heard. She'd done everything he asked, except stay back at the compound. He'd tried again, telling her to wait with the zipper, and she'd ignored him totally, swinging out of the zipper's cockpit and sliding her goggles and the sand mask into place over her nose and mouth.

Good thing he already wore his so she wouldn't see his annoyance.

He fell into the run, his footsteps pounding the sand below. They had a few hours, maximum, before a storm came up, and that didn't take into account the very real fact that random storms happened all the time out here, which was why it was pretty much deserted. Still, there had been a smattering of the low, curved abodes the settlers had lived in out this way. They dug into the rock foundation below the sand, keeping the abode in place in heavy winds. Still, it had to be a fairly hair-raising experience with the winds and sand trying to get inside to slice a body to pieces.

As they ran he planned his trip to Mirage. It would be better to just go without word. Cleaner. He'd come back most likely, at least to be sure they were all safe. But he thought of her face as she'd told him how it had felt when he'd gone without a word eleven years before, and he knew he wouldn't be able to do it to her again. It wouldn't be right. Her whole family had been good to him. Had helped him with this mission, and it wouldn't be fair.

So he'd tell them all right before he left for the Portal. That would work.

She tapped on his door, impatient, but set on her goals.

"We don't need to leave for some time yet," he murmured when he answered.

"I know. Come with me." She held out a hand. "Bring everything we'll need for the run. We'll leave directly from where I'm taking you."

He narrowed his gaze a moment.

"Trust me."

He snorted but reached down to grab his duffel with his free hand. The other remained in hers.

Expertly, she flew past the closer canyons and toward the caldera. When she reached the spot, she landed on an outcropping she'd have been nervous about only a few years before.

"Nice flying."

She didn't hide her smile at his compliment. "Thanks. Took me about a thousand tries to get it right. But it's worth it. Follow me, and watch your step."

The blast of heat wore away as she drew him through the narrow, sloped passage. And the dry was replaced by moist air. She broke some glow sticks and tossed them near the water to reflect the light.

"Pools?"

So very glad she'd brought him, she nodded. "Fed by underground springs. The saline is high here, so it's easy to float. The dark blue ones just beyond"—she indicated three small pools to the southern end of the cavernous space—"are cool."

She began to strip, leaving her things in a neat, folded pile. "Brought some drying cloths. These here"—she dipped a toe into the nearest pool—"are warm. Not too warm. Just right."

When she turned to face him, she found him partially unclothed, his gaze snagged on her body.

Flattered, she smiled and moved to him, making quick work of getting him all the way naked.

Andrei couldn't say why, not totally, but emotion flooded him when he saw the space. Water bubbled slowly up, seeping into the pools, lending a tranquil air. All his worries ebbed, and he grasped this moment. Just the two of them.

He watched her as she stepped into the largest pool. Everything in his body tightened at her groan of delight. Even more when her breasts floated so prettily.

"I'm liking the high saline in the water right about now," he murmured as he swam lazily toward her.

Her laugh was easy as she came to him, her arms around him, lips pressed against his throat.

"Do you like the pools?"

He ducked under the water, kissing a trail up her belly and neck. "Yes."

Laughing, she swam away, flipping to her back in a most alluring fashion. "I'm glad. I found this place a few years ago. Got caught out in a storm, and I needed the cover of the canyon. It's my secret place."

He smiled, swimming after her like a predator. "Thank you for sharing it with me."

She splashed him, scooting just out of his reach, teasing. "There's a story. About your hair. You said something about not cutting it unless you had to. Your face says more to me than you do with words. There's something there. I want to know it. Will you share it with me?"

He paused, and she moved past him, a phantom touch of her fingertips against his shoulder. "I want to know you. Fill in those spaces in my head."

What else could he do but give her what she'd asked for so honestly? "In my first year, during training for Phantom Corps, I got into a lot of fights. Stupid, insignificant stuff I wouldn't blink at today. But I wasn't the same then."

He'd been nearly feral. Away from everything he knew. At first he trusted no one. Then slowly he'd built a kinship with Daniel. A bond he felt to that very day.

"All of us, all the operatives in Phantom Corps come from tumultuous backgrounds. We lacked discipline. Lacked self-respect." He did a backstroke, trying to pretend it wasn't a problem to tell this story.

"I got into one too many brawls." An understatement. He'd nearly killed another trainee. The boy, now one of the few people Andrei could always count on to get his back, had nearly lost an eye.

She never said a word, just treaded water, moving her gaze with him as he continued to swim.

"My punishment was to tend to the soldier I'd wounded." He'd gone to his barracks every day, three times a day, to help administer medications and to change the bandages. Had seen, firsthand, just how much damage could be done with his fists. Every day, over and over, he was confronted with the hurt he'd caused.

"Ellis had been off-'Verse at the time. He called me to his office." His gut clenched at the memory of Wilhelm's face, so full of disappointment. That had shaken Andrei more than anything else. He wanted Ellis's respect, and he'd only earned his disdain.

"He said I had too much pride for all the wrong reasons." Said Andrei had no self-respect or understanding of how teamwork could save a life. "My hair was part of it. So he had it shaved off."

She gasped, unable to stop herself. She knew he didn't want pity, but it was there in her belly. What would it have been like for him so far from everything he knew? Cutting all his glorious hair would have left him utterly exposed, body and sprit.

"Don't. I deserved it." He flipped to his back, cradling her against him as he swam them to the ledge.

"And you grew it all back to prove you could have both." And, she'd wager, the first step he'd taken to controlling his anger.

The hands he'd had roving all over her body paused a brief moment. His way of agreeing with what she said, she imagined.

"Love me," she murmured as she turned to face him.

He swam them over to the shallows, his palms sliding over every part of her he could reach. The silk of the water created delicious friction. Weightless and caressed, she let him carry her, gave herself to him, willingly going wherever he wanted.

Slow and sexy, he glided around to face her once her feet touched the smooth rocks. He kissed each eyelid, over the bridge of her nose, across her cheeks. Feather-light touches that echoed through her like an earthquake.

He devastated with tenderness, surprising her when she'd expected ferocity. He had a way of doing that. Of sneaking past her expectations and touching her when she least anticipated it.

The pad of her thumb brushed over his lips, against the soft bristle of the scruff on his face. "What a glorious sight you are, your hair slicked back away from your face." He turned his face into her hand, first kissing and then catching her thumb between his teeth, licking and then sucking.

An echo tugged at her nipples, around her clit, and she took a deep breath, relaxing in the warmth around them, letting herself give over fully to this moment between them.

He dipped just a bit, licking across her collarbone. "I just had you a few hours ago."

Her head fell back as she let herself float, boneless. "I'm always happy to be had again, you know."

Instead of speaking, he let his hands and mouth do the work. A tug of teeth on a nipple peeking just above the waterline. The tease of fingertips along the seam of her labia and then a tickle against her clit.

He drew her to the farthest end of the shallows, so that she rested on her back, reclining on rocks warmed by the water. Only her calves and fingertips remained immersed.

Taking her foot in his hands, he kneaded her instep, giving a hot, openmouthed kiss at her arch and then just behind her anklebone. So tender it brought a strangled sigh from her lips. Gentle, but firm hands continued to massage up each leg, his thumbs sliding along the place where thigh met body.

Such a tease.

She loved every moment of it. Every bit of time they could steal, just the two of them like this, sharing and growing, was a gift. A secret side of him she was thrilled to be shown. Made her feel special to be part of it.

His finger made a swirl around her gate, just barely dipping inside. "Tender?" He bent his head, reverent, to place a kiss on her belly, just below her navel.

"I want you."

He laughed, the sound tight with need. "You'll get yours, greedy girl."

Tugging on his hair, she brought his gaze to hers, searing her to her bones. "I want all of you."

He settled between her thighs, kissing up her belly and to her nipples, teasing the already stiff nipples to throbbing.

She couldn't tear her gaze from the flash of his teeth as he nipped the sides of her breasts and then back down her belly, settling between her thighs long enough to take a nice leisurely lick.

"So much talent." She sighed happily as he licked and sucked, his tongue, teeth and lips all working in concert to blow her apart.

His knuckles brushed against her rear passage just right, with just enough pressure to spark her nerve endings, the water barely lapping against it. But when he dipped his mouth to her, his tongue replacing his knuckles, she nearly hit the rocky ceiling above them.

The shock of not only how naughty it felt, but the pleasure he brought with it, made her stomach muscles tremble as she gasped.

His fingers fucked into her cunt as he licked at her rear passage. So much she nearly came until he held back and made his way to her clit again. Over and over until she was senseless, needing so badly to come, and yet never wanting this delicious tension to end.

When he pushed her over, her clit between his lips, two fingers hooked and stroking against her sweet spot, it was a long groan of his name.

"Gods," she managed to say around her tongue, "that was some of your best work. What next?" She used her elbow to prop herself up to see him properly. He flipped around, like an ocean creature, swimming out, submerging and coming right back to her after a nibble of her toes.

"Next, I do believe I'm going to fuck these and come on you." He said this as he heaped her breasts together, sliding a thumb over her nipples.

He straddled her body as she held her breasts for him to slide his cock between. He made a sound, a grunt, a growl, an entreaty. Whatever it was, all that it was exploded, sending shards of the need to please him all through her system.

Each time he thrust all the way, she managed to lick the head and crown of his cock.

Such a bounty to look at she wished she had brought more glow sticks. His muscles and the wet strands of his hair stood in shadow, his features cast in the blue-green glow.

Above her he was a demigod. Strong. His thigh muscles bunched against her sides as he fucked the fleshy space she'd made for him.

Though if it had been bright or they'd been anywhere else, it wouldn't feel so very intimate. Just a place for them alone.

She licked across his cock again, tasting the spice of his semen. Knowing he was close, even after they'd been together at her house, knowing he'd have her again when the situation presented itself. This knowing, the power of it, humbled her even as it titillated.

"So fucking good to see my cock between your tits. Your nipples so hard." He nearly stuttered the last bit and pushed hard, his hands on hers to hold her breasts tight.

When he came, his head didn't fall back; instead, his half-closed eyes snapped open, gaze locked on hers. She saw it come over him, the exact moment when desire took over, glossing and blurring the sharp warrior's eyes, and orgasm held tight.

He pulled back, fisting his cock, coming on her breasts. The heat of each pulse of his seed sliding over her nipples and chest was a shock and yet ridiculously arousing.

After running his fingers through it, teasing her nipples for a few moments, he pulled her back into the water.

"Let's get cleaned up and try the cool water next."

She smiled, throwing her arms around him.

Two hours later, they finally approached the rise, beyond which the open pit mine lay. He slowed down and used a hand signal to get her to do the same. Crouching behind an outcropping of rocks, he pulled out his field glasses and surveyed the area. Three guard towers to the east. Stupid to only guard one side, but they must have figured only crazy people would come from the direction they came.

He urged her to stay, and she shook her head. He made the same hand gesture again, and she sent him one of her own back, indicating her refusal to keep her ass in place. With a growl, he pointed off in the distance and used a finger to indicate the guard towers.

She shrugged and pulled her weapon out.

Damn it.

He had no choice other than to let her accompany him or knock her out and leave her there. He knew the latter would be better, but again, she got under his skin, and he couldn't do it.

They crawled, pausing and moving again every few minutes. From the top of the rise, he noted the lack of guards on patrol around the pit and shook his head. Lazy security. He'd keep cautious, because one never knew what could be thrown at an intruder. What he needed was video and measurements. He used the cameras and the special geographic plotting device to note the space. The moon was up, casting plenty of light on the pit.

Rolling close to her, he removed his mask and spoke quietly in her ear. "I need to go down there to get samples and to see what sort of surplus they have. I need to do that alone. Don't argue with me, or I'll knock you out and leave you up here behind those rocks. I won't take you. You can get my back from up here. Use your head. Only shoot if it's dire. I can talk my way out of most trouble."

She growled quietly but nodded. Relief flooded as he made his way silently down the hillside.

Piper was in awe of how he worked. He made no sound at all as he moved. Not a single speck of dust rose as he made his way down to the pit. How that was possible when the daily facts of life in Asphodel meant dust and sand blowing around all the time, she didn't know. But he did it. He would pause and look, waiting. And then begin to move again.

Her heart stuttered a few times as someone would move in the area below. She prayed fervently that he not be discovered. And then they'd move on, and Andrei would continue to crouch and get closer.

She thought the trip down was bad, but she was not prepared for the long, pulse-pounding minutes he was down there, among the stacks of containers and the crew still working the mine. He had a way of easing through, avoiding any contact. He didn't stalk or walk; he flowed.

Through the field glasses she watched as he took video and grabbed samples, putting them in the bag at his waist.

And then there was movement as four guards began to sweep the area. Did they know Andrei was there? She switched from the field glasses to the scope on her weapon. She'd kill every last one of them if she had to, to protect Andrei. Did he do this alone all the time? How could they send him out without backup? It seemed criminal of these people in the Federation.

Her heart beat wildly as they continued to search and Andrei simply eased past, around them, as they looked. From her perch, it was nearly magical as he did it. As if he had some sort of second-sight to know which way they'd turn.

And finally, he began to skirt the edges of the pit area and make his way back to her. But it seemed so very exposed. She took very shallow breaths as she watched his progress. He seemed in no hurry, which enabled her to relax a little, but it was still nerve-racking the way any of them might have seen him and killed him on sight.

When he finally rolled over the lip of the rise, she grabbed him, holding on tight. He hesitated a moment, and then returned the embrace.

"We have to run hard to get back. They know something is up. I used a jammer so their surveillance video won't have worked the whole time I was down there. But now they'll be on higher alert. I want out of here before they figure out I was there."

He handed her a piece of the protein cake they'd snacked on before and some water before they got down the rise and hit the sand below at a full run.

Even at a full run, she knew they wouldn't make it to the zipper. The wind had risen. A storm was on the way and headed toward them.

She took his arm and jerked her head toward the abode they'd seen earlier. In the desert, the rules were different. A traveler wouldn't be denied shelter in the storm. It was life-or-death out there.

She didn't need for his face to be uncovered to know he frowned, but he had to have scented the storm, too, and they headed toward shelter. She'd covered the zipper well, tying it down, and she hoped it would be enough. But she'd deal with that later. For now it was about getting the hell out of the open for safety from the weather and from detection.

At the front doors, Andrei stepped in front of her. He pounded, pulling his goggles up and the mask off so the inhabitants would see they posed no threat. But no one came, even after he pounded a second and third time.

Without waiting any longer, he fiddled with the seals and locks until the doors opened, and he went first, looking right to left. She closed and resealed the door, waiting in the dim for him to deal with whatever he needed to.

"Hello? Is anyone here? We were caught out in the storm." Andrei walked around the small one-room space, noting the lack of human activity for some time. He pulled some jammers from his pockets, though he doubted he'd need them. Out there the storms were heavily laced with ambient electricity, knocking out listening posts and other tech.

"I think they've abandoned the place."

"Don't move. I want to be sure there are no traps before we get too comfortable." He checked cabinets and drawers. Most were empty, though there was enough food to get them through if they got stranded longer than a few hours and some water in the tanks that appeared to be potable. "All right. Looks like we're in for the duration. No one is going to be coming back any time soon, and those Imperialist soldiers would have turned back long before now. Make yourself comfortable."

He tossed himself into a seat at the table and tried to get a message out to Daniel, but the storm was disrupting the signal too much. "Comm traffic is down."

The storm outside took shape and began to slap at the exterior of the abode, and the walls trembled. He'd checked the seals and the anchors to hold the place together when they'd first entered, so he was fairly sure they'd be in one piece when the storm let up. Still, he hated having her out here in this, exposed, should the Imperialists find them.

"You're bouncing your knee. Haven't seen that in a very long time." She shook out the bedding, using her pack as a pillow. "Are we going to be all right? Should I be worried?"

"I'd never let anything happen to you. I'd die before I allowed that."

She sighed with a small laugh. "You try so hard to remain aloof, but then you say that, there's no way to not be affected. When you show me so much care, you move me, Andrei. No matter how hard you try, the connection between us is there."

"Don't. I'm not that man, Piper. Don't romanticize what I am."
He broke out a map and pored over it.

She rolled her eyes. "I know exactly what man you are. I don't
have to know exactly what your job description is to understand
what you are. I know you so much better than you assume."

"I'm a killer. Gods know, you've seen it enough since I arrived.
You'll do well not to forget that."

Interesting. She cringed when she heard the emotion in his
voice and wondered how it was he could blame himself or see what
he did as anything but heroic.

"Do you think I could see what is happening out there and
judge your response negatively? When you kill someone who is
trying to destroy the lives of hundreds of millions of people, *you're*
not the bad guy. The person trying to kill all those people is the
villain. Seems to me someone has to slap them down, or they'd
keep coming. And then what? Who will protect them if you don't?
Hmm? I heard, oh, I think a few turns before you showed up, that
some Imperialists were trading humans again. Slavery. We eradi-
cated that after Varhana, and they're bringing it back. That is das-
tardly. Your response is not."

He turned to her, all his focus on her face. "What?"

"You're painting yourself as a horrible person when it's not you."

He made a cutting motion with his hand, impatience on his
features. "Not that. Slavery?"

"One of the merc pilots from the Frontier said he'd heard rumors
the Imperium had a slave auction. He'd been asked to run human
cargo, he imagined, for that purpose. He told them to fuck off."

"Did you report it to anyone?"

"Who am I going to tell, Andrei? Who would believe the likes of him or me? I don't know anyone high up." She cocked her head. "Well, didn't know I did. And now I do. I'm sorry I hadn't mentioned it before. I only remembered part of that now."

He sighed heavily, and she ached to fix it. Ached to share his burden. "I'm not going to tell anyone if you want to talk about this stuff. Sometimes you need to unload when it gets too heavy."

He closed his eyes, just briefly. "When we get back, I have to leave."

She sprang from the bed. "Why?"

"They've got a full-blown operation here. I set some explosive packs, but there were crews working inside, Federation citizens, and I won't risk them if I can help it. So I have to figure out a way to get them to evacuate, and then I'll blow it. I need to get the samples and the data chip I found in the conveyance earlier to my people in Mirage. I can't trust anyone else to get it there."

"Will you be back?"

"Of course. If only to say good-bye."

"Bullshit. I'm coming along." She put her hands on her hips and glared his way. "Don't waste your time arguing. I am coming, and you can't stop me. It'll be easier if you just agree up front and we can avoid the trouble."

"Trouble is right. From your toes to the top of your head, you're made entirely of trouble. It isn't safe for you. I'm trying to protect you, and it makes it a lot harder when you insist on throwing your pretty little ass into the thick of it over and over." He scrubbed his hands over his face.

She stalked over and knelt before him, removing his hands, holding them in her own. "You think my ass is pretty?"

He snorted. "Leave it to you to grab on to that one."

"We have something. You can pretend you don't think so, but it's insulting for you to do so. A mockery of what we share."

"Perhaps if this was a different time and place . . ."

"Oh fuck you, Andrei Solace. It isn't another time and place. It's right now, and you are here with me. You have been inside my body. You've saved my life multiple times. You've taught my people how to fix things and how to defend themselves. Do you think you can come here, give and give and no one will notice?"

"Gods damn it!" He pushed to stand and pace. "What have you seen that makes you moon over me so? Was it the way I sent pulse rockets into a conveyance, killing everyone inside? Or how about the way I snapped a few necks the other day? All those head shots maybe? Oh, I know, it must have been the stench of burning flesh."

She watched him as he moved, listened and heard the anguish and guilt in his voice, and it broke her heart. "Why do you think I'd see those things and judge you as anything but someone defending innocent people? I live on that line between law and not, in the place where I make comfortable excuses for my behavior. I run cargo. Illegal cargo. Sometimes into the Imperium. I understand the place where nothing is clear, nothing is black and white. I live in the gray, Andrei. I understand you because you do, too. I love you because you exist in the gray and are still a hero." She stood and pushed past his outstretched palms. This had gone on long enough.

"I've put you in danger just by being here."

"Of course. Because I wasn't in danger at all out here near the Edge with Imperialist soldiers bent on destroying Portals and killing everyone in sight. So what other horrible things have you done? You weren't nice to the elderly a few times? Did you break the velocity

limits when you came out here? Oh, I know, you sent three containers of books to the children in my compound because you had an
evil ulterior motive of some sort."

"I'm not the boy you loved."

"Of course you aren't. Not entirely. Who is the same person
they were at nineteen?" She snuggled into his body, and he remained stiff, but she continued to hold on. "You've changed, but not
in the way you seem to think. You've changed for the better. The
Andrei of your youth reacted. You spent every waking moment surviving, and it pissed you off. How many fights have you been in over
your life? I bet the huge majority of them were before you turned
twenty-five. So, no, you're not the boy I loved. You're the man I
love, who used to be the boy I loved. He's still in there. Sometimes
I catch a glimpse of him. A flash of anger. And you've managed not
to break anything. You haven't hit any walls. You haven't been
hauled off to lockup the entire time."

"I get in bigger fights than barroom dustups pretty much every
day. It's sort of my job. Anyway, you can't love me."

"Men are so silly sometimes." She kissed his neck, and his spine
lost its rigidity as his hands moved to her waist. She didn't hide her
smile as she kissed just below his chin and then to the other side of
his neck, under his ear where she knew he liked it most. "I can do
lots of things. Loving you is merely one of them, though one of the
most important."

He growled, and she laughed, stepping back and giving him a
good hard shove toward the bed.

"What are you doing?"

"Good gods, what do you think?" Reaching out toward him, she
grabbed his cock through his pants and squeezed.

He shuddered, in a good way, she was pleased to note.

"I love you, and I will get your back whether you like it or not. So let's just agree to let me do whatever I want."

One-handed, he unbuckled and unzipped her pants, shoving them down, hobbling her. "How about I agree to make you come instead?"

He flipped, using his leg to hook around her and topple her backward.

"I can definitely agree to that. In addition to the other."

"Gods, don't you ever just quietly agree with anything?"

Delighted, she laughed and then moaned when he shoved her shirt up and licked over her nipples. "You can always put something in my mouth to keep me quiet."

His eyes darkened as one brow slid upward.

"Yes, that's what I mean."

He unzipped and pulled his cock free. Her gaze was frozen on the way he fisted himself a few times, smearing the bead of come all over the head. She licked her lips, swallowing hard, imagining how it would feel when he finally let her at it.

"All right then. Suck my cock, Piper."

She managed to kick her pants off and crawl to him, pushing him to his back and scrambling atop his body to look down and wonder at his beauty. His belly called, and she gave in, kissing over the flat muscle, licking the hollow at his hip after she shoved the pants open.

"Easy, take it all."

She wanted to rub all over him like a cat when he talked that way.

Eager to please, eager to bring pleasure, she took him deep, breathing through her nose. He urged her closer, not more than she could take, but right at that edge. She paused to swallow, and he let go.

Pulling off, Piper looked up into his face. "No. I want all of it. If you go too far, I'll tell you."

He took a deep breath. His mouth quirked up at one corner. "Fine. Get back to it then."

She did, licking up the long line of him, cupping his balls in her palm as she angled his cock with her other hand to keep him just right. She sucked. She licked and even nibbled, taking her cues from the way he sounded, from the pressure of his hands urging her onward.

Andrei was delicious in so many ways. Swirling her tongue over the head, she sucked slow and hard down, over the crown, deeper and deeper as his nails dug into her shoulders.

Winning emotion, words and deeds from this man who never wasted any of those things, turned her on beyond bearing. Each time she took him all the way down, her clit got squeezed by her movements, labia pressed against the swollen, slippery knot, giving friction. Not enough. Enough to bring a tremble in her knees, enough to know she'd be begging him only too soon.

He snarled and arched up, pressing deep, so deep her eyes watered as he came. She took every bit of him, everything he gave her, his essence filling every part of her senses.

She pulled off, locking her gaze with his, licking her lips.

He'd been so lazy there as he recovered she hadn't expected the way he sprang up and pounced. She found herself on her back, her shirt buttons flying everywhere and a hungry mouth on her nipple.

His need for her was fierce, a full-blown grass fire though his system. Heating, blinding, bringing nothing but need and a drive to fill it. To bring her pleasure. To drown himself in her taste and feel.

He nipped her velvety skin, laving the sting. He gave her love bites, reveling in her surprised cry and the way it wisped into a moan. And finally he reached her pussy. Pressing his face against her mound, he breathed her in, pulling her pants all the way down and off.

The wind picked up, the sand against the outer walls like the harshest of caresses, a roar of white noise. He lost himself in it as he settled between her thighs and spread her labia wide.

More.

He licked through her, tasting every fold, every slick dip and curve. Her geography, the map of her intrigued him. He teased and tantalized as she dug her fingers in his hair, tugging. He liked that, too. Liked the way she boldly grabbed her pleasure from him. Demanded he give it the way she liked it.

Bold was his Piper. Bold and brave and beautiful.

Shoving the rush of emotion away, he pushed her, mouth on her pussy, tongue rimming her gate. A bit more and she'd beg. A breath over her clit, the lightest touch of his tongue. She moved restlessly against him, rolling her hips to get more contact.

And he'd happily give it to her. Once she asked for it.

Her groan vibrated through her body, her breath catching when he gave her clit a little more attention. And then he brushed his knuckles through her cunt, twisting his wrist a little, placing pressure over her gate and then down again, over her rear passage.

This time her moan was ragged, hesitant at first, and then she relaxed again, widening her thighs. He'd take her there, too. Before he left and she went back to her life without him, he'd bury himself in her ass.

"Please, pleasepleaseplease, Andrei, make me come. I can't take it anymore." Her words slurred, her breath stuttered. He opened his eyes and found her looking down at him, bottom lip caught between her teeth, skin aglow with sweat and exertion.

He gave her what she so prettily asked for, sliding two fingers into her cunt as he sucked her clit between his lips and pressed ever so gently.

She sucked in a sharp breath, her body leaving the bed as she arched into his face, hips rolling as he fucked her with his fingers while she came in a hot rush.

One last kiss and lick, and he pressed another to her belly as he got to his knees, helping her get her pants back in place.

She said nothing, only put her palm to his cheek. An act of such aching tenderness his heart seemed to expand. Only she got to him like this.

They puttered around each other, neither wanting to disturb the peace that had settled between them. He listened to the storm outside as it raged on. He thought of taking a risk and making her tea, but he wasn't entirely sure if they could trust the foodstuffs there or even the water. Chances were, it was fine, and if they were stuck there much longer, he'd consider it.

Instead, he made sure she ate some more of the protein cake, knowing she'd need the energy and the boost to her health. His legs were a little sore, so he was sure hers would be as well. Her strides were shorter, so she'd had to put more power into her run than he had.

At last, the wind died down, and he broke the seal carefully. "Stay here. I want to check to be sure we're clear, and then we need to get out of here and back to the zipper." He hoped it was still there and in one piece in the wake of the storm. If not, they faced a great deal more walking and running to get close enough for them to call for a ride.

"I'll tidy up and get ready. Be careful."

Outside the abode all was still and utterly quiet. The storm still raged off in the distance, in the direction of the mine, and he hoped it kept them grounded long enough for him and Piper to make their escape.

She waited at the door, weapon in her hands, and pride burst through him. He'd seen his share of strong-willed women. His best friend had married one, and the man's sister, another strong-willed female, was married to the most powerful man in all the Known Universes. And yet Andrei knew both women, though tough as pikes, were not trained as warriors, not trained to deal with the harsh realities of life out here near the Edge as Piper had been.

Tough, ball-busting bitch was what she was. Unapologetic about it. He loved that.

"Can you run?"

"Yes, but I'm going to expect a lot more orgasms for this, because my legs will surely fall off."

They took off after resealing the door and leaving some credits for the shelter. And ran.

Chapter 11

"I'm going away with Andrei. He says we should be back shortly." Piper announced it as if the two of them had decided together. Andrei's brows drew together, and Taryn looked to him and shook his head.

"Should we be worried?"

"She's your sister. If I were you, I'd be worrying all day long, every day. Why don't you tell her to stay here? I've been telling her exactly that for hours, and she won't listen to me."

She looked over her shoulder at him. He packed things into his bag, already having secreted the data chip on his person and the samples in different places between the bag and his body. He'd done this in his room while she wasn't looking. If she'd known, he knew she'd have insisted on helping and carrying some of it herself.

"You've met my sister. Does it look to you like anyone tells her anything?" Kenner shrugged.

"Stop talking about me as if I am not here. I made my mind up, and that is that. Anyway, Andrei, Kenner and Taryn know I love you. My place is with you. At your side. Getting your back. I can't believe they'd send you out on such a dangerous mission all alone." She shook her head, and Taryn groaned.

Andrei reined in his smile at her moxie. The woman was a law unto herself. Intractable. He should not be amused by it, damn it. She was a handful, and now she was his handful. Then again, he'd have her to himself a little while, and what harm could there be in that?

Taryn was made of sterner stuff as he attempted to rein her in. "Piper, leave it be. I'm sure Andrei is quite capable of doing this on his own. It's his job. You should stay here. We need you."

"Don't try to make me feel guilty. It won't work. And weren't you just telling me a few turns ago how much I needed to go off-'Verse for a holiday? Well, here you go."

"This isn't a holiday, Piper." Andrei hefted his bag onto his shoulder.

"Of course it isn't. Which makes it even more important that I go with you. What if you get lonely?"

Kenner snickered, and Andrei gave a long, put-upon sigh.

"Let's just quit it. She's not going to do what she doesn't want to. She's made her mind up." Kenner shrugged. "Andrei will keep her safe, and you know she'll do the same for him. We can manage without her." He looked back to Andrei. "What do we need to know while you're gone?"

"Listen to me carefully. Those soldiers are Fardelle's most dangerous. They will stop at nothing if they think you're getting in their business. Stay away from them if you see them in town. Tell them the zipper is broken down." Andrei held up a part. "This disrupter will take a while to order a replacement for. If they ask, this is why you can't do any runs for them. Don't try any of this on your own. We'll be back as soon as we can." He paused. "In your personal comms I've placed a special contact. You'll know what it is when and if you need it. The people on the other end will get to you as soon as possible to help." Andrei sighed. "There will be an evacuation and then a very loud explosion. Be sure to keep as far away from town as you can."

He held a hand out to Piper and opened the door with his other hand.

She kissed and hugged each brother and grabbed her bag from him. "I can carry this. I'm not useless."

She loved the Portal. It was, without a doubt, the finest thing in Asphodel. That she had access to, anyway. The Portal itself stood, ringed by loading platforms for arrivals and the lower set for departures. Carts were being guided along the baggage and freight corridors.

Below, as the town spread out at the foot, were food hawkers and stalls selling every ware imaginable.

She'd been off-'Verse many times as she ran cargo, but had only used the official Portal three times in her life. Once when they'd arrived from Earth after three months' travel. She couldn't remember any of it, having been less than three years old. The next time had been when they'd traveled to Borran to check in for military corps training. She'd been assigned right back to Asphodel shortly after their basic training had been completed. The last had been a trip to Sanctu for a joining ceremony of some friends she'd met running cargo.

This was different. She was traveling with Andrei, who kept a protective arm around her at all times. With her man, she'd travel in the sleek private transport tethered just ahead of where they'd climbed the blue departure deck. She'd never been in this part of the complex before. It was one with lots of security, far more than the norm. He showed his papers only once. Whatever they'd been, no one even asked for hers.

She held her tongue as he led her through the area, weaving around the crowds, and she marveled, not for the first time, at the way he moved with a grace she'd never seen in anyone else. He was magic when he moved like this. Flowing through the place as if it were natural to move with such silence and stealth all while in open view. She supposed it was an asset to his job.

The captain met them at the docking doors. "We will be leaving shortly. There's some sort of problem out in the Wastelands, I hear. Just caught via comm traffic that there'd been a massive storm and damage to some operation out that way." He shrugged. "Never knew they did anything out there these days."

Andrei guided her past, his hand at the small of her back. "Interesting."

Crew showed up and began to unlock the tethers holding the transport in place. "Get settled then. We'll be on our way momentarily."

The transport was as fine as the Portal to her eyes. Public transports were more stripped down, but this was not so at all.

Sumptuous fabrics covered lush seating areas as they made their way to the staterooms.

And when he opened the door and motioned her inside, she stood, still beyond impressed with the lodgings.

He locked the door and dropped his bag. "Sit down. We'll be shifting soon toward the Portal and get moving."

The flutter in her belly was partly due to that but mainly due to him. To his presence so very near.

True to the captain's word, they were under way and sliding through the Portal not too very long after she'd settled on the bed, her stocking feet up.

"I'll order some food and drink once we get the green light." He moved through the room, looking at everything. Running scans.

"Aren't these people on our side? Why do we need to look for listening devices?"

"I trust very few people. Least of all total strangers." He continued to work, and she continued to watch.

"Where did you learn to move like that?"

He finished, putting the scanner away and settled at the small table, bending to remove his boots. "Like what?"

"You . . . I don't know how to describe it really, but you're sort of a shadow. All these people all around you, and you glide through them like water or a wind. They don't even see you, and you're right there! When we were . . . out last night, there were four men looking for you. They walked right past you as if you weren't there. I don't remember you having that before."

He shrugged.

"Do you need to imbibe a great deal of liquor before you say more than four words at a time? Or, your cock in my mouth?"

Oh, she loved the way he paused and straightened, his gaze locked on her like a hungry predator.

"I don't know where it came from."

"Did they train you to do that?"

"They trained in surveillance and the avoidance of detection. Stealth is necessary for what I do."

"But with you, it's more. Isn't it?"

He licked his lips. "It's something I'm good at, yes."

"What do you think when you do it? Is it something you do on purpose?"

His smile was quick and bright and gone within moments. Piper loved his smile, loved evoking emotion from him.

"What? I'm curious, Andrei. I want to know. You left as this boy, barely a man, who had so much anger. Always moving. And you came back thoughtful, accomplished and with this amazing capacity to do all the things you've done. I'm . . . I'm amazed by you."

How could he resist it? "I don't think about anything. I just turn it all over to my instincts. If I think on it, I stumble. I let the white noise swallow me up, and I flow through it. My gut understands exactly where I should step, how I should move and when. I give myself to that."

Her eyes lit, and he didn't regret sharing.

"You're a gifted pilot. Did you ever consider staying in the corps?" He changed the subject as he keyed in an order for refreshments and sent a coded message to Julian, letting him know they were on the way and that the mine had had an explosion. He'd fill them in when they arrived. He hesitated and then added that he wasn't traveling alone. Better to not let her presence be a surprise.

"Not really. It was very—I enjoyed the things I learned, but

that life wasn't for me. And they couldn't guarantee I'd get an assignment as a pilot. Without that, why not go back home to my
life and my family? The skills were transferable." Her grin was
quick and beautiful.

"Forever? I'm not judging what you do, so get that look off your
mouth, it's too lovely for you to mar it with that grimace."

She relaxed, looking quite satisfied.

He found himself saying things he hadn't intended to around her
a lot. She did things to him, made him want to please her and make
her happy.

She shrugged. "It keeps us fed. Keeps the power working and
our people clothed. Not a lot of options out here, you know. I tried
to get hired on as a pilot for the Portals, but the wait list is years
long. I'm still on it."

He'd look into that, because running cargo might be lucrative,
but it would be increasingly difficult to do as this thing between
the Federation and the Imperialists was heating up and travel would
be restricted. It had already started, and it would only continue to get
worse. He didn't want her caught up in any raids or other nonsense.

She deserved a life free from want. Free from strife. He'd spent
a lot of time—years of his life—doing the right thing, putting by for
that time when he'd need the power and credits he'd accumulated.
Now was that time, and he meant to use it to make her life better.

"We should arrive in half a day's time."

He leaned back in the chair, trying not to think about taking her
again. And failing.

"Do they know I'm coming with you?" Her voice was so casual
he suspected her instantly. There was nothing casual about Piper
Roundtree. She was up to something.

"I sent them notice of that, yes."

"How did you describe me?" She fluttered her lashes, and he groaned.

"I should have told them you were a beautiful pain in the ass. They know I'm working with you. They know you have some details about what we're doing."

"Beautiful? Do you think I am?" Her face held no teasing, and though he could have made light and the hurt would have given her some distance from him, he hadn't the will to intentionally harm her.

"Yes."

She smiled, satisfied and totally female. "Good. Now, tell me about them. Or is this a top secret thing, and I'll have to wear a blindfold and be taken to a hidden facility with retinal and DNA scans? Will I have to take an oath?" She didn't bother hiding her amusement, and he rolled his eyes.

However, a blindfold, well now, that was an alluring idea. Had merit. He tucked it away for the moment.

"They'll assume that as you're with me, you can be trusted. You won't be privy to everything, naturally, but you won't have to take any oaths. It's a private residence where my friends are staying."

"No top secret headquarters?" She mock-pouted.

"Maybe next time."

"Will you get in trouble for bringing me? I'll wait in town if that's the case. I don't want you to be disciplined or anything."

His wrist comm crackled as Daniel's hail burst through. He looked to her and then back down, answering.

"You're on your way then? Good. Get those samples and that disk to Vincenz immediately. We've got some movement out there.

The Imperialists have filed an official complaint with the civilian government in Asphodel. Apparently some of their people have disappeared, and they're claiming it was a military corps operation."

Andrei lifted a shoulder. "By the by, there was an explosion in the early hours, just before sunrise. In the Wastelands, I'm told."

The corner of Daniel's mouth lifted. "Did the symbol get left?"

Roman Lyons, the leader of the Federation Universes, the most powerful man in all the Known Universes, had ordered all Phantom Corps operatives to leave a lion's head coin at the scene any time they'd put a stop to Imperialist trouble. He wanted them to know he would wipe them all off the face of all the 'Verses if he had to.

As such things went, Andrei thought, it was spooky and took the sort of aggressive tack the situation needed.

"Delivered via courier." Straight to Jan Karl's apartments in town, left on his doorstep.

"Good."

He relayed some more information and signed off.

"He's your boss?"

He looked up to her. "Of a sort. Yes."

Before he could break out the kerchief to create a makeshift blindfold, the food arrived, and they ate in companionable silence.

She reached out to draw her thumb just beneath his eyes. "You need to rest."

He did. Exhaustion, no real stranger to his life, had sapped his strength, and he was operating on the last dregs of his stores.

"Come, let's nap. I promise your virtue is safe. For the time being, anyway."

He allowed her to draw him to the bed, putting her closest to the wall so he could lie on the outside, being the barrier between the door and her safety.

She pressed against his back, her arms around him, face against his back. Taking care of him. Making sure he ate and rested. It had been a very long time since he'd felt this way.

Sleep came fast and deep with her scent in his system.

Chapter 12

Julian answered the door and instantly locked on to Piper. He smiled and held his hand out. "You must be Piper. Come in."

They followed him inside and down the long entry hall toward the office and labs.

"I'm Julian, and that over there is Vincenz. He's had his head in those calculations and the code for days, it seems." He took Piper's hands, squeezing them. He called back over his shoulder, "Vincenz, come and meet Piper."

Andrei noted the easy way the two had, feeling less worried when he saw Julian's sadness had ceased carving runnels of pain into his face. The sadness was there, but it wasn't stamped over him so desperately.

"While he finishes, why don't you two settle in? The guest room is all ready. I had a meal ordered, so we can eat while you debrief. Ellis will be joining us."

That took him by surprise. "Via vid?"

"No. He's taking care of some business in town, but he'll be back shortly. I'm surprised you didn't bump into him when you were at the Portal Station."

With a nod, Andrei led Piper, *quiet* Piper, down the corridor until they'd reached the guest sleeping quarters and they dropped their things off.

"Clean clothes in the closet," Julian called out from the other side of the door.

He needed them. He hadn't even changed when they'd returned from their trip to the Wastelands. He'd need a long, hot shower, but with Ellis there, it meant something big—bigger than usual—was happening. He'd need to keep on his game and save the relaxation for later.

"Drop your clothes in that basket there, and we'll have them cleaned up." He told her this as he did it himself.

"Who is Ellis?"

He sighed, wavering on what to tell her. Not that he didn't trust her, but each thing she learned put her in more danger. At the same time, it was robbing her of information that could actually save her in the future if he didn't tell her.

"He's the boss. The big boss."

"I thought Roman Lyons was the big boss." She stripped her shirt off, and his gaze roved over her upper body, especially her breasts and the love bite on the swell of her hip.

"He's just one size down from that."

"Should I be afraid?"

Knowing Ellis, he'd love Piper the moment he met her. The man had a thing for women like Piper. Hells, Roman's wife, Abbie, had the nearly seven-foot-tall Ellis wrapped about her finger. She even called him Wil.

"No." In any case, no one would harm her as long as Andrei could draw a breath.

"Andrei, how much stuff do you have in all those pockets?" She watched, eyes wide, as he pulled all the samples and the chip from various places. "You're like one of those animals with a pocket on their body to carry their offspring in."

He sighed inwardly, moving to the closet to grab the clean clothes. Julian hadn't missed a detail. Clothing in Piper's size hung there as well. He tossed a few things her way.

"Nothing luxurious, but certainly clean and comfortable."

"How long had he known I was coming? Did you tell him my size?"

She peeled the rest of her clothes off, and he leaned back against the door to watch. He should have taken her in the transport. It would be hours of debrief and work before he'd have her alone again, and they had no time just then.

"Makes me feel better when you look at me that way." She smoothed her hands down the front of the blouse she'd just put on. "This is lovely. Thank you."

"He's detail-oriented." Andrei left it at that. Of course her personal information, including photographs, was in a file some-where, and that's most likely where Julian had gotten the idea of her size.

She moved to him, putting her arms around his waist and tipping her chin up to look at his face. "If you need me to leave the room, just ask. I promise I won't give you any guff in front of these men. I know this is important."

Before he could stop himself, he dipped his head to taste her mouth, staying for a while because she was too delicious to resist.

The front door opened and closed, and he straightened. "Let's get you fed. You'll have to come back here, or there's a screening room upstairs if you want to watch a vid. A library, too, if I remember correctly. I'm to be debriefed, which, as you've pointed out, is top secret."

"Are you laughing at me?" She grinned and opened the door.

"Yes."

"Good." She looked at him over her shoulder as she walked ahead of him. "You need to laugh more."

Piper tried not to gape when she nearly ran into a man the size of a tree trunk. She looked up and then up some more and into the startlingly handsome face of the man who had to be the boss Andrei had just mentioned.

He smiled down at her, taking her hands.

"Welcome. You must be Piper Roundtree. I'm Wilhelm Ellis, and I wanted to extend my appreciation, and that of Roman Lyons, for all the help you've rendered Andrei."

"Thank you, though you need not thank me. Andrei is like my family; I'd do anything for him."

Ellis's left eyebrow rose over intelligent eyes. "Lucky Andrei."

"Come on into the work room. I've got the food out, and we can get started." Julian waved them all toward the room they'd been in earlier.

"Sit, Piper. You must be tired." Vincenz poured her a mug of kava, still steaming. She took it gratefully, adding a few drops of sweetener. The table held several platters of meat, cheeses and vegetables. A lot like home, and she felt better for that bit of familiarity.

No doubt about it, though she tried to act nonchalant, she was overwhelmed and way out of her element. Still, she wanted to be with Andrei as long as she could in any way possible, and there was no denying how amazing it was to watch him in his many varied guises.

"Eating and talking." Ellis nodded at Andrei. "Good job on the sample."

"Thank you, sir." Andrei handed over several tubes, packets and a data chip. "The samples are from the mine. We went to survey it all." He tossed another chip to Vincenz. "Video footage of the mine and what distribution and processing system I could see."

"We went to survey it?" Ellis turned to Piper, who raised her chin and stared back. Of course she had to pretend she was dealing with Taryn, who was scary but nowhere in the same league as Wilhelm.

"Yes, sir. Piper rendered much-needed assistance to me. Has done since I first arrived. She monitored the situation from high ground with a weapon as I was down at the mine site. Her superior piloting skills have been integral as I was able to infiltrate the merc community in Asphodel on the weight of her reputation."

"Sounds like we should offer her a job." Julian said it, and he didn't much sound as if he was joking.

Vincenz tucked the chip from the destroyed transport into a data receiver and began to unlock the coding. The samples were similarly loaded into test trays for analysis.

"The mine is well staffed?" Ellis asked.

"Was."

The smile Ellis gave Andrei chilled Piper down to her toes. Andrei ran his foot along the back of her calf to comfort her, and it worked.

"We need to debrief. Piper, will you excuse my terrible rudeness?"

She stood, holding a roll in one hand and the kava in the other. "Andrei told me you have a vid screening room upstairs?"

"Top of the stairs, second door on the left. Please help yourself to whatever you find to watch. The kitchen is down here. The pantry is fully stocked, and there are juices and some ales in the cold case."

All four men stood when she moved to the door. She wanted to say something flip and silly to Andrei but knew it wasn't the time for it.

She settled on one of the large, overstuffed chairs in the room, tucking her legs beneath her. Choosing an action vid from the screen menu, she tried not to think about anything but enjoying the show.

Instead, the sound of explosions and weapon fire was her music as she thought.

She'd spent her life surviving. There had been times when she'd truly wanted things, and she'd worked hard to attain them. But somehow, new blast doors for the house and a better engine for the zipper did not really equal what she felt right then.

Being with Andrei had brought her need for more to the surface. Not more things. Not more credits. But a life with a man at her side. A life with Andrei in it.

She wasn't stupid. She knew he wasn't the kind of man who would be home each night by the time the glow lamps went on. She knew there'd always be his job, and sometimes it wouldn't include her.

And she was all right with that. She accepted who he was, and more than that, it was part of what she loved so much about him. His dedication to something more than himself.

It made him into what she considered to be a real-life hero. In his quiet way, he was larger than life. Much like the way she loved him.

Somehow, she'd always imagined falling in love with the man she'd consider her mate would be miraculous and startling. It was, indeed, miraculous, but as she'd already loved him eleven years before, she wasn't so much startled by it or by him. No, she was startled by how easily she simply accepted it right then. Accepted how much she loved him.

There were things she'd been undecided on, things she wasn't quite sure how to feel about. Not so this thing between her and Andrei.

She was old enough to know what it felt to love someone. Old enough to know the difference between a fleeting infatuation and the depth of love. And she believed, quite strongly in fate.

Oh, she knew others would laugh and think her silly, but there were things in the world that could not be explained. Things a body just knew or did. Her future wasn't one path but limitless possibilities, branches and connections.

She'd lived her life making choices. Not always the ones she wanted to make, but she'd made them and dealt with the consequences. She'd existed and survived, and on the continuum of joy and sorrow, she'd had much more of the former. Her life was filled with love. Love she'd made the deliberate choice to open her life to.

And now, this was one of those branches in the road. Her path was Andrei; she saw that clearly. She walked exactly where she knew she was supposed to be and would choose him with everything she had.

She smiled, leaning back in the seat, wiping away the tears, knowing her future would only be one with her life twined with his.

"Thanks to the information you've gathered, I believe we've stemmed the flow of Liberiam into Imperialist territory." Wilhelm paused as he looked through the data before him on the table. "As of this morning, we learned what Parron was being used for. A substance used in super-machines to keep them from overheating. A gel used in the firing mechanism. It's more complicated than that, of course, but the details aren't relevant. Only that the material's flow from the Federation Universes has been cut off."

"Processing plants." Vincenz looked up from his work between five different screens of data. "It has to be. The part Mirage plays. The other two 'Verses had raw materials. They've got to be processing it somehow. They can't possibly smuggle that sort of mass and not be detected."

Ellis leaned back. "Get Daniel on the comm. Andrei, I want you here looking for these processing plants."

He'd have to leave her, send her back to Asphodel.

"Yes, sir."

"Go talk to her while we wait to get Daniel on line. Roman should be involved as well."

Heart breaking, he ascended the stairs and headed toward the screening room. That broken heart stuttered when he saw her there, tears on her face. Never had he needed to fix something more in his entire life.

He moved quickly and ended up on his knees, pulling her into his arms. Over and over he'd done it. He'd tried to hold back, tried to erect defenses against her, but there weren't any where she was concerned. He needed her.

"What is it? Are you ill?"

She hummed her pleasure, nuzzling his neck. "No. Not that I'm complaining about this lovely cuddle you're giving me. Why do you ask?"

"You've been crying. Are you unhappy? Do you miss your brothers?"

"Oh that. I'm the opposite of unhappy. I'm overjoyed. Because I've chosen you." She said it as if it made sense. She had a way of doing that.

"What are you talking about, Piper, and why are you crying over it?"

"Women cry when they're happy, too. You cannot tell me you've no experience with the emotional wiles of females. They moon after you everywhere we go."

At his confused expression, she laughed, kissing him quickly before she went on. "I've chosen you to be my man. To be very old-fashioned, which I am in some ways, you know, my mate. I already loved you of course, but this is different, a deliberate choice to love you and be with you."

"Piper, we can't be together. Especially right now. There's a war starting. I have to stay here, and you have to go back to Asphodel." He paused at her silence, wary. And he didn't want to hurt her. "When this is over, I'll come to you. I don't know if I have anything to offer you. But I'll come to you."

Her brows rose and she cocked her head to the side. He was still on his knees, so they were eye to eye. "I'm not going back to Asphodel if you'll be here."

"You'll be safer there. Or, you, Kenner and Taryn all go to

Ravena. Stay in my house while I'm gone. It's the Center, no place better protected." He nodded, making his mind up, and still she had that face. "What? Woman, why are you looking at me that way?" he thundered, and she jumped up.

Instead of fear or sadness, she jumped up and down, clapping her hands, grinning.

"There it is. Now I know for sure you love me, too. You have a lot of fire inside you. But you keep yourself so controlled. You lost that control for me. Oh, stop looking at me like that. You and I both know you love me, and that is that. What kind of woman would not know a man loved her when he shielded her from dead bodies and jumped in the line of fire for her? And you nearly broke someone's hand because he was snotty to me."

Still wearing that grin, she crossed her arms over her chest. Like a lunatic.

"You love meeee. You love meeee." She sang it, dancing around the room as he watched, shaking his head.

"You may never say it, being the stoic body you are." She shrugged. "But I know it and you know that I know it. You show me you love me, which is better than telling me. Now, are you going to tell Ellis that I'm staying to be your backup, or shall I?"

She headed down the stairs at a very high rate of speed as he made it to his feet, yelling her name.

By that point, everyone had gathered at the base of the stairs.

"Mr. Ellis, I do like you, and you've been very nice to me so far, but I have to tell you I have no intention of going back to Asphodel while Andrei stays here."

Andrei moved to take her hand and yank her backward, but Wilhelm stopped him.

"And why is that, young woman? Are you under the impression

that an operative's lady friend should be allowed to accompany him around like a camp follower?"

Andrei would kick her ass if she picked a fight and Andrei had to jump in to protect her. Of course, Ellis could fell him in one hard punch, but he'd go down protecting Piper.

"Camp follower! What an interesting example. But you see, I don't intend to sit around and wash Andrei's clothes and make his meals, though I do like to cook. No, he needs backup, and I'm it."

"I think we've got plenty experienced operatives to handle that. You're a civilian."

Andrei took a step forward, expecting Piper to leap on Wilhelm's leg and bite him for being so condescending.

"I am a civilian. But I have military training, which you have to know because you had me looked at like I would if I were in your shoes. I'm also a damned fine pilot. I know the land here. I know how to fly in canyons and over deserts. I know stealth. Probably as well as many of your operatives." She looked to Andrei and smiled, patting the hand on her arm. "Not this one, of course, but I doubt you have anyone better either."

Ellis stood there, frozen in shocked silence.

"I love him and we work well together. All his silence doesn't bother me one bit, and he's a good navigator. I can shoot well, and I will when I need to. You can ask him about that."

Ellis's gaze shifted to Andrei. "What is your perspective on this?"

"Sir, I'd apologize, but, to be honest, I always find myself amazed when she's this way." Everyone gaped at him. "It is my preference that she go to a safe place in the Center. But it is my understanding and my belief that she will not allow herself to be sent away. *Tenacious* is a nicer word than *stubborn*."

"Andrei, you made a joke." She winked, and he sighed.

Ellis laughed and shrugged. "Fine. Don't get killed, or he'll be useless to me. Come on in, we're about to brief on the escalation we've seen recently and Vincenz's very astute answer to a question we'd been pondering."

Chapter 13

They filed into the room, and Piper was very proud that she'd held back her impulse to jump into Andrei's arms and laugh when they'd let her stay. It had been, she thought, a very fine bluff. Oh sure, the things she said were true. She was a good pilot; she knew how to shoot and be sneaky. But they were so much more than that. She could see it simply in the way they all moved.

These four men in the room with her moved like predators. She could have walked by Julian on any street and despite the handsome face, the way he held his shoulders, the way he listened, she'd never have chosen to cross him or even interact with him. They were all this way. Still, they were all quite delicious to look at, especially Andrei. Though the others seemed to talk more, her attention was always on him. Even when she was listening to Vincenz set up the connections to the other people who'd connect in by comm, a corner of her mind was on him, the way he sat next to her.

Probably to keep her from doing or saying something crazy. She hid a smile. This was serious business, and she knew it. She needed to prove herself to Ellis and these other men. Prove herself worthy of protecting Andrei and of their trust, too.

Two men showed up via remote, one with hair dark like Andrei's, though his was thick and just to a collar's length. The kind a woman would love to run her fingers through. He wore a band on his intended finger. A committed man then. The other man, well, this was a predator, too. Pale hair. She thought of the right shade, gold. Yes, the color of her favorite ale. Arrogant features. Ramrod-straight spine. This man was used to giving orders and having people follow them to the letter. This man was, she knew, Roman Lyons.

Turned out Andrei was even more important than she could have imagined. Pride warmed her.

"The samples Andrei brought back are indeed Liberiam. None of them are processed." Vincenz spoke as he dragged the data up to the main screen they all faced. "We know the gel is also unprocessed. At least what we've found. So the key is Mirage. Here. We've got two sources for raw materials and none are processed. Taking that sort of mass over the line into the Imperium would be impossible."

"Why not assume they'd use unregistered portals instead?"

"None of those go directly into Imperialist territory." Piper spoke up, feeling on solid ground at last.

"Roman, Daniel, this is Piper Roundtree. We've brought her on as a special attaché to Andrei. Her knowledge of the cargo running business will be quite useful." Ellis actually winked at her when no one was looking. Why, the cheeky man! Piper bet he'd intended to have her part of the team from the beginning.

Daniel looked at Andrei, who gave that shrug of his. Piper might have been insulted, but there had been the ghost of a smile on his lips. For her. About her. She knew enough from how Andrei spoke of Daniel. Knew Daniel was his closest friend. Which made Piper want him to like her.

"How do you run cargo to the other side then?" Roman spoke up. "Thank you for your assistance, Ms. Roundtree," he added, remembering his manners.

"No problem. Understand that what cargo I do run to the other side is not munitions. Never that. But I don't run it into their territory. I almost always run it to the Frontier. Ceres or Nondal. There's a completely other sort of cargo runner who takes it from there."

"You said almost always. What about when it's not almost always?" Ellis's gaze sharpened on her as his fingers tapped over the keys of his comm unit.

"Twice I've taken a run to the Waystation."

Daniel leaned toward the screen as the rest stared at her.

"Go on, please. How does it work from there?"

"The stationmaster's nephew takes it over. At least that's what I understand. We dock, they confiscate the cargo and make us leave. I assume they run it from there, but I don't know for sure."

"What did you run those two times?"

"Botanicals for perfumes and enhancements for women. You know, for face creams and that sort of thing. The botanicals are not on any restricted list. I told you, I don't run the bad stuff.

"Both times you ran this same load of botanicals? What was different that you took it to the Waystation?" Roman asked.

"One of the largest companies in all the Federation Universes was what was different. Anyway, I know others—other mercs, I mean—have dropped at the Waystation, too."

"Wyath Labs?" Daniel began to type, as did Vincenz.

"They must be involved. Look up what they're making. Those botanicals might be a key."

They all began to talk around her, and Andrei took her in, noting the way she shook her head.

"What is it?" He leaned close, all his attention on her.

"I don't think Wyath has anything do to with this mess. They're just a big corporation who wants to make money. They make glosses for lips and hope in a jar for women who wouldn't have considered the extravagant price on their anti-aging creams even just a year or two before. They're certainly evil, but in the same way most large businesses like that are. This is a whole different kind of evil. I don't think this is connected."

"Do you remember the specific botanicals?"

"I don't. But I swear to you I checked to be sure none of them were banned. Mainly because I didn't want some girl's nose to fall off or her lips to get blisters. I can ask Kenner. He remembers everything."

Andrei took her personal comm and keyed in several lines of coding. "Contact him and get the exact cargo manifest."

"Do you trust my feelings on this?"

"Yes." He answered without a pause of any kind.

It wasn't more than five minutes or so before they had all the information, and it looked very much like Piper had been right. Though she didn't gloat. Certainly they knew way more about this sort of thing than she did.

"All right. So it appears to be nothing more than greed because

Wyath has begun to do business in the Imperium and they didn't want to pay the tariffs." Roman's expression, even with the distance of space and the screen, didn't bode well for Wyath at all.

"One of my people just went to speak with their owner. He didn't much like being woken up. But I don't care what that bastard feels. However, I don't very much like to hear the Waystation being involved in this. At all."

"Could explain the problem we've had with our intel being leaked." Andrei brought up the files on the Waystation master and then the man's nephew.

Ellis sucked in a breath. "Daniel, on that. Now."

Daniel got up to speak with someone else, returning shortly.

They spoke, discussing the probability of a processing plant being somewhere on Mirage and how they'd go about finding it. Mirage was one of the largest 'Verses in the entire system. It was covered in geography of several types, but mostly it was hot, dirty and filled with giant cracks in the ground and sharp-faced canyons. It was entirely possible to have set up a processing plant, several of them, and remain undetected.

They had been in the process of signing off when someone burst into Daniel's office with a wail. Ellis's comm began to ping, and Vincenz's screens froze and began to fill with data.

"Gods above and below," Ellis breathed out as he read his comm. "Roman?"

"It's true." Roman turned to look at someone just off the screen. "I need an emergency convention of the entire Governance Council. I want every last member to be available either in chambers or via vid, and I want it to happen within the hour. Wilhelm, I need you back here."

Piper, wide-eyed, knew something bad had happened, but Vincenz's screens were tilted so he could see them best, and the glare kept her from reading whatever it was.

"Parron has just been hit. Massive airships came from the Portal without warning. They carpet bombed pretty much the entire surface. Initial data shows at least five thousand have been killed, but that's just the early data." Ellis looked back to them as he stood.

Piper went very, very cold, and she was grateful when Andrei reached out to take her hand, squeezing it.

"Did we have people there?" Andrei asked.

"Yes. I don't know if they made it. As you can imagine, information is slow to get to us. We've sealed the portal traffic to all but official Federation transportation. I have to go and get this meeting set up. Keep Marcus apprised of your situation there." Roman signed off.

"I must get back to Ravena." Ellis turned to Piper.

"Sir, I know the location of two private portals in Parron." She had to tell them. If the Imperialists were using them to kill people, mercs be damned, there were things far more important than running illegal liquor and black market conveyance parts.

"Thank you, Ms. Roundtree. I appreciate the data. I would ask you for similar information on other Edge 'Verses if you have it. I fear that if we do not close up these back doors, we're far too vulnerable. And, Daniel, when you have that Waystation master picked up, along with his nephew, bring them directly to me. I want to know how Imperial airships can get through that many 'Verses without detection."

Ellis jogged from the room.

"I need a drink." Andrei stood.

"Let's open up the big comms and get the data from the attack streaming in. We're closer, so we should be able to pick information up."

$\mathscr{B}$y the time Andrei stumbled into the room, it was long past moonset and only a breath or three from the rise of the first sun. Piper had tried to stay up with him, wanting to help in any way, but after she'd given them the coordinates of as many private portals as she had access to, she was pretty much just in the way.

He'd been devastated. They all had.

But that night he'd been swimming in the data. Two-thirds of the surface of Parron had been destroyed. Nearly ten thousand people had been killed. Close to a hundred thousand had been injured, and the number of missing rose more with the passing minutes. Utter and total devastation. An open declaration of war.

And for what? This is what bothered her so much. What purpose would there be to this choice by the Imperialists?

They'd sat and watched the footage from the meeting of the Governance Council. Had watched Roman Lyons announce he was sending troops to the Edge in great numbers. All portal traffic, other than medical and essential, to Parron would be rerouted past. The airships had been a huge strain on the system, slowing down even the essential travel needed to deliver medical supplies and personnel.

He stood there, and she turned to face him. In the dark she couldn't see his features, but the tension in him vibrated. She knew what he needed so she got to her knees in the bed. "Come. I'm awake. Let me make it better. At least for a while."

He was there, ripping at his clothes, naked in a few moments. There was no gentleness this time. His need was ferocious. Their coupling was hard and fierce, a thing of teeth and nails, of fingers and nails dug into flesh, of the hard slap as he thrust into her body, of her muffled cries of pleasure and his growls. His growls roamed over her senses like his hands on her skin.

The barely leashed desire, the way he snarled his need for her, it did her in.

When he'd finished, after he'd made her come twice, both times so hard she probably couldn't move her legs for an hour, they lay together, her head resting on his shoulder as he drew a gentle line up and down her arm.

"I'm sorry."

He paused, clearly surprised. "For what?"

"For all this pain. Not sorry because I caused it, sorry that it happened. Sorry you're carrying their weight. All ten thousand dead, all the wounded. I know you better than anyone. I know you feel like you failed them in some way."

"We should have known. It's inexcusable that we did not know. It's inexcusable that four airships—*four* airships—used a Federation portal to attack civilians. Why didn't we know about the Waystation? Why didn't I ask you about it? How could I have missed that?"

"You were a little busy finding that mine and destroying it. Getting the information you'll now use to stop them. You will. I know you will. Stop blaming yourself for not being omnipotent. Even Andrei Solace can't read the future. Maybe it's my fault for not telling you up front. I'm the one who didn't tell you. How is it not my fault?"

"Bullshit." He swung from the bed and began to pace. "This isn't your fault. We're the ones who are supposed to know this stuff. You weren't even involved until a week ago!"

She waited for him to wind down, these occasional bursts of intense emotion somehow making her feel better.

"So then, can we agree that neither of us willingly caused the murder of ten thousand civilians? That we can now move forward and stop them from doing it again?"

He growled, spinning, and she patted the bed beside her.

"Come back to bed. You need to rest. So do I. Let's sleep a while so we can be ready for what the morning will bring. It's not very far off anyway."

He obeyed, turning to face her. "You're facing the wrong way."

She snorted and turned over, backing into the shelter of his body as he curled it around her. Sheltering her from harm, surrounding her with himself. Despite the sadness, the severity of the situation, they were together, and she couldn't be anything but satisfied about that.

Andrei awoke after three hours' sleep. He needed more, but there wasn't time for it. But she didn't need to be up, so he carefully eased from bed after pressing a kiss to her shoulder. She looked soft and feminine in sleep. Her face relaxed, one hand under her cheek. The ropes of her hair spread on the pillow and over her shoulders.

A shower first and then great amounts of kava. That's what he needed to face the day, so he set about getting it.

Vincenz was already up and working when Andrei got downstairs. "Kava is hot. Grab a mug. Julian should be down in a bit. He was up even later than we were."

Andrei realized he was hearing a lot more than just friendly concern in Vincenz's words. "Is he all right? He's seemed better when I've commed with you both. Calmer, not so prone to those long stares off into nothingness."

"He's recovering. Marame was his best friend. They were like siblings. He feels her loss deeply."

And, Andrei knew, Vincenz understood what it was to lose people he loved dearly. To feel utterly alone. "What he feels is responsible. When it was not about Julian at all."

"And now he's feeling responsible for those ten thousand people. He was just on Parron two days ago."

Andrei knew their friend, knew he'd be feeling that he missed a clue of some type.

"There's more." Andrei sat, watching Vincenz.

"Yes. But that's between Julian and me."

Ah.

Andrei shrugged. "If you expect judgment of a negative sort, you'll get none. Not from me. Work wise or personal, if you need me for anything, you have but to ask."

Vincenz nodded and moved on. "Today we should work out some logistics. I've been comming with the people in the labs on Ravena. They find more each hour, it seems. We learn more about the destabilizing device and then have more questions. But we're narrowing it all down. If we can just isolate the key to reversing the destabilization process, then we could have them in place just in case."

"The Imperialists on Asphodel need to be taken into custody and questioned. I can handle that part." Andrei found his silence and surrounded himself with it, seeking the calm to make better decisions.

"Ellis sent a team to do that. He says he doesn't want Piper or her family exposed. Sera, Ash and Brandt's team will handle that."

Andrei had to admit he was relieved to keep Piper and the others on the compound out of this mess. Well, her brothers anyway, since she'd launched herself right into the heart of the storm and made no moves to escape safely. Just to drive him mad in the interim.

"I feel sorry for them then. There won't be much left after Sera gets done." The three made up a special team, intelligence gathering usually, but Sera, Brandt's wife and also Ash's wife in all but title, was not a woman to be trifled with. She'd been part of the first teams to uncover the Imperialists' first forays into Federation territory, and with her, this was nearly a holy mission.

"At least we can cross Parron off the list now. I know that sounds merciless." Vincenz scrubbed his hands over his face. "They must have gone in to destroy all evidence of what they'd been using. They have to know we're on to them."

"We have to find the processing plant here." Andrei drank the kava, reading the reports that had come in during the last few hours. More death. More destruction, and he had no idea why.

Piper came into the room, and Andrei found himself drawn to her, needing to touch her. She smiled at Vincenz, patting his arm on the way past, moving unhesitatingly toward Andrei and into his arms.

"You should have woken me up."

He kissed the top of her head, not caring who saw. After the tragedy of the last day, the fact that the world was so fragile that any day could be his last had hit. She was important to him, and acting as if she wasn't would have been an insult to them both.

"You needed the rest. There's kava over there."

She walked over and poured herself a mug. "It's nearly empty. Shall I make more? Have you eaten at all today?" She shook her head as both men grunted at her while reading data screens and plotting maps. "I'll see to it."

The kitchen was so large she stood just admiring it when she first entered. Her kitchen at home was open to the rest of the house, so it was a kitchen, a dining area, a place for the kids to do their work, where they had meetings and relaxed at the end of the day.

She smiled at the memories. And she still loved the sleek, large cooking space with high windows that sent the light streaming down into the room. So much counter space and dozens of the latest cooking technology. A large oven, she discovered after peeking, just for making breads of all sorts. A grill, a cooktop, ovens, large refrigerated bins and hot drawers, too.

"Amazing, isn't it?"

Startled, Piper looked up from where she'd been pulling together the ingredients for a hearty morning meal.

Julian Marsters stood nearby, his hands in his pockets. Even exhausted and under a great deal of pressure, the man was still handsome. Close-cropped hair the color of the kava boiling on the cooktop. His eyes were a lighter shade, the brown in a glass of brandy with the light behind it.

She smiled. "It is. I hope you don't mind that I poked around. I wanted to make something to eat for everyone. This is the most beautiful room I've ever seen."

When he smiled, he was even more handsome. "Thank you. I can't take credit for it, I'm sorry to say. This is Vincenz's house. He lives here part of the standard year."

The way he said Vincenz's name was interesting. "How long have you two been together?"

Julian sighed as he moved to wash his hands and stand next to her at the counter as she sliced root vegetables to fry up with the aromatics she found on the windowsill above the double sink.

"It's complicated. And new. And I don't quite know what it is anyway. But he . . ."

He blushed.

"Is he why you look so sad? Or why you look happy right now?"

"I can see why you and Andrei connect so well. I lost someone recently. She was my best friend. A woman who we all worked with."

"Marame?" At his nod she began to whip the eggs. "Andrei told me about her."

"She and I always worked together. We were closer than friends." At her questioning brow, he shook his head. "No. She was with Andrei a while, and after that she declared she'd never get involved with soldiers of any kind. Oh, my, I shouldn't have said that about Andrei."

Piper laughed. "You thought I'd be jealous or angry that he might have loved someone else before he and I came together again? Don't be silly."

"All right. I'm glad to hear it. But he didn't love her. Not like he is with you. I've known him for a long time. He and I came into the corps within a year of each other. He's never looked at anyone the way he does you. Before he went back to Asphodel, I figured he'd always be one of those men who lived and breathed the job and would be happy with the occasional woman when he thought of it. You're different. He's different with you. Marame wanted that and knew he'd not be that for her, so she moved on. They remained friends, but that was all."

"Julian, thank you for telling me that." She knew it, but it helped to hear it, too. To know others saw it. To know she was different.

He bowed slightly and began to pull out plates and tableware.

"As for me and Vincenz? He knows what it is to be alone. He lets me be, and right now, that's all I can handle."

"That's certainly fair enough."

He paused and then smiled a little. "Yes, it is. I'm trying to just, you know, be."

She couldn't really help with whatever they were doing out there. They ate quickly, each man on his personal comm while the screens in the background streamed data. Daniel had checked in several times.

She volunteered to go over some aerial film the drones had taken over the last days. She could do that. And she could bake some bread and keep them eating. When all she really wanted to do was punch Ciro Fardelle in the face before she shot him and left him in a ditch to rot.

She wondered how it would feel for Vincenz. Knowing it was his father who'd done these terrible things. Andrei had told her he'd been arrested and transported to a death camp by his father. Some of the men assigned to move him were loyal to Vincenz and with the help of his grandmother, helped him escape. He'd worked for the military corps since then and was recently given operative status with Phantom Corps.

Phantom Corps. That had rocked her back on her heels. She'd known Andrei was some sort of specialist, but this was so far beyond that. This group of men and women who had been waging war with the Imperialists for standard years. A constant push and shove that had held the status quo until Fardelle had escalated to open and all-out war on the Federated Universes.

Now they walked on the very edge, past the place where they

could prevent war. The costs had risen with real, deadly consequences. She knew Roman Lyons had launched a similar attack on
Imperialist military targets.

So there would be no avoided warfare, but they still sought a
way to stanch the bleeding and then push back so hard they'd never
make the mistake of attacking the Federated Universes again.

The main comm system hailed an incoming transmission, and
they all gathered around facing the screens, Daniel and Ellis on one
and Roman Lyons on the other.

Piper's stomach cramped as she saw the look on Roman's face.
The toll of the death of his people, she knew, weighed heavy. His
wife was in the very last stages of pregnancy, and she couldn't imagine how that would feel.

Lyons was in a lab of some sort. "There's no way to reverse the
destabilization process." He said it hard and fast, and Piper watched
Andrei stand straighter, taking on the heavier burden now on them.
Love—so much love—filled her for this man of honor she'd been
blessed with for most of her life. Even when he wasn't physically
present, he'd been with her.

"It's worse." Roman nodded toward the technician he stood
next to.

"Without a duplicate machine, the portal not only collapses, but
it would weaken the fabric of space/time all around the portal until
nothing was left."

Andrei started as if he'd been slapped. If this happened, the
Known Universes would be completely in chaos. Trade would be
interrupted, because once it wasn't just that the portal would burn
out, but the 'Verse itself would simply cease to exist. 'Verses on one
side or the other of whatever 'Verse was destroyed would be cut off.

Universes on the other side of the one destroyed would be utterly cut off from the Center. The Federation Government could not defend anyone on the outer side of a portal collapse, leaving them vulnerable. Entire 'Verses could die out because they wouldn't be able to get their needed supplies via portal. Depending on what 'Verse was destroyed, the parade of horrible possibilities was endless.

"Yes, I see you all understand why this news is so unwelcome. All portal stations are under martial law as of last evening. There will be no more express transports. All transports will stop and be scanned at every Federation Universe Portal."

Which was helpful, except there were private portals all over the place.

Roman spoke again. "We need the rogue portals working."

And Andrei knew. "We need to get the parts to make our own device. The exact duplicate of the one they have."

Ellis nodded. "Look to your comms on this. We've updated with more intelligence. After we plugged in the data from the Liberiam samples, we achieved enough to crack the rest of the code. The data is unlocked. We know what we have and can get there, and we know what we need from there."

Piper nodded her head, and he wanted to toss her over his shoulder and lock her in a closet until everything was safe, but she'd never allow it.

"We will not, I repeat, we will not be going into Imperialist territory for these materials unless we have no other choice. Let's get them to smuggle them out for us."

"We can't go through Asphodel at this point now that we've removed the Imperialists who'd been there." Julian continued to read the data as he spoke.

"No. But I have some sources here in Mirage." Piper hesitated and then continued to speak. "I think I can get us an invite to meet with the Imperialists here. You know they're around somewhere."

"Good idea. Andrei, keep cover as one of her crew. Let's get this process moving, people. Every moment that passes means he's closer to finishing his device. Use the private portals to avoid the checkpoints." Ellis sighed heavily. "It would behoove you all to be extraordinarily wary and observant at this point. By that I mean to say, kill these motherfuckers first before they kill us."

The meeting ended, and Andrei looked to Piper when she spoke. "Let's get started. We'll head down to the Market. I take it you'll have a pile of credits so we can get this process moving at the swiftest of paces?"

He waved toward Julian and Vincenz, and followed her out. "Yes. I have the ability to handle a problem however it is necessary to do so."

She put on her sunshades and looked back over her shoulder as they headed outside. "Do I get that, too? Say I bump into one of those Imperialists who were in those airships, and I could shove him out the window screen of my zipper at full speed?"

He shook his head, but she saw his smile.

Chapter 14

The streets were full of soldiers.

Soldiers who bore the same look of shock and anguish many of the citizens had. This part of Mirage was stylish. The kind of neighborhood a man posing as a tech consultant for a large multi-'Verse company would live in.

They walked the long way to the public transit stop and headed to the stretch of the Portal City called the Market. A body could find anything to buy in its long rows of shadowy stalls, at long lunch and dinner counters, past the houses of prostitution and the ale vendors.

"By the way," she tiptoed up to whisper in his ear as the tram began to slow down for their stop, "it's best that you pose as my lover, too. Elsewise I'd never share all this loot with someone not my family."

She hadn't expected him to take the role so wholeheartedly. He slung an arm around her, holding her to his side. Not that she was complaining. It was actually quite delicious, so she went with it. They had good rhythm when they worked together.

Subtly, she led him to the public house she and Kenner drank at when they were in Mirage. In the old days on Earth, bars like this one catered to pirates and brigands, to highwaymen and all those who lifted tankards with them.

They pushed their way through the doors and took a look around before heading to a table on the far side of the room. Andrei rolled his smokes and watched the room while she patiently drank some ale.

Soon enough they were approached, but before she could speak, Andrei stood and clasped forearms with the woman he then invited to sit with them. Piper tried to indicate with her eyes just how much she wanted to kill the woman for being so friendly with Piper's man.

"Piper, this is Aya. She is the wife of another friend. Aya, this is Piper Roundtree."

The woman turned her gaze to Piper, taking her in carefully. "Benni sends his well wishes. I can't stay, but I wanted to say hello while I saw you."

Andrei finally released the breath he'd been holding, and Piper figured this Benni had to be important to him.

"Of course. You're welcome to share a drink with us if you've a bit of time."

She blushed, and Piper, now charmed by the woman, wanted to pat her hand and tell her not to feel bad, that he made all sorts of women respond that way.

"I appreciate the invitation." She turned back to Piper. "And I'm glad to have met you, Piper. But I have an appointment. I expect I'll be seeing you here and there."

She left quickly, and they settled back again. They'd need to be seen first. No one just rushed up on a body to seek their skills to run cargo unless they were desperate and therefore trouble, or the polis working undercover.

She knew many of the faces in the pub that afternoon. A few very good avenues to make some connections with the Imperialists. She'd bide her time and then make the move.

"You know," Andrei spoke low as he moved his chair closer, "it's so dark back here I bet I could make you come without putting my hand into your pants."

My. She took several swallows of her ale, but it did nothing to cool her off. And then his hand slid up her thigh, over the material of her pants. Up some more until he reached the notch between her thighs.

Piper couldn't believe she was not only allowing a man to make her come in public but also pressing her clit against the knuckle he had pressed against it. Even through the pants it felt good.

Being so totally exposed while having an incredibly intimate moment with him was so hot it made her a little dizzy.

He looked so casual there she knew no one suspected anything, but still, the thrill of possible discovery made her entire body tingle, especially the part he rubbed over with his knuckle.

She pushed harder against him as she scooted her chair in, and it took everything in her not to scream out when the sharp shock of climax hit her hard enough to jar her teeth.

He loved the way she looked right after he made her come. Loved the relaxed muscles and the gleam of pleasure in her gaze.

"Now I'm ready to go say hello to a few people." She pushed to stand, and he followed, keeping his attention on the crowd. Most weren't anyone he'd have worried about. Common thieves mainly. None of them would get close enough to Andrei or Piper to pick any pockets. No, it was the man near the back bar, the one with flat eyes and an expensive pair of boots Andrei would watch closest.

Which was easy enough when Piper's rather greasy compatriot invited that man over after Piper had made the query about running goods for him. After Piper had paid a referral fee, of course.

"This is Arge, and he just might be able to help you." The other man made his good-byes and left the three alone.

Arge ignored Andrei and put his focus on Piper. Andrei said nothing but moved to stand between them until Arge got the message. He told himself it was all in keeping with his cover, but it sure felt good to mark his territory in any case.

The chrono he wore was a fake and not even a very good one. The kind soldiers often wore because they couldn't afford the real thing. His hair was short, regulation short. His clothes were nice, but not too nice. The boots were genuine, though. But Andrei was a soldier, too; he knew what a truly well-made pair of boots could do for you when you were on your feet all the time.

Piper fenced with him, being cutting and clever. He kept an eye on the rest of the room, all while being totally confident in the way she was going about this transaction.

This Arge hadn't the brains to be as important as Cheney and his like, but he was here in Mirage and clearly a soldier and that in and of itself made his life less than worth a damn to Andrei. His only use was to get those ingredients back to them so the lab could complete a device of their own.

His haggling showed a man with more debts than brains, but

before long, Piper had finished the transaction, and they had walked away, both breathing easier to be away from that place.

The plan was in motion now, the cargo engaged. They'd hear soon when they could expect to receive the goods.

Nothing else to do then but go back to Vincenz's house and check in.

Andrei checked over the new data and sent his report on the meet to Daniel. He needed to run some recon in town, and he anticipated reticence from Piper on being left back while he did.

So he waited until after they'd checked in and had eaten dinner. He caught her alone in their room.

"I need to do some work. Alone."

Her eyes hardened and her spine went rigid. It annoyed him, even as he found it attractive. And then he wondered at himself for finding bossy women so hot.

"Why can't I help? I'm your backup. That's what Ellis said. I remember that even if you don't."

"I remember it, but some things I do, I need to do alone. I know my job, Piper, and I know I'm damned good at it, especially with reconnaissance. I need to go see what's what. I need to seek out people in far seedier establishments than the one we were just in, and I need to do it alone. None of my sources will talk to me if you're around. They don't know you."

She snorted. "All right. Fine. I understand that. I'm going to wait up. If you aren't back by the moon set, I will come looking for you."

He growled, shoving his hands in his pockets. "Gods above and below, no. If there's trouble, leave it to Julian and Vincenz to deal with any extraction."

"You think I can't handle myself?"

"I know you can. But that doesn't mean I'm going to drag you along to a place so dangerous your simply being there would put you in danger. I can't have my attention shifting. And if you were there, I'd be worried about you the whole time."

She hugged him. "From you these little statements are the most passionate of love sonnets."

"Stay in the house."

He shed her as he left, not wanting any part of her to be sullied by what he'd be dealing with. Moving silently, steadily and down toward the part of town where law and order were a long distant memory. Where murder was common, fights like communion. He moved, letting it all roll off him, slicing through the crowds, barely noticed.

His quarry lay in an establishment full of the worst society had to offer. As such, he had the information he needed within a few minutes and headed out again.

He climbed the exterior fire stairs to a one-room, coldwater flat above a whorehouse. Inside it was the man who'd been trading credits for Imperialist access to the Waystation.

Andrei dropped to the floor and shook his head at the man who rose and made toward the door. The man didn't listen, and so Andrei used his blaster on the man's left knee.

Then they came to an understanding.

True to her word, she waited up for him, tucked into a chair next to a monitor, reading aerial film. She saw him and began to rise, but he held a hand out to stay her.

Julian put a hand on her forearm. "Give him some time to clean up."

Andrei tossed a disk to him and went up the stairs.

"He's up there feeling guilty and dirty for whatever he did out there tonight. I need to go to him."

"Piper, being with someone who does what we do every day can't be easy. Most of us don't have long-term relationships."

"I understand what you do. Don't you see that? We can't all be pilots or bakers or bricklayers. There are dark characters about who mean to be the end of us. You face that every day, and thank the gods for it."

"Doesn't mean we can't wash the blood off sometimes. Doesn't mean we don't feel as if what we see and do taints those we love. We want to shield you from the ugliness."

"But sometimes, Julian, it's better that the person you're with faces that ugliness, too, and stands with you to fight it." Vincenz spoke, startling Piper, who'd forgotten he was in the room.

She stood. "I'm going to him."

"Good for you." Vincenz waved her toward the stairs. "Sometimes if another person is holding the mirror up, we see ourselves more clearly."

A quick check of the laundry showed a shirt with blood at the collar. Panic ate at her insides for the time it took her to get to their room. Had he been hurt and hadn't said?

No, if that were so, Julian and Vincenz would have said so. Would have stopped him and made him get treatment. These warrior men she found herself surrounded by looked out for each other.

No, the blood wasn't his.

She went to him, standing outside the door to the bathing suite, gathering her wits and removing her clothes.

He stood under the water, head bowed, motionless.

Moved beyond words, she stepped in with him. She hugged him tight, pressing against his back, pushing her own emotional response away because he so clearly needed it himself.

"Baby, no. I'll be out in a little while."

The way he'd whispered *baby* had torn at her. He wasn't the sweetheart name sort of man. She couldn't recall him ever calling her baby. With a voice trembling with emotion, she said what he needed to hear. What he needed to know. "I love you, Andrei. There's no other place I should be right now."

"I don't want you near me when I'm like this."

"Like what? Ashamed?"

He turned and backed her against the wall. Her heart pounded, but not from fear.

"I'm not ashamed. I do not feel bad when I kill them. Is that what you wanted to hear?"

"You shouldn't be ashamed unless you've used your power to harm someone who didn't deserve it. Did they deserve it, Andrei? The person whose blood was on the collar of your shirt?"

He cursed.

"What, you didn't think I'd look in the laundry?"

"That I didn't shows how much you distract me. I needed to wash the violence away before I touched you."

His face was suddenly very close. She was rabbit to his wolf, and it thrilled her to her toes.

"He's not dead. That part wasn't my choice. He would be if it were up to me. But he's in custody, and he gave us the information we needed."

"Why, then, are you trying to push me away when it's so clear you need me?"

"You don't need to be exposed to blood on my clothes and my

hands still sore from beating someone enough to spill the details of how he betrayed his own people."

"Did he tell you?"

He nodded.

"Good. Andrei, do you hear me? Good. Yesterday, these people engineered an attack that destroyed nearly an entire 'Verse. They murdered ten thousand and injured eighty thousand. How many are homeless now? How many families are wondering if their sons and mothers, daughters and fathers will come home? For what? Credits? Power? Do you think I could feel anger at you for doing your job?"

"There's a darkness in me, Piper."

She nodded. "I know. And I love you. Despite that darkness. Because of it. You're who you are, darkness and all. I love the entirety of you, Andrei."

With an anguished sound, he kissed her, holding her tight against his body.

She realized she'd needed him as much as he had her. His body, strong and solid, took her weight as she wrapped her legs around his waist.

His hand at the back of her head saved her head from a nasty crack when it fell back at the sheer pleasure when he sank into her in one, hard thrust.

Ground quakes of pleasure rolled through her as he thrust and thrust again, filling her up and retreating.

His touch was urgent, covetous, possessive. He knew what to touch, how to touch it, how she liked it when he held her down on his cock with one hand at her hip, staying deep as he swiveled just a small amount.

He'd given her a climax at entry and now he built her up again.

Relentless as he fucked her, pushing every button he could, pushing more and more until she leaned forward with a gasp, her teeth sinking into his shoulder as she cried out against him.

"Gods above and below," he snarled, increasing his speed and coming as he pushed deep.

On trembling legs, he put her down, going to his knees before her to soap her up. Her hand at his shoulder for balance was his anchor, holding him there, in the stall with her instead of in his head with his memories. She was the memory that counted.

He wanted her to understand that, even if he didn't have the words for it just yet. Wanted her to feel it through his touch.

Her pussy was soft and slick, swollen from her climax, from his cock. He angled the stream of water to her cunt. But became ensnared by the beauty of it when he spread her open wider.

She gasped softly when he pressed a kiss against her clit. Gently and, ever so slowly, he licked and kissed with featherlight touches, slowly giving her pleasure, feeding it in increments so that when her fingers dug into his shoulders and she came, she did so on the sweetest of sounds.

He was lost to her. Lost in her and in letting go and admitting it; he realized it was far more that she'd found him and had given him something worth holding on to. She wasn't a country or a job, but she was everything anyway.

She didn't speak as he bundled her in a drying cloth and rubbed the water away. She looked at him with eyes full of nothing but love. Only acceptance. She was his light. Evidence that he was capable of more than just killing and fighting. She was the finest thing he'd ever had. She'd been so eleven years before, and she was right then as well.

"Come to sleep. We'll go exploring tomorrow." She led him

back to their room and got into the bed first, holding the blanket back for him.

"I need to check in with them to be sure they didn't have any trouble retrieving the data from the disk. I'll return shortly."

"If you don't"—she yawned hugely—"I'll come hunt you down."

"I know." And thank the gods for it.

Chapter 15

He seemed better, she noted, as they took one of the borrowed zippers, a sleek little beauty she'd have loved to own, toward the canyons to the south of the Portal city.

Vincenz had come up with some sort of program that mapped as they flew above, taking into account mass of a type found with manufacturing.

"I bet Ciro Fardelle rues the day he thought to simply toss his son away the way he did. Vincenz is a genius."

"Maybe. Not the genius part, I agree with you on that. But I met Fardelle. I've seen him in action and I don't know that he's got the capability to rue any of his mistakes." He adjusted their path slightly.

"One of the reasons I'm keeping you is the way you navigate."

"Kenner can navigate."

"He can. But he doesn't like it. Taryn doesn't like it."

"Doesn't like navigating?"

She could tell by the way he said it that he knew the answer.

"They don't like the cargo running. We're good at it. Good enough to have some credits saved up. Good enough to keep everyone fed and clothed."

"Is that enough, Piper?"

She shrugged, though he couldn't see with his gaze fixed on the screen.

"I'm good at it."

"You are. You're good at flying. You're good with people. You have a lot of skill in general for all sorts of things."

"You think I should stop running cargo, and then what? What else is there to do on Asphodel?"

"I think you should do what makes you happy. Survival is good. An important instinct. But your whole life can't be about that."

"That so? What were you then, before I came along?"

"I find it hard to remember what I was before I saw you again."

She closed her eyes a moment.

"You do things to me. You make me want more than I've wanted in a long time."

He adjusted again.

"Do you think I'm wrong?"

He snorted. "About many things like your insistence on coming with me during all this danger. But about who you are? What you might want? No. I think you're perfect."

Argh! He was so wonderful without trying, and the more stoic he was, the more frowny and solitary, the more it got to her when he tossed it aside. For her.

"If you're trying to make me love you more, you're succeeding."

He hmpfed.

"Villain. Brigand."

He hmpfed again.

Her comm hailed her to show an incoming from the pig they dealt with the night before. Andrei took over the flying while she handled it. They'd do a meet the next day in Ceres.

"We'd better get moving immediately. Via private portal, it's going to be close."

"I'll get us there." She took the controls and headed them back to the hangar.

Julian was waiting for them at the house. "I took the liberty of packing you both up. Hope you don't mind."

Andrei nodded his head in thanks.

"There's a fast private transport waiting for you at the portal. I take it Piper knows where it is."

"How is it on supplies?"

"Fully loaded. Weapons behind the usual panels. It doesn't look like much on the outside, but appearances mean nothing."

Piper tried not to grin, itching to give it a try.

The private portal had been controlled by the loosely affiliated group of mercenaries out on the Edge territories. They maintained it, regulated traffic and made sure no one burned it out with too much use. The same couldn't be said for all the private portals, but those are the ones that got burned out fast. And those were the merc groups who lost power because of it.

Only now, two days after the horrible attack in Parron, the

traffic had slowed to a trickle because of the checkpoints at the main portals. Not much general cargo running, she imagined, at least not for a few days more. But business was business and the transport was there, as promised, and the dock was still under the control of the mercenaries. Though she doubted they had any idea they were being used by the Federation Military Corps to run missions.

The ship wasn't much to look at, just as Julian had said, but once they'd boarded and sealed up again, she fired up the engines, and the raw power echoed through the platform her feet rested on. Andrei hopped into the nav seat and began to plot the course.

Another Phantom Corps operative, Carey, got settled in the back. Carey had shown up just as they were making to leave for the portal. He and Andrei had nodded at each other, and Carey then pulled Andrei into a hug, laughing and patting his back. Piper had tried not to gape, but Julian had tipped his head closer and told her that Carey was one of the men Andrei had trained when Carey came into Phantom Corps.

It was hard not to be impressed and maybe a tiny bit jealous of the way Carey looked at Andrei. Andrei, for his part, seemed to be befuddled by all the affection and respect people paid him. It mostly amused her to see him try to deal with it, but another part of her felt sad that he seemed to have no real idea of how much people saw him as a leader.

"Andrei, being the chatty guy he is, hasn't told me much about you." Carey moved to the seat just behind hers once they'd gotten under way. "Clearly, the way he looks at you means you're special. And you're here being a civilian and all, so Ellis must also think you're special."

Andrei gave a long-suffering sigh, one of her favorites.

"We grew up together. He's been mine since I declared it so when I was eight. He saved me from a beating." Wasn't the last time he had either.

Carey looked to Andrei, who kept his focus—or pretended to keep his focus—on the nav screen.

"Yours, huh? All right then."

"How did you two meet? Obviously through work and all, but what's the story?"

"Five years ago I ended up in lockup. Going nowhere fast. This giant of a man came to my cell and made me an offer. Knowing I was bound for permanent prisoner status if I kept it up, I took the offer, and on my first day after my six-month basic training, they told me to report to Operative Solace."

He laughed, and Piper did, too, imagining what it must have been like for him to have dealt with Andrei for the first time.

"He barely spoke to me. Sent me out on these mini-missions all over the place. Made me qualify on three different weapons before he'd have a mug of kava with me. I thought he was an asshole at first. And then I found out he'd paid the medtech bills my sister had racked up."

Andrei looked up from the screen. "Enough. Carey, be sure those blasters are good to go. At our current pace, we'll be arriving in Ceres in four more hours. Take a nap. Read the briefing material. Do something."

"Already did. Weapons are green. You know Julian would never arrange for anything but. But I checked anyway, so don't go to step two where you explain the difference between a live operative and a dead one is not taking anyone's word for anything. Read the briefing material on my way to Mirage. So anyway, I'm sure he didn't tell you this, but he also underwrote her education. She wanted to be an engineer. My sister, who had nearly lost a leg in an industrial accident and thought her life was over, now has a degree and a damn fine job. My whole family thinks Andrei is theirs. But we're willing to share."

Piper smiled. "He sent credits to me and my brothers for the last eleven years. He's the reason we have greenhouses that can feed everyone. When he stayed with us recently, he drew up plans for two new cisterns for water, fixed the seals, taught the group how to shoot better and how to make explosives. He left us better than he found us."

"Seems to me, he considers you his, too."

"Enough." Andrei got up and moved to the back of the transport.

"He's embarrassed to be seen as a good guy. You'll find us, you know. In every few 'Verses there may be some guy or gal, once on the path to being a professional loser until Andrei came along and helped them be something better than they were before."

She thought of Aya and Benni and realized they were some of his people, too.

If she hadn't already been in love with him, seeing him through Carey's eyes would have done it.

Piper left him be, knowing he needed the time alone. She didn't need to tell him he was being silly. Part of why she loved him was the way he simply did the right thing and never expected to be thanked or recognized.

The hours passed quickly as the transport hurtled through portal space, bypassing the 'Verses in between Mirage and Ceres.

"We should be approaching the deceleration lane soon. Here."

Andrei handed her a blast-proof tunic. "Put it on. It won't show outside your clothes."

"They're scratchy."

He simply stared at her until she sighed and obeyed. And it was scratchy.

The Imperial mercs waited for them in the nearby field surrounding the portal.

"Andrei, check it." Piper didn't look at him when she said it, not wanting to take her gaze from Arge. She hadn't gotten as far as she had all in one piece without listening to her instincts, and they were very agitated.

"It's all here," Andrei called out. "Get them loaded," he said to Carey.

Piper tossed the bag of credits to Arge, who grabbed it from the air with a leer in her direction. "Nice doing business with you. I could make it nicer." Again with the leer. She didn't suppress her shudder of revulsion.

"Thank you, but no. We need to be on our way."

He made to reach for her and she stepped back. "*No*. Don't touch me."

"Fine. If you're too whipped by your girl-haired keeper over there, it's your loss."

She made it a point to stay out of reach as she kept an eye on the loading of the pallets of goods.

"Anything else I can do for you? I'll be on my way if not."

"Not today."

He hailed the three with him, and they all turned in unison.

The hair on the back of Andrei's neck had been up since they took the stairs to leave the transport. This Arge was up to something. There were too many men with him for such a reasonably small transaction. They were carrying, he could tell given the way they moved. Not unusual, they'd have to in their business. But the sum total of it was something overdone.

Carey saw it, too, making a hand sign indicating they not get flanked as they handled the cargo.

And then the man had the audacity to reach for her. She jumped back and told him no. He'd sneered as Andrei imagined breaking his fingers. And then the hail. He knew that hail.

"Get down," he snarled and in one easy movement, threw one of his knives, which won its goal, landing in Arge's throat.

"Do you honestly think you can rob us?" Piper, who'd recovered enough to get behind the stairwell, called out.

"No. I think we can rob you and then kill you. Maybe after we get a little taste of you. We're hungry men."

Andrei stalked over, blaster shots raining around him. He headed straight for the one who'd told Piper they'd gang rape her and kill them all. "No. You'll be dead." Without pulling his weapon, he reached out and snapped the man's neck.

That's when he felt the cold, painful slice of a plas-fire to the back.

Piper screamed in the background, but he told her to get in the transport. Soon enough the field would be filled with people alerted by the sounds of the firefight. They didn't need the exposure.

"Get the bodies in the transport," he called back to Carey as he rolled, the pain from his back nearly making him bolt his last meal. He blocked it out and, grabbing the dead man's plas-rifle, hit the last man who'd been standing.

Piper had started the engines; the hum of the thrusters heating up rumbled through the ground. Andrei grabbed the body of the man he'd just neutralized, tossing him over a shoulder as he scooped the weapons into a pack. Carey came to grab Arge, and they did one last check and got onto the transport and sealed the doors.

"I unlocked the docking clamps. Go." Andrei slumped into a chair in the back, strapping in right before he was flatted by the gravity of reentry into the portal space.

Carey unstrapped and moved to him. "You're injured."

"We have to dump this trash first."

"We have four hours until we reach Mirage. We have time. Let me help you get this shirt and vest off so I can treat the wound, or I'll use a tranq, cut it off and leave you unconscious until we arrive."

Andrei growled but let Carey peel the clothing from his upper body. The air hitting the burns, especially after the clothing that had been melted to it was removed, hurt like a motherfucker.

"What's going on back there?" Piper called out from the cockpit.

"Nothing. Just dealing with our friends." Andrei had intended to sound in control, but even he heard the pain in his voice.

Moments later she ran back. "What's wrong?" She skidded to a halt, stepping around the bodies and knelt next to where Carey was busily tweezing bits of fabric from the wound. "Why didn't you tell me you were injured? Why isn't he out? Surely this has to be incredibly painful."

"No need to tell you. We were a little busy back there. Go"—he paused, pushing the nausea back—"back up front. I'm all right."

"The hells you are." She shoved her sleeves up. "Let me sanitize my hands and then I'll be back to help you."

Carey chuckled as he worked. "No one is going to think you weak if you took a little pain reliever. At least that, Andrei. I won't knock you out, though I think you'd heal better that way. I know you want to watch over her."

By the time Piper had returned, he had no choice as she simply injected the pain relievers at several spots around the wound. The gray at the edge of his vision began to dissolve as he could breathe better again.

She knelt, holding one of his hands as they spread the nanite gel over the worst of the damage and wrapped him up.

"Are you all right?" She held his face in her hands, not allowing him to look away.

He swallowed and nodded. "I was stupid to let myself get flanked. It's a lesson I won't forget."

"Gods forbid you have any flaws, Andrei Solace. If you get hurt again and try to hide it from me, I will kick your ass, no matter how spectacular it is." She kissed him hard and stood. "Should we search the bodies to see if we can find anything useful before we dump them?"

Carey laughed. "I like you, Piper."

"Go fly the damned transport." Andrei managed to stand. "I can do this part. You fly, I do body disposal. That's how this thing between us works."

"Since you're sort of charming, I'll let you get away with it for now."

The worry etched on her face tore at him. He moved to her because he couldn't do anything but. Wincing, he adjusted his hold on her. "I'm all right. I promise."

"I don't like seeing you weakened by anything," she whispered before she tiptoed up to kiss him. "Just do this, because I can't stop you. And then rest. Promise me that."

He sighed. "Unless something pressing surfaces, I promise to rest after we've dumped this offal out into portal space."

She smiled. "See how easy it is to just make me happy by doing what I ask?"

When they arrived back in Mirage, Julian was waiting to have the cargo hauled. "We've set up shop at the military installation outside town. Reinforcements have arrived, so we're well-defended, should anyone figure out what we're doing there. Can't say it bothers me much to have manned guard towers protecting us. Removes the stress. Well, at least that stress."

Andrei tossed him one of the packs they'd taken from the soldiers back on Ceres. "Have a look in there. Arge, the one who ran that cargo, has been dealing with more than just us. His logs show a lot of travel to Mirage and Parron."

"Why do you look like someone ran you over?" Julian looked him up and down.

"Took a plas-blast to the back. Caught him at the edge of the vest he had on." Carey hopped up into the conveyance.

Piper kept a close watch on Andrei, who despite the appearance of being run over, looked a far sight better than he had only two hours before.

Julian held an arm out to Andrei from his place already up in the conveyance. Andrei grasped his forearm and let Julian help him up. Piper smiled her thanks and followed him up.

When they arrived at the military camp, they were given new credentials and badged through all the security checkpoints. And though Julian had mentioned reinforcements, Piper had to admit it was unsettling to see the surge in numbers of troops not only on the streets of the town but at the installation as well.

"Any word from Ravena?" Andrei asked as they settled into the workroom. Their sleep dormitories were attached on either side.

The labs were steps down another hallway. The place lacked the warmth of Vincenz's house, but it had better equipment.

"Yes. In fact"—Julian paused as he looked Andrei over—"they want us to bring part of the cargo you picked up today straight there. The top scientists feel that we should have more than one site working on building the device."

"And being the Center, Ravena is a natural choice for the second site." Piper sighed. "I'll fly it. The run to Ravena. The transport we used needs fuel. The trip will be three days via the private portals. Get Andrei looked at and treated here before I leave."

"You're not going anywhere without me." Andrei had that look, the one she knew meant he would not be swayed. The fear she may have felt was mitigated by the sheen of sweat on his upper lip. Her stomach hurt knowing he was in pain.

"You're injured."

"*You're* a civilian. You're not running any trip to the Center without me. Period."

Julian slammed a fist on the table. "Stop it, both of you. Neither of you is going, though I appreciate the way you volunteered, Piper. Andrei, the doctor is waiting just down the hall. He *will* treat the burns and get you some pain relief. Don't argue. You know Ellis himself would order it so. We've got a better transport waiting, and Carey will go with Sera and Ash. Ellis wants you here, Andrei."

Andrei obeyed in his way, but there was nothing obedient about him and the look on his face.

"He's going to be really mad at me for letting you go. So don't get killed, all right?" Julian looked at Carey.

Carey snorted. "He'll want to have gone himself to keep anyone from getting hurt. But he'll soon accept he's an asset better used here. Anyway, there's a great deal of cellular damage on his back.

He had a lot of painkiller, so he was able to walk. But he's messed up, Julian. He should be put in a tank for at least a day to get it all healed."

"What can I do, then?" Piper wanted something to keep her mind from Andrei being treated just down the hall.

"We have plans for you. Now that we don't need to worry about Parron, I want you and Andrei with the teams scouring the surface to locate this processing plant. After he gets rest and treatment. He'd hunt me down and kill me if I sent you out with anyone but him."

"Oh, he'll get the rest. If I have to tie him down and sit on him, he'll get it."

Vincenz chuckled. "Better you than me trying to insure that. He's not so easily managed."

"No, he isn't. But he isn't stupid either. He'll rest because he has to. He needs to, to complete a mission. In the years I've known him, I've never seen him fail his orders. Ever." Vincenz stood. "I know this isn't optimal. But it's necessary, and he understands that. You're a good pilot, and you'll get his back. We are all doing what we have to."

Suddenly very tired, she indicated the endless line of screens. "Put me to work while I'm here."

It had taken so long, Julian took pity on her and took her out to the firing range and worked on her shooting skills. Anything to keep busy and to stop thinking about how they'd put Andrei into a gel tank to repair the damage from the plas-blast. It had been worse than he'd indicated, and the doctor told Piper it had been a miracle Andrei had kept conscious after being hit.

Finally, he came into the lab, moving right to her. Heart skipping, she leapt up and ran toward him, careful not to jump into his arms, though she wanted to.

But she realized he'd come right to her. He'd come to her seeking comfort, and her heart sang with it. Burrowing into him, she sighed. "You're all right."

"Tired. Which seems silly, given that I was in coma-state for twelve hours, but I am."

The doctor followed him out and spoke to them. "He needs to rest now. His body has done a lot of work. A good nap should help. High-protein meal when he wakes. He should be ready to get back to it in the morning."

Andrei growled, a scowl on his mouth.

She forced herself not to be charmed by his resemblance to a toddler who'd had his sweets stolen.

"Come on then. We're through there." She thanked the doctor and marched Andrei to their rooms.

"I don't want to be in bed."

She shook her head. "Don't be a baby." She grabbed a blanket and pointed toward a lounge chair. "There. Not a bed. Don't make me call the doctor again."

Julian had put them just down the hall from the labs. They had privacy and proximity to work, the best of the situation. Even a private galley. Piper meant to coddle him as long as he'd allow it.

He began to argue, probably automatic, she thought. But he shuffled to the lounger and got in, putting his feet up and allowing her to cover him with the blanket.

Alarm sharpened the headache she'd had since before they arrived. His lack of argument at being told to rest was not like him at all. On the one hand, that was a positive, because she knew he took care of himself to do the best he could at his job. On the other hand, it meant he'd been hurt enough to know better than resist. But as his color had improved greatly after being treated, she figured his body was doing what it was supposed to.

He fell asleep very quickly, and it hit her that it had been over a day since she'd slept. The worry weighing her down hit hard. Piper grabbed another blanket and stretched out on the small couch near his lounger. She got the feeling she'd need all her strength to manage him once he woke up.

The stench of burning flesh filled her dreams. The way her stomach had dropped when she saw the mess of Andrei's back, the blood soaking down his hip and into his pant leg. She had a moment where she had to truly face the reality that she could lose him. A moment when she imagined the desolation of life without him in it after she'd finally found him again.

It was Andrei's hand on her arm, the gentle way he shook her and said her name that brought her free of the fear holding her. She surfaced to find him close, worry on his face.

"Bad dream?" He brushed fingertips over her jaw.

"Yeah. I'm all right." She straightened and took a good look at him. "You look much better."

"Feel much better."

The dead of night had passed, speeding toward the first sunrise. They'd both slept for nine hours. She felt it. Felt refreshed.

"Good."

He hugged her tight, and they swayed for long moments. Just

readjusting to each other. They remained silent for some time before Andrei stood and headed back. "I'm hungry. Would you like a meal?"

"Let me get you something. I had a lot of time on my hands while you were being treated, so Julian worked with me on target practice, and then I made a stew. The doctor said you needed protein, so this should do the trick. Come on and let me get you some."

He ate the meal she'd made, feeling better than he had since the firefight earlier. The gel had done its work, along with the massive infusion of antibiotics and immune boosters to speed healing.

The skin was taut, healing. Another good sign, he knew. New cell growth was exactly what he needed to heal. It made him antsy though, to feel less than totally at full speed and strength. He couldn't protect her as well as he liked.

Still, as always, simply being with her calmed him.

She moved about the galley as he read through the new briefing materials.

"Andrei?"

He looked up as she put a bowl of thick stew before him. "Yes?"

"How long will we be here, do you think?" She sat, near enough for him to touch her. "I'm fine with however long it is, as long as I'm with you. I just wanted to keep Kenner and Taryn apprised of where I am and for how long. Taryn worries."

"He should. It's not safe around me, Piper."

"It's way safer around you than not. You've saved my life a few times now."

"Yes, and how many times did your life need saving before I walked back into it?"

"It doesn't matter, because you weren't in it." She handed him a piece of bread, slathered in butter. "Stop being so determined to be villainous. I told you already, you're not."

The way she was so affectionate used to knock him off balance, but he'd quickly gotten used to it, and now he was pretty sure he'd hate it if she stopped.

"Piper." He licked his lips, determined to forge ahead. "I just wanted to tell you thank you." He looked to her, into her eyes. In the gel he was under, but he did a lot of dreaming and thinking. Of her. Of them. It was vivid when he'd been brought out, enough that he knew he needed to tell her how he felt.

"For what?"

"For everything."

He shoveled the stew into his mouth. He owed her more than seduction talk. More than platitudes. She'd given him so much, had saved him from that yawning darkness his job drew him closer to every day.

"Of course. Everything I am, everything I have is yours. I love you, Andrei." She took his hand, her fingers intertwined with his.

"Before I came to Asphodel, things were . . . not bad necessarily, but just, well they just were. I did my job. My friends, the few I trust, are all connected to the job in one way or another. It's hard to do what I do and to walk away without feeling—"

She said nothing, simply letting him find the words he needed.

"Feeling like it contaminated everyone around me. Being with the others in Phantom Corps is easy enough; they carry the same darkness inside them."

She stayed silent, but her frown telegraphed everything she felt. She thought it was bullshit, and it made him feel better.

"I know I don't flatter you all the time. You deserve that."

Her grin was quick, and his own was pulled to his lips in response. "I don't need flattery. I could have that if I wanted it. You're with me. You protect me. I don't need the words. I need the deeds."

Inside, her belly was warm and her heart overflowing.

"You don't need them, but you do need to hear them from me. I'm not good at this."

This hardened warrior actually blushed, and she couldn't resist leaning in for a kiss.

"When I walk into a room, you're all I see." He sat back, drinking tea.

Stunned by the way this man who barely spoke had opened up to her this way, she was also worried about his back, so she moved closer, watching his face for signs of pain. He cocked his head, watching her, knowing exactly what she was doing, and he smiled again. "Look at you. How did you happen to me?"

Gods, she was going to cry if he kept this up.

"I just . . . there's no one else. Ever. It's you until I no longer draw breath."

Yep, going to cry.

She hugged him, trying to be gentle. But he surprised her by grabbing her and pulling her into his lap, facing him. "You make me feel like I could do anything."

"You can." A line dug into his forehead between his eyes. "Why are you crying? Did I upset you?"

"Didn't I just tell you about happy tears not too long ago?" She smiled as he thumbed the tears away.

"I think I might be able to make you even happier."

That pulse of thick, hot desire spread through her, making her limbs heavy.

Not that he seemed to notice when he stood, bringing her with him, putting her on the table in front of them.

"You're injured." Even to her own ears it sounded totally feeble.

"Don't hit me in the back with a pike, and I should be all right." He said it as he made quick work of her shirt and bra, leaving her upper body bare, her nipples so hard they throbbed at his attention.

He kissed her neck. The underside of her jaw just at her ears where he made her tremble. He tasted, drew it out, little touches, hot and wet as he nibbled on her shoulder, licked down the valley between her breasts, his hands all over her. Often his lovemaking was hard and fierce, urgent. But just then, he sampled. Meandered, dropping kisses and licks.

She struggled to get closer to the leg he had wedged between hers, brushing against it, enjoying the sensation.

As if he read her thoughts, he pressed his thigh against her harder, adjusting her body so she rocked against him.

"Take your pleasure," he murmured around her nipple.

The roar of white noise subsided as she began to rock against his thigh. His hard, muscular thigh. She knew she acted like a wanton, and she didn't care. She could be anything with him. Demand her pleasure and know he'd give it to her without hesitation. Without judgment.

Even better, he seemed to enjoy it when she fully engaged with him sexually and emotionally. It was the one place he was free with her. The one time he seemed to give himself to her in the most unvarnished way. And how could anyone remain unmoved by that?

Her breath came shorter as her climax drew near. She was wet, so wet the friction against his thigh was delicious.

He straightened and brought her closer, embracing her as she continued to stroke her pussy against his thigh, needing it, needing to come as his mouth sealed over hers, stealing her breath.

The kiss was sweet and hot as he took his time, sampling her lips and tongue. Seducing her with that small thing as she held on to his upper arms for purchase, to keep herself from floating away when he rolled and pinched her nipples. It was too good, and she gave over to it, orgasm rolling through her in a welcome rush of heat.

He laid her back gently, pulling her boots and pants off as he stood above her. His hair tickled the skin of her belly as he moved.

Sliding his palms up her thighs, he grabbed her panties and pulled them away from her body, leaving her totally naked while he was still totally dressed. She didn't know why, but the sight of him there that way while she was bare did something to her at an elemental level. It shook her with the intensity of sensation. With the way she felt totally owned and bound to him in all the best ways.

He fisted the cock he'd freed from his pants. She licked her lips and widened her thighs, needing him in her.

"Please fuck me," she whispered, not wanting to wait to beg. Needing him right then.

He pressed slowly into her body as her inner muscles stretched and fluttered all around the invasion. On and on it went as he tortured her inch by inch until he was seated fully within her body.

"So good."

Beyond words, she nodded her agreement.

Hands everywhere, caressing, soothing, inflaming and pleasuring, he continued to fuck her hard and torturously slow. He touched her as if she were fine and delicate. It brought the sting of tears—the happy kind—to her eyes. This hardened man who'd seen so much showed her nothing but gentleness and love. Oh, she knew he thought the hard and fast fucking wasn't as loving, but that was just silly.

Hard, fast, slow, sweet or with teeth and nails, he always touched her with love.

Little ground tremors of climax shuddered through her over and over, leaving her a boneless mass of pleasured female. Unable to take her gaze from him, from the way his pale blue eyes darkened when he was inside her. The brush of his hair against her skin like a caress. The way he was so big and battle hardened, a feast for her eyes. So fierce and beautiful, her Andrei.

"I need you to come inside me," she managed to whisper through suddenly dry lips. She arched and he groaned. She tightened herself around him, and he groaned again. She used the table to get some balance and rolled her hips to meet his thrusts, putting her legs around his waist, a favorite no matter the position because it took him even deeper, the head of his cock brushing over her sweet spot repeatedly until he reached down to flick a fingertip over her clit and she rocketed off, orgasm surrounding her as she cried out his name.

He watched her, keeping slow and deep as she writhed against him. Once she'd relaxed, he bent to kiss her and then sped up. Fucking so hard and deep her breasts bounced and she had to reach behind herself to grab the edge of the table to keep from sliding off.

"Yes." A snarl from him as he grabbed her hips and held her, his cock jerking as he came deep within her.

He sighed and pulled out carefully, helping her to her feet.

"Off to clean up, and then we begin the second round. We'll be flying later today, so I'll need to get my fill of you before then or I'll be distracted all day. And, Piper?"

She paused before heading into the bathing suite.

"I'm going to fuck your ass very soon."

A shiver ran through her at the way he said it. Commanding. In charge.

She swallowed hard. "O-okay."

The bathing area was as sleek and full of delightful tech as the rest of what she'd seen. Enough water to clean up, nice and warm, with the added benefits of the decontamination lights and the ultrasonic embedded in the water to get even cleaner.

"Andrei, come in here so I can help you," she called out.

She plugged the large tub in the corner of the room and began to fill it with hot water.

He stalked through the doorway, naked. She paused to take him in. Unbelievable, still, that he was hers.

"Shameless with that body," she teased. "Come on and let me get your hair. I'm sure raising your hands up to do it yourself will be uncomfortable."

"I was trying to stay away so I didn't ravish you again for a little while."

"Here, sit in the tub. Hair first." She knelt behind him, using the removable sprayer to get his hair wet enough and then poured the aromatic soap into her palm.

He groaned when she began to wash his hair, massaging his scalp and the back of his neck. Ministering to a man who had made a career of taking care of everyone else. He relaxed fully, moaning occasionally, his eyes closed as she washed and then rinsed his hair. Which, granted, took a while because he had so much of it.

The time was lovely, just the two of them. Quiet but for soft breath and his occasional sound of pleasure.

"Why did you grow it so long?" She squeezed the excess water from it with a drying cloth.

"Because I could, mainly."

She took the wash cloth and the soap and moved to where his feet were, massaging them as she cleaned. "Knowing you, that makes sense. I like it. I didn't recognize you at first that day. You came from the smoke and dust like a ghost. An avenging spirit, more like."

"I've had to—oh gods, that feels good—cut it from time to time. Luckily most of my work is solo and covert enough that I can tuck it into my collar or change the color, and it's enough."

His personal piece of rebellion.

She kneaded the muscles in his calves and then up his thighs. So complicated, her man. Even in his job—and special ops or not, the military demanded a certain type of rigidity and order—he had his own spin on duty. He wasn't one to be up every day at the trumpet song, wearing the same thing his neighbor wore, having the same hair to the exact specifications. At the same time, he sought out the order, clearly having some need filled by it. Fascinating. She could happily spend the rest of her life just thinking about him and why he did what he did.

His gaze caught hers, snagged as she got higher and higher, brushing his cock, which was reviving quite nicely, before she moved up again to his belly and chest.

"Where did you learn this?" He nearly purred at her as she pressed all the right places in his hands. Between his fingers, over the heel of his palm, over his wrists and up first one arm and then the other. Carefully, she attended to his back and then told him to stand so she could rinse him.

"When I did my compulsory time in the corps, I learned the ancient art of reflexology and massage from one of the other soldiers in my unit. I can get rid of headaches and stomach pains, too." She grinned.

His features, though, stayed serious. "No one has ever taken care of me like that. No one but you."

His quiet words lodged in her heart as she smiled up at him. "I love taking care of you." She tipped her chin toward his cock. "And you return the favor plenty."

He got out and stood still as she dried him off. When she turned to grab another cloth for his hair, he grabbed her, hauling her body to his. Skin to skin, and she sighed, melting into him. "I could have lost you."

"But you didn't. I'm hard to kill, Piper. Count on it. I will be back to you after every op, even if I have to crawl to get there."

"I get all ready to be angry with you, and then you're so sweet. You undo me, befuddle me, leave me breathless and tingly."

He sent her a smile closer to a leer, and she laughed, leaving the room, off to find some clothes.

She found him in the small living space, looking over the briefings that had come in when he was in treatment. He wore underpants and a snug, dark colored tank. She wanted to lick him from head to toe and back again.

"Your hair is still wet." She touched his shoulder, leaning down to kiss him. "Why didn't you come in to shower with me right away? You couldn't possibly have thought to bathe yourself without my help."

"It wasn't difficult, and if I'd had you nearby and we'd both been standing, I'd have nailed you again. And again for good measure." He turned, cupping her cunt in his palm, the heat of him nearly scalding her. Instead, she jutted her hips forward.

"I'm available for all and any nailing you'd like to administer, sir."

He quirked a smile. "That so?"

She nodded, swallowing back anticipation.

"I'll keep that in mind for later."

Happily clean, fucked, warm and dry, she settled into her seat, curling up to face him so she could watch him work. And then she stood. "I'll be back in a moment."

In the sleeping quarters, she found exactly what she needed.

"Here." she stood behind him, her thighs brushing the back of his chair. "Let me brush the tangles free."

She brushed and remembered the times he'd braided her hair back then. She'd sit on the floor between his knees as he braided and talked. Braided and sometimes smoked. With his hands on her, she'd always felt better, stable, adored.

"Feels good." He nearly purred it, leaning back into her touch.

"I'm sure your ladies do it for you all the time."

He snorted. "Piper, I told you, there's no one else. And before"—he shrugged—"I didn't stick around to get my hair brushed."

"If you try to not be around *this* lady, you'll walk with a limp forever more."

"One of your most charming qualities."

His hair was soft and cool against her hands and arms. So much of it. She pressed her face to it, breathing him in, taking in the scent, his scent, a mixture of weapons lubricant, sex, power and warm skin. No one and nothing else smelled like him.

"Can I braid it? Just one long braid, I don't think you'd look as pretty as I do in my braids."

He spun, catching her by surprise. "You please me."

She tumbled into his lap, laughing and wrapping herself around him. Totally, utterly flattered and happy.

"Good. You please me, too."

"Let's get this update finished so we can go to bed. And eventually sleep." He looked at her then, one brow raised.

Grinning, she nodded. "All right. I have some vid footage to look at. I'd finished most of the southwestern quadrant. It's got to be somewhere." The processing plant couldn't be so totally hidden. She'd comb over every single inch on the surface to find it so they could get rid of it.

"Take some breaks. You'll get a headache if you don't."

Touched, she hopped to her feet. "Braid first." She made quick work of it, standing back to admire her work. His face was exposed that way, showing the masculine beauty there. "Gods, you're even better looking this way. Clearly I need to be with you just to keep all the other ladies from putting their hands on you."

"My hero."

Chapter 16

Andrei planned, step by step, how he would kill Julian for barging into their room and waking them up. He'd had plans for her—detailed, filthy plans—and instead he woke up to Julian's voice, telling him Ellis and Daniel would be comm conferencing within the hour and to get up.

Now he sat in a briefing room with a bunch of other people and most definitely not back in his bed with Piper's pussy wrapped around his cock. Contrasted with this room filled with agitated soldiers, he preferred the way he'd been waking up since she'd come to his bed. And, he supposed, it brought home just how used to her he'd grown. How much he'd come to expect that time with her, naked and snuggled up into his side, her snuffling little snores.

He dragged his thoughts from her soft, creamy pussy and back to his job.

"The materials have arrived safely in Ravena, and they're currently in the process of building the device." Daniel looked at the papers before him. "We need to find that processing plant. I want it triple time to find it. Andrei, you're my second-in-command; organize the Federation soldiers there at the installation. Get them combing every rock, every stream and tree, every grain of sand. I want that processing plant."

"So we're just giving up on Parron as a possible location for a processing plant?" Piper sat forward, tapping her pen on the edge of the comm keyboard. Andrei heard the tension in her voice.

"We've got twelve thousand confirmed dead. Eighty-five thousand injured and three million homeless. They have enough problems. They've moved on. We're not concerned about Parron in any way other than humanitarian aid at this time."

"Respectfully, sir, I disagree with this angle. I worked around these Imperialist types for years now. They're not the kind who'd hesitate to destroy two-thirds of an entire 'Verse to keep people away from their work. Why else would they do it?"

Andrei didn't necessarily agree with her, but she had a point.

Daniel took a deep breath. "It's not our belief that this is the case. We want the focus on Mirage."

He signed off, and Piper sat back, clearly unhappy.

"He's wrong."

Everyone stared at her, and she shrugged. "What? I didn't say he shot anyone in the face; I said he was wrong about Parron. Vincenz"—she turned to face him—"you've lived out here a long time. Long enough to know how things go here."

Vincenz laughed then, startling Andrei.

"Thank you, Piper."

"For what? You agree about Parron?"

"Not necessarily. But you didn't assume I knew because I was *one of them.*"

Her expression said it all, and Andrei couldn't help a smile.

"Because you're not. You're one of us." She waved it away.

At that moment, Andrei was very proud to be loved by her.

Vincenz continued. "I agree to a point that the Imperialists are totally capable of carpet-bombing an entire 'Verse to keep people away. Then again, I'd agree that the Imperialists would carpet-bomb an entire 'Verse to hide evidence of what they'd been up to before moving on."

"We haven't found it here."

"We haven't looked everywhere," Julian countered.

None of them downplayed her opinion, but if she wanted to be taken seriously as a member of their team, she'd have to learn to hold her own, even when Andrei wanted to handle it for her.

"No, but it's a processing plant. It would have to be either near a portal or near some method of transport to a portal."

"What makes you feel so strongly about it? If we're thinking it's not here, then why not Asphodel?" Andrei was interested in her logic.

"I think the atmosphere on Asphodel is too harsh to have a processing plant of that sort. Most high-tech gear is made off-'Verse because of that. They can't keep the clean rooms sealed. Dust finds a way."

Andrei nodded. That much was very true.

"I've felt strongly about this since we heard about the bombing and everyone lost the focus on Parron as a possibility for the processing. I just don't think we should write it off."

"No disrespect intended, but, Piper, there are people with more expertise at this who think otherwise." Julian said it, not unkindly, and still Andrei kind of wanted to punch him in the face.

"None taken, even though you should dial back the condescension more if you truly don't mean for anyone to take offense."

Andrei didn't hide his smile of amusement.

"What I mean is—"

"We know what you mean, Julian." Andrei sent him a look, and Piper shook her head.

"No, it's all right. If I'm to be taken seriously, I have to back up my opinions. I don't have the training you all do. But I have expertise nonetheless. It is my opinion that ruling out Parron without a comprehensive check for the processing plant is lazy. You want to cross it from the list because it *seems* logical at first glance. But it's not. You looked at Parron without knowing what you were looking for, and then you isolated the gel. Before anything else happened, the Imperialists bombed it, effectively shutting down all further investigation." She shrugged. "Which is a good thing for them, don't you think? To be left alone to keep working on making material for the device? All while we scour another 'Verse. Totally out of their way."

Andrei leaned forward and hit the hail button on the comm. "Get me Wilhelm Ellis and Daniel Haws. It's urgent."

"Do you believe me?" she asked him.

"I believe you have some very good points, and I believe you should be able to make them to people who'd have the ability to make the decision to send some teams to Parron. Or not. Either way, it needs to be brought up."

Ellis got on first, clearly busy and agitated. He was short, and his instinct was to brush off what she'd said. Surprisingly, it was Daniel, who'd discounted her only minutes before, who'd picked up her points and had underlined them, getting Ellis's attention.

"We need to discuss this. For now, status quo." Ellis's word was final. "Get out there today and find that fucking plant." They both signed off, and Andrei stood.

"Julian, work with the lieutenant. I want those soldiers sitting around this installation doing something. Send out teams of three. Break it down quadrant by quadrant. Let's search every fucking bit of this 'Verse until we find that plant. Piper, with me. Vincenz, stay back here and work on the device. You'll be my liaison between the field work and the Center."

He stalked out, Piper at his side.

"I'm not mad, you know." Piper said this as they moved at a very quick clip to the hangar.

"Good. You won't always get your way in this job. Sometimes you'll have to follow orders you're sure you'd have given better. Anyway, he listened to you. Daniel. He's very influential with Ellis. If he thinks your idea has merit, he'll find a way to open the door for some investigation. Until he can do that, we need to focus here."

She nodded, not missing his *this job* comment and the base assumption that she'd be there permanently. "Don't be mad at Julian."

"He acted like an asshole. But he's hurting, and you're a new-comer. And you handled yourself just fine without my punching him in the face. It would have discounted your point if I had."

"I don't think he meant to act like an asshole."

Andrei snorted, underlings scurrying out of the way as they strode in, heading straight for the most beautiful aircraft she'd ever seen. She skidded to a halt and gaped. "Wow."

He turned, the hardness of his features melting away as he reached out to cup her cheek. "I thought you'd like it. It's got all the best mapping tech in the camera system on the underbelly."

All that ferocity within him, and he touched her with such

exquisite gentleness, awe sometimes. She felt special every time he looked at her. Every time he showed her the Andrei most never saw.

Knowing he believed in her abilities enough to stand back and let her make her own arguments filled her with confidence.

With his predator's grace, he hopped up into the cockpit and took the nav seat, leaving her to do her own checklist. Knowing that's how she preferred it. He let her be. She smiled as she went about her ritual.

That he got it and respected that, deferred to it when he needed to, only made her love him more.

It was full dark by the time they came back for the last time and had quit for the day. Andrei had gone to the briefing room, but she'd begged off, needing to be alone.

She stood under the spray back in their room some hours later. Four sorties and nothing. Well, not entirely nothing, they'd discovered a small unit of Imperialist soldiers in a forested area within walking distance of a private portal. They'd called in the coordinates, and those soldiers were now being interrogated.

Another day of nothing only made her more convinced Parron was the key. Her gut was so very sure about it. Patience wasn't her strong point; Andrei had the lead on that one. But she managed to take his words to heart, holding out hope that Daniel would be able to convince Ellis to at least send a team or two.

After she dried off and got dressed, she headed to the comm unit in their rooms and pinged home.

Taryn's smiling face lightened her heart when he took the hail. "I was just thinking of you. Tell Andrei we send our thanks, by the way."

She laughed. "For what? Taking me away so you can get some quiet?"

"For the credits. He paid all our outstanding bills. You didn't know?"

She didn't know whether to be angry or relieved. Her being gone would have stretched things tighter than she wanted. Which, she thought, brought her to the question of whether or not the situation at the compound was sustainable over time, and even if it was, if that was what she wanted for the rest of her life.

Eiriq could run cargo. She could give him the aircraft and the compound. Or Taryn and Kenner could take over, but she wasn't sure they would if she didn't come back.

"I didn't. He didn't say."

"That's how he is." Taryn cocked his head, peering at the screen. "You all right? Do you want to come home?"

"I love him, Taryn. I want to be with him. Things are crazy and busy and I'm out of my element a lot, but he's here, and every day I am more sure of what I feel."

"Home is where he is."

She nodded, smiling. "Yes, I suppose that's the way of it."

"Piper . . ." He hesitated, choosing his words carefully. "You know it's not a terrible crime to want a life with your man." He'd always known her so well. She wished she could hug him just then, hug him and thank him for always knowing.

Kenner plopped into the chair next to Taryn. "What he's trying to say is, this place is a dead end. We can run cargo until you and I are too old to outrun the polis, and we'll still be stuck in a pile of dust in a compound filled with broken and aging tech. Your future is with Andrei. You know he'd do anything for you. Hells, look at how he's taken care of all of us over the years. Choose yourself for a change."

Taryn shrugged. "Right now you're telling yourself that we need you and you couldn't possibly leave Asphodel because how can we get along without you?"

They knew her so well. She sighed heavily, torn. "You're my family. I don't want a future without you in it."

Kenner rolled his eyes. "We love you. We need you in our lives. But you don't need to raise us. Taryn and I are adults. We are perfectly capable of life without you picking up after us. In fact, you know, who's to say we won't move to Ravena or wherever you end up? What I *am* saying is you can have your own life and still be a good sister. We aren't going anywhere."

"What about the others?"

"Piper, they're not incapable of moving on and carving out a life for themselves. The foundation for everything is right here. The cisterns are done. We're guarding the place far better. You and me and Kenner aren't the reason the place works so well, though we're part of it. But there are others who could step up and run the compound."

"The point is, you'd be throwing away your life to only come back here out of obligation. You'd die bitter. And alone. Don't do that. Don't make me and Taryn watch you turn into that."

She talked with them a while longer, feeling much better by the time she signed off. She couldn't share any details about the job, but she could reconnect with them, which she realized she'd needed very much.

They were part of her home as well. Regardless of where she was in the world, she had part of her heart with her brothers, always. And suddenly, what she was choosing to do, both with Andrei on a personal level and on a professional level, took on a great deal more importance.

* * *

*A*ndrei had fallen so deeply into the data he didn't realize how much time had passed until her hand rested on his shoulder.

He looked up into her face and was struck, deeply so, by how essential she'd become. Perhaps always had been in some way. The sight of her, the familiar weight of her touch, her scent, all of it simply rolled through him, soothing and exciting all at the same time.

"How are you doing? Need some help?"

He closed the document and stood, stretching. "No. It's all running together right now. How are you? Hungry?"

"Better now that I'm looking at you." She grinned. "I can definitely eat."

He looked her over. Tired. He leaned down to brush a kiss over each one of her eyelids. "You need something hearty. Come on, there's a mess hall here. Julian said it had good food."

She took the arm he offered, snuggling into his side as they walked out into the courtyard. The sounds of machines, of conveyances and aircraft hummed through the air as they moved. Lights from the buildings gave them enough to see, along with the moons high above. One big and heavy, the other one smaller, brighter.

The mess hall wasn't extremely full at that time of night. He caught sight of a newcomer and tipped his head in greeting.

"Who is that?" Piper asked, taking a tray.

He looked back to the woman in the corner. "That's Odette. One of our operatives. She and her partner Ilse arrived a while back, while you and I were still out." He ordered the special, taking a moment to put some of the energy drink he knew she needed on her tray.

She put her head on his shoulder for a moment. "Thank you for taking care of me. Now, what's her story?"

"What do you mean?"

She made the sound very male dreads. That sort of derisive snorting hum of disapproval. Almost always concerning another woman. "Oh, that. No. After Marame, I made it a point to only see women who were not in the military corps." He kissed the top of her head. "Until now."

"You're so smooth."

"Keeps me alive."

She laughed, and he couldn't help but smile.

When he began to sit at a table off in the corner where they'd be alone, she shook her head, looking at him as if he'd done something terribly wrong.

"Andrei, really. She's there all alone. You're the boss, right? I mean, second-in-command under Daniel?" At his nod she rolled her eyes. "Then we definitely need to go over and sit with her. If she wants to be alone, she'll say so."

"She has a partner. They seem to be friends. It's not like we're all alone here and she has no one else. I want you to myself."

The way he said it pleased her. "There's time for that, too." And she could make sure the heart-stopping, gorgeous Odette would understand Andrei was not on any menu but Piper's.

When they reached the table, Odette had been gathering her things. "Hey there." She smiled up as they sat.

"Odette, this is Piper Roundtree. Piper, this is Operative Odette Small. Piper is newly assigned to me."

Piper found it endearing that he attempted to sound so businesslike but when he said her name, he softened, saying it like a lover. Well, for him anyway. Most would hear it and think he was introducing a coworker.

"Oh, we've heard all about it." Odette laughed, but the sound was nothing more than good-natured, and Piper relaxed a little.

"How so?" Andrei seemed genuinely confused, and Piper met Odette's gaze and they both rolled their eyes.

"Andrei, of course people talk about the gorgeous new operative who now serves as your partner. In more than one way."

Piper snorted as she ate, feeling better with each bite.

"I can't imagine why anyone would care. I only worked with Daniel before anyway, and he's not in the field as much. Not like she took anyone's spot."

Odette tipped her head back and laughed. Piper shrugged, amused.

"But the point is she took *everyone's* spot. The one all the ladies made up in their heads. No offense, Piper, but Andrei has been the object of desire within the ranks for years. Only once did he get involved with another one of us, and that wasn't very long. So when you finally chose, everyone had to admit there'd never be a chance, no matter how slim."

"None taken. I look at him every day. Hells, I'd be thinking the same thing." She popped a piece of bread into her mouth and grinned. "But I get to see a lot more of him than most. He's been mine since I was a girl."

"Childhood sweethearts. That's a nice story to tell your children someday, eh? Julian said you were perfect for him. I can see he was right. It's nice to meet you, Piper. You're going to fit in just fine. After we've taken care of this mess, we'll be sure to invite you along when the female ops go out. There are only four of us, so we tend to be tight. Luckily, none of us are idiots, so it keeps the fighting down, even when there's been alcohol."

Andrei groaned and Piper just smiled. Once this was over, she planned to hoard him all to herself for a while. Just the two of them somewhere. Naked and sweaty. No interruptions. No work.

"Thanks. I appreciate it."

Odette stood. "I'll see you both tomorrow. I'm off to bed. The trip through the private portals kills me every time."

Andrei leaned in to speak in her ear. "Hurry up and eat. I have plans for you, and you'll need your energy."

She turned her face into his chest, trying to hide her smile.

"I'm full."

He narrowed his gaze and pushed her tray back to her. "No, you're not. Eat, Piper. You need it. Not just for what I plan to do to you, but in general. Your body and mind are your best weapons. Don't let them run down."

Sure she looked like a ravening beast, she demolished the food he'd put on her tray and sat back, blinking. "Done. Now, please do filthy, unspeakable things to me."

Fascinated, she watched his pupils swallow all the color of his eyes. His demeanor changed from protective to predatory in a shift she barely caught.

"I love a challenge."

He hurried her back to their rooms. Her heartbeat quickened with each step, knowing he would have her any way he wanted once they were alone. Knowing she'd give him anything he wanted. Knowing she'd love it.

"Stop that," he murmured. "I can feel your pussy getting wet from here. I know your heart is pounding. I know how much you want it."

She swallowed hard, looking up into the masculine beauty of his face. The knowing passed between them. Hot. So hot she felt feverish, his eyes on her like a caress. No one could turn her inside out the way he did just with a look.

"Not now, unless you're on fire or bleeding," he snarled at a tech who hailed them. She tried not to laugh but did when he swung her up and into his arms, carrying her with those long, ground-eating strides.

"I feel as if you're a pirate about to ravish me." She'd meant it to be a tease, but it was more. When he snagged her attention and focus, he gave her the smallest lift at the left corner of his mouth.

That part of her descended from small, furry animals froze and then showed its belly in utter surrender. His snarl only thrilled her more when he pushed through the door to their rooms and slammed it behind him.

"On your knees," he said as he lowered her to her feet with exquisite care.

Hoo.

She dropped to her knees as he'd asked. No. Ordered.

"You know how I like it."

Swallowing hard, she reached and lowered his zipper, one snick at a time. The sound snagged her consciousness, drawing her deeper into his spell.

As if moving through warm honey, she reached into his pants and drew out his cock. Beautiful, like the rest of him. Feral. Just then so hard he'd have tapped his belly with it if it weren't in her hand, angling for her to take a taste.

And she did. Dark. Spicy. Salty and utterly male. Breathing deep, she let herself fall into the spell. Licking over and around the head, she moved down little by little with each swipe of her tongue.

His taste filled her, need itched along her skin, she wanted to drown in him. His hands slid over her shoulders, the tips of his fingers brushing against her neck and then down her back to either side of her spine.

When he dug his fingertips into the muscle there, she groaned around the cock in her mouth, and he moaned in response.

Those massaging fingertips dug in deeper, urging her closer. She gave in, taking him deeper, needing more, needing to give him all she had, all she was.

"*Piper . . .*"

The whispered sound of her name on his lips drove her mad with desire. To know *she* drove him to that sort of pleasure, that sort of desire and abandon, made her feel invincible. Beautiful and magical.

Andrei made that happen, made her feel as if no other woman in all of creation was for him. But her. Only her and always her.

To watch him better, she tipped her head back and looked up at him. Watching the way his eyes went hooded, the light in his eyes, the avarice in his gaze when he took her in, it swirled around her, snaring her in the power of their chemistry.

"Mmm, yes, look at me, Piper. Give your gaze to me. So fucking beautiful and all mine. Like a dream."

When he did that dirty talking muttered snarl thing he did, she'd let him do anything to her, she'd do anything for him. There was something so intimate about it. And to add the flattery at the end?

A shiver went through her at that sort of power, at the power of what they were together.

She licked down the shaft, dipping to lick over his balls as her fingertips played against the sensitive spot right behind.

He tried to spread his legs, but they were still in his pants. He arched toward her, and she took him back into her mouth over and over, loving his taste and scent.

She was wet, her clit swollen and sensitive as she rolled her own hips to get some sensation.

"Enough," he said softly, pulling her up to her feet. "Bed. Naked. On your back." She got three shaky steps away, and then he added, "For now."

She nearly stumbled but managed to cover it up. Or he let her pretend anyway.

With shaking hands, she pulled her clothing free of her body and got on the bed to wait. Her naked skin raised and pebbled from the cool air and anticipation. Even the air in the room seemed too much stimuli.

It was something she'd done with him before. Sometimes four times a day. And yet, each time with him was a new experience.

He walked in some minutes later. "I've wanted to do this for a while now. Since you first mentioned it as a joke." He held up a piece of vivid purple material. "A scarf I saw at the Portal station and thought it would look even better over your eyes."

No words.

He moved to her, sure of her response. Her nipples thrust out, hard, begging for his attention. He got up on the bed, straddling her body. "Last opportunity to slow things down." He waited, and she shook her head, emphatic.

"Please, yes. More."

He smiled, his gaze raking over her breasts. And the world went soft and purple when he leaned down and tied the scarf over her eyes.

Sensation leapt to her skin like a million new cells were created right at that instant.

"Do you have any idea what I see when I look at you?" he whispered against her ear. "You're so beautiful. Your skin is like the afternoon sun on the grain fields. Bronze with a bit of gold. Kava with milk."

A kiss on her neck, where it met her shoulder. She shivered.

"Your breasts make my mouth water." The ghost of a touch across one nipple and then the other.

Deep inside the dark, soft place he'd bound her in there was only sensation. Only his hands on her skin, the hot brand of his mouth on the curve of her breast, the hollow at her hip, the nip of teeth, the brilliant shards of pleasure/pain as his short, square nails scored down her sides until she let out a shaky moan of entreaty.

"Do you need it?" His voice, a whisper against her skin.

"Yes. *Please.*"

"I can smell you. Your pussy calls to me." He kissed down her belly, and she wondered if she'd burst into flames when he finally reached her cunt.

She didn't.

He spread her thighs wide and settled in for a long lick, and she shuddered, jutting her hips forward, needing more.

And he gave it to her.

Two fingers in her pussy and another teasing her rear passage, he played against her clit until she nearly screamed.

Instead she managed to inarticulately beg for more.

He'd reduced her to whimpers and grunts, and she loved it. Wanted more.

"More," she thought she said, but who knew, maybe it was only in her head.

Whatever it was, he responded with a dark chuckle and then a mouth sealed over her clit, suck and draw, suck and draw, over and over, until her thighs trembled and beads of sweat broke over her from want.

And then she was sucked beneath, no longer struggling for air, simply giving over to what he delivered.

Digging her heels into the mattress, she used it for leverage, pushing her cunt into his face with naked yearning.

He licked and sucked, eating her like he was starving. Eating her until she exploded all over his mouth and hands. Eating her as her nails dug into the blankets on the bed beneath her. All the while rubbing herself over his face as wave after wave of climax hit until she was senseless with it.

He kissed her mound. "Your taste lives in me, Piper."

His words wrapped around her, caressing, squeezing. It was as if the blindfold had freed his tongue—literally and figuratively—setting her on fire.

And then he rolled her over, kissing a hot, wet line down her spine, his tongue swirling in the slight dip at each side when he reached her ass.

She smelled the lube right before she felt it, warm and slick down the crack of her ass. Drawing a shaky breath, she willed herself to relax as his thumbs massaged against her asshole, pressing just a bit more with each touch.

It was . . . new. Taboo. Dark and sticky. She'd been fucked in the ass three times. All the same man who had a big hard-on for it. She wasn't overly impressed. Once he had gone, she'd never felt any compulsion to have a dick in there ever again.

But with Andrei things were different. He touched her like a man who knew every part of her body, knew how to excite and ready her for anything he wanted to deliver.

He drew her in with each brush, each caress, until she practically thrust herself at him, pressing herself back on his fingers. It was uncomfortable at first.

"Shh. Push against me as I press in. Finger your clit, get yourself wet and hot, and it'll be better."

She nearly lost her mind, mad to have more from him.

He stretched her. Slowly and carefully. There was no haste in him as he scissored his fingers, making way.

He slipped all the way in with his fingers. At first there was that burn, the sharp sting of unexpected penetration. And then it warmed as she made the effort to relax.

"You don't know what it does to me to feel you relax. Knowing you're ready for me to put my cock in your ass."

Raw desire edged his words. Her nipples brushed the blankets beneath her as she thrust herself back at him. "In me. Andrei, please."

"Please what?" He pulled her up so she was on her knees, her head down and her ass up.

There was no hesitation in her, no shame with him. Never. "Fuck me. Put your cock in my ass."

He nipped her left cheek hard. Enough to make her gasp a breath, and then he was pushing in.

So patient was her Andrei. Pressing carefully but consistently, past the first ring of muscle. She blew out a breath. A cock was an entirely different feeling in one's ass. Fingers couldn't compare.

Trying to relax, she breathed through it, pushing out as he pushed in. But once he reached around and flicked a fingertip over her clit, she was just fine.

There was nothing but sensation. Overfull. Too much. She wrestled back her panic that it was too much. He petted her flanks, uttering soft sounds until she relaxed again.

With her eyes covered it was hard to gauge time. She let go and

floated as he began to thrust in short, feral digs, all while his fingertips played through the folds of her cunt, keeping her hanging
on the edge of climax.

His hands on her were covetous. Jealous and greedy. In his
touch she was a goddess. The embodiment of sex and desire.

Not entirely unexpected, climax hit her as her pussy clenched,
empty. He grunted and then snarled as he came, filling her as he
said her name like a prayer.

And then she was on her side, his hands caressing, soothing.

"I'll be right back."

She felt his weight leave the bed and heard him pad through the
main room and into the bathing suite, running water.

And then he was back with a wet cloth and cleaned her up with
so much tenderness and care it made tears spring to her eyes.

Eyes he soon uncovered, and there he was when she opened
them again.

"Only you."

He smiled. "Always and forever."

Chapter 17

"Operative Haws and I have decided Operative Roundtree's ideas have merit. With the way things are going, we need to be sure not to leave any stone unturned. Therefore, two teams will head to Parron. You'll arrive with the relief troops. Once there, you're on your own. You have two days to find something. If not, get back to Mirage and keep looking."

Andrei looked to Piper, and they both nodded.

"Transport leaving to Parron within the hour." Vincenz looked up from the screen. "I've booked you both passage. Come back here before you leave for the portal, and I'll have identification and papers for you."

Piper hoped she was right as the transport shuddered to a halt in Parron's massive Portal station. The wait wasn't long, given that the only incoming transports were humanitarian, with food, medicine and other essential supplies. Their papers had identified them as geologists. Vincenz had said it would give them the opportunity to split off from the rest of the workers once they arrived, and he'd been right.

Outside the transport was utter devastation and chaos.

If the Imperialists had meant to destroy everything on the 'Verse, why leave the Portal standing? It only made her more convinced when she noted how the damage had ended within a few clicks of the Portal itself.

Andrei guided her through all the checkpoints, his accent perfect as he identified them as geologists sent to take readings of the tremors near the equator. After the last one, they were on the ground, and crowds milled around. In the distance there was simply nothing. Smoke and rubble. The damage was simply too massive, too thorough for her brain to take in and make sense of.

Andrei took her hand, leading her to a tent with supplies for the workers. He grabbed two packs and some water before heading toward the gates leading away from the Portal.

It didn't take very long. Once they'd left the gated area serving as the base camp for the relief effort, the area was pretty deserted.

"We'll take this road"—Andrei highlighted it on his wrist comm—"and head north."

A long walk.

"I wonder if we can commandeer a ride, just at least to that ridge"—she indicated the spot she meant on the comm screen—"and then we can hike the last part." Without that ride, it would take them at least two days to get there. Even if they ran, it would take that long, and she had no idea how much damage there'd be in between.

"Stay here." Andrei left her, jogging off, the crowd swallowing him again.

A few minutes later he popped up again. She thought of getting him some sort of bell or other noisemaker, because he was so quiet she didn't even see him until he was right in front of her. She really needed to work on that, or she'd get killed.

"I've got a ride. Can you helo-jump?"

She blew out a long breath. She hated jumps. But there was nothing else to be done, she supposed. They had to use the tools available, the distance was too much to manage on foot in the time they had.

"I can."

"Don't worry, I'll be right there," he said quietly as he guided her around the edge of the gates until they ended up in the midst of a group of helos. The sun was going down so they'd have some extra cover, and she supposed it wouldn't be as easy to see the ground hurtling toward them faster than she wanted.

He spoke Sanctinese to the pilot, who indicated they get in as he flipped the switches and fired the blades up.

Andrei helped her into the chute and she him, each checking the fit, making sure the straps were strong and tight. The pilot told them over the mic that he'd been there since the day after the bombings, and he'd been making runs out to all the outlying areas where relief stations had been created.

As they flew over, Piper choked back tears and bile at the damage below. She'd never seen anything like it. In some places there was simply nothing there but piles and piles of bricks and dust where buildings once stood.

There had been war in the Known Universes. Small skirmishes between 'Verses and even between groups in the same 'Verse. There had been the last war with the Imperialists when the Federation Universes had pushed them back, taking all the Frontier that had been part of the Imperium. As a child she'd learned of the devastation then when the Imperialists had dropped null bombs, the kind that killed everyone and everything but left the buildings standing. And when it was clear they were losing ground, they set fires with chemicals that could not be extinguished, they'd used large-scale bombs called 'Verse killers that had leveled hundreds of miles of cities, towns, ocean, whatever.

But it hadn't touched her life here. They'd escaped Earth for that reason. Had escaped war and famine, and though Asphodel hadn't been perfect, she'd never worried about fire raining down on her home and friends.

This is what the Imperialists had brought them. And that was why they needed to be stopped.

The scene from horizon to horizon was a nightmare. The dust still smoldered in places. Underground fires, the pilot had explained.

"They hit schools and hospitals. Violated every single law of engagement. Then again, they did it last time, too. Just not this far in. No fucking honor, those Imperialists." The pilot's rage tautened his voice, adding to how ill she already felt. "Lyons sent troops. I like that part. But he has to man up and meet this force with force."

Piper knew he had, but said nothing.

"T minus three minutes. I'll drop you to the east of the ridge. There's too much damage otherwise. There's a relief camp about three clicks to the other side of the ridge, toward the lakes. If you get in trouble out there, and you might, because there's no one else around, just hit your call button. It's a public channel, and they can extract."

She moved to the doorway, sliding it open and standing at the ready. Andrei was right behind her. He'd asked, though quietly so no one heard but her, if she wanted him to go first. She'd refused, wondering if there was anything in all the Known Universes he was afraid of.

It had to be done, and she'd do it. So when the pilot called out a go and gave a green light, she jumped, letting her body take over, knowing her muscles would remember what do to.

Landing hurt more than she remembered, but she managed not to break anything and to roll out of the way as she retracted the chute back into the pack. She reined in her fear and the swell of relief that she survived to jump from aircraft another day. One she hoped was far in the future.

Within moments the sound of the helo had faded, and Andrei had retracted his chute and had joined her.

"What do you see?" he asked quietly, pulling his own field glasses from his pack.

"Nothing much. We need to take readings to get a baseline. I see some camp lights about five clicks to the south and what looks to be a heat signature from a small group about four clicks the other way. Looks like it matches up with the data we had about who was out here."

"How are you? Tired?"

"I slept on the transport. I'm good, and I know we need to get some ground covered before first light."

He touched the side of her neck. "If you need to stop, give me a double tap." He demonstrated, and it sounded in her ear where she'd tucked the receiver.

"Got it."

"Let's go then." He led the way, and she followed.

Every hour or so she stopped to get readings. Vincenz had created a spectrum analyzer of some sort. It would show a spike in either the material that made the gel or the Liberiam or a rise in the electric pulse usually found near labs using processing equipment. They might get false positives, but that was easy enough to check and better than having nothing to help them narrow their search at all.

He stopped her at the edge of the canyon floor where it flowed out onto a plain that once held a small city. Now there was simply nothing but rubble.

"We'll have to get through that open area up ahead. There'll be no cover."

"Moon is setting. Lead the way, and we should be able to clear it by the time the light begins to rise."

"And then we need to find a place to strike a camp."

She shrugged, trying to remain nonchalant, but boy oh boy, did it sound like a dream to be able to stop and get off her feet.

He saw right through her, of course, but said nothing more about it. Which she appreciated.

He paused, taking her hand. "This is going to be difficult." He handed her a mask. "We have to wear them. Don't go near any dead, all right? The ones not cleaned up and disposed of properly are high risk for contagion. They're beyond our help now. Do you understand? We're doing what we can for them this way. Just hold on to that."

Running with a mask on? She took a deep breath and put it on, setting the regulator and engaging the tox and bacteria screens.

And they ran.

It had been hard; he hadn't lied. From the distance it had looked like just rubble from buildings, but up close it was bodies and pieces of people as well as rubble. Everything broken. Everything destroyed. She pushed the gorge back, focusing on running and keeping from tripping over the bricks and the dead.

She'd always considered herself strong, jaded even. But those two hours they spent passing though the rubble of the city that had once marked the entrance into the back country had corrected that misperception. She wasn't jaded. She was shaken and sweaty and trying not to gag or cry. Incredibly thankful for the mask, which blocked the stench, and for Andrei, who led her, keeping her focused and moving.

When they finally got not only free of the outer edges of the city but began to climb into the foothills beyond and into some cover, she wanted to fall to her knees, but she kept moving until Andrei finally held a hand up for them to stop.

He pulled the mask off. "Go on. It's safe now. Let's set camp here."

There was a gulley. They couldn't drink the water for fear of contamination, but there was a small rock overhang, and the switchback would give them excellent cover and also the high ground should anyone try to approach.

"I'll set the alarms while you get the camp up."

He gave her a long look, but then shrugged. "They're in my pack. Do you know how to set them?"

She just looked at him before pulling the small proximity alarms from his pack. "I'll be right back."

Andrei listened to her through the mic system they both wore. Her breathing had calmed at last. Back in the city below, she'd been panting and not from exertion. The devastation had rocked back even the likes of him. He'd had years of training to get used to the dead, and it hadn't been enough to stop his horror at what he'd seen.

He'd wanted to pick her up and put her face to his chest to shield her from it all. He had wished, every step of the way down there, that it had been Julian or Daniel who'd seen the damage and not her.

But now she moved with more stealth than he'd given her credit for, placing those alarms in pretty much the same places he'd have chosen. He smiled to himself as he got the shelter up. This high in the hills his breath misted as he moved. Chilly. They'd get some rest and get moving again.

Shelter up, he tossed the sleeping bags inside and pulled some food from his pack. They'd eat, he'd wrestle back his constant need for her and they'd sleep a while.

Her being in Phantom Corps had been a completely unexpected turn. Wilhelm had never surprised him so much. The man was *not* given to rash decisions of any sort. There were waiting lists years and years long to apply to the special teams.

But, as usual, Ellis had known what even Andrei hadn't been overly sure of. Piper was a natural at this.

She was good at the job. Would get better as she trained. Daniel had asked him the prior day if he'd be interested in being her trainer. Normally, it wouldn't be something he'd take on, but they worked well together as it was. They had that sort of intensity of unspoken communication it takes years to develop with a partner.

He had it with Daniel, but then again, they'd worked together for years. And he had it with Piper. She'd need others to help her, others who could help her develop skills that weren't Andrei's strengths.

Piper being Piper, she'd simply made a place in his life and had no plans to give it up. He should encourage her otherwise, and they'd need to have that discussion at some point that wasn't wrought with urgency and disaster. But he liked her there with him.

She came back to him, wiping her hands on the front of her pants, which were probably dirtier than her hands. Wisely, he kept that part to himself, tossing her the pack of special cloths he carried with him.

"You're the finest man in all of creation." She eased onto a nearby rock with a groan and began to clean up with the cloth.

He handed her a food packet.

She looked at it and laughed. "Haven't seen one of these since my days in the corps."

"Still tastes like the bottom of a boot, but it's got all the stuff you need to keep working and thinking."

"It feels so good to sit down, I don't think I have the energy to care what it tastes like just now." She tore into the package and began to eat, sipping her water from time to time.

"We can kip for three hours, maybe four. Then we'll continue east. Unless or until we get readings that take us in another direction, I think the areas like this one, with so much destruction all around, relatively deserted and still close to the private portal in the valley, are our best bet."

"I didn't see much when I set the alarms. Used the heat scope, no human life within sight. Some small birds though, so there's hope. Life finds a way, I guess."

She crawled into the shelter and toed her boots off. "I don't want to sleep if you're not with me."

He heartily agreed with that point, following her, settling in the bag along with her. She snuggled into him, and within moments, they'd both dropped to sleep.

Chapter 18

Her muscles had stopped aching about two hours into the hike after they'd broken camp. She was grateful for the way she'd had to be so physical before, because she sure as seven hells couldn't have kept up with Andrei if she hadn't.

He was a machine. He caught everything. His awareness was nearly superhuman. She watched him carefully, learning. His patience with her endless questions seemed limitless. He answered in detail, often opting to show her how to do something instead of telling.

They'd been inching through a culvert, both of them unsettled, making small progress for the last hour. There was something not entirely right in the air. They'd stopped a few times already because of her feeling and found nothing.

But the air was wrong. Different than it had been before. She double tapped the mic, pausing to pull the analyzer from a pocket.

He turned, pausing to grab his water and drink, keeping an eye on the area as she took the data.

A spike.

"Andrei," she whispered, and he turned, focus totally on her. And then he was there, hand on her arm, looking down at the screen.

"Motherfucker."

She nodded. The screen had lit from traces of the off-gases frequently used in processing minerals.

"Enough that this isn't an echo of what was done before the bombings," she muttered as she pulled up the map of industrial sites pre-existing the attack.

He kissed her, hard and fast, leaving her head spinning. "You got some gut on you, my beautiful criminal."

She grinned, and then the sickness came back. "I could still be wrong. We need to get closer to see just what we've got."

"Let's get in closer, get some more documentation. We'll need an extraction. And most likely some backup."

He forwarded the data back to Mirage, and they headed toward the source of the readings.

The air was close, humid, clinging to Piper's face as they crept through the undergrowth, checking the readings periodically to keep their direction true. Another click, and the reader pinged with more data. Liberiam.

He halted, sending the data to Daniel.

She caught her breath and mopped her face off as they waited for a response.

It came soon enough. "He wants us to get visual confirmation. They're sending reinforcements now."

He shoved his water at her, and she took it gratefully. He

watched her, those careful eyes roving over her face. "Are you all right?"

"All things being equal, I'd far prefer being eighteen 'Verses away from here. You and me. No war. No stench of death in my nose. But we're here, and we have a job to do. I'm fine. The water helped."

"Eat this." He procured an energy bar and passed it her way. It wasn't a fine, fancy meal, but it was what her body needed, so she made quick work of it before standing again.

He paused, his fingertips lighting on her collarbone, making her shiver. "You're doing a great job. I've been impressed with your stealth. And your gut. You're the reason we just found the processing facility."

No praise could have affected her more deeply than those few words from him. He didn't say things he didn't mean. She smiled and hugged him.

"I have a good teacher."

He snorted.

"Let's see how fondly you feel for me after I tell you that I am in command here. My orders are to be followed to the letter. We can't afford to engage them unless there is no other choice."

She rolled her eyes. "How is that any different than how you are any other day?"

"I'll take point." He moved away with that nearly inhuman, magical grace, and she did her best to follow, though by comparison she felt like a giant beast trampling through the brush.

Time seemed to crawl as slowly as they did. The sweat was a fabulous magnet for all the dirt they seemed to gather.

There was no more banter back and forth, and after a while, the hum of activity rose through the air, and her stomach fell as nervousness bit her skin like thousands of insects. Fear that they'd fail. That *she'd* fail him when he needed her most.

And there, below them, tucked in a hidden little valley, lay the plant she knew without a doubt processed the ingredients the Imperialists would use to create a device that would destroy the foundations of everything she'd ever known.

She took vid coverage as Andrei commed with Ravena. His fingers moved fast and furious as his features darkened. She imagined there must be a flurry of activity in several 'Verses to get a response in motion.

Clearly upset, he motioned her back, down from the edge where they'd been perched. They said nothing as he led them back up the ridge and into some cover.

Andrei let out his breath and indicated she sit. "We'll make camp here. A team is already inbound." He paused, not wanting to say the next part. "Kenner is with them."

She stood. "What? What? Why? Is Taryn here, too?"

"Taryn is back in Mirage. They both showed up, and Ellis thinks Kenner can help by piloting."

She shook her head so hard it made him dizzy to watch. "Bullshit. No. Andrei, *no*. Julian is a top-rated pilot. Why not him?"

"Julian is being put into play elsewhere. Vincenz will be here, but we need his skill set with all the science and tech."

"He's not trained for this. This is for experts. Why can't someone else do it? You can fly; I can fly. Why the fuck are they involving Kenner?"

He took a deep breath, unused to not agreeing with Ellis. He'd argued harder than he'd ever done, totally opposed to letting Kenner come along. Military training and cargo runs aside, this mission was complicated and dangerous, and he didn't even want Piper there, much less her twin.

But he'd been overruled, and he couldn't deny it had left a sour taste. He'd been put in a position of protecting her and her family from his other family. It soured his stomach that he'd been reminded of the gravity of the situation and told to get back to work or risk permanent lockup for insubordination in a time of war.

"An entire battalion of Imperialist soldiers has engaged our troops in Ceres. Julian is dealing with that. Kenner was there and pushed his involvement. Whatever he said pushed Ellis to send him here."

"I've not asked you for anything. Not other than your commitment to me. I'm begging you, please send him away when he arrives."

He hurt so much for her right at that moment that he'd have ripped his heart out and laid it at her feet if it would have helped.

"I'm sorry. I'll do what I can when he arrives." He'd risk decommission if he had to. Anything to wipe the pain from her features.

Her eyes, filled with tears, found his. "He wouldn't stand for it, even if you tried. And you could risk lockup for refusing an order during wartime."

She was in his arms, and he held her tight, murmuring his apologies.

"It's not your fault. I know him. I expect he saw the opportunity to help and took it. It's who he is."

His heart ached for her.

"How long till they get here?" Her voice was muffled against his chest.

"They were already in transit with priority clearance and a fast transport. They'll pick up the helo at the portal. Two of them, actually. You'll fly the other." He hadn't liked that much, either. But if she was at his side, at least he could keep a closer watch on her.

"Why didn't you tell me that earlier? When I was so mad about them sending Kenner?" She tipped her head back.

"You needed to run through it all. Needed to get it out. You didn't need more details. Didn't need excuses or explanations."

She wiped her eyes on his shirt, and he tried not to laugh. "Tears, yes. Anything that comes from your nose, you use your own shirt for. I draw the line at snot." He tried to look stern, but she only laughed, as he'd hoped she would.

"You know me better than I know myself it seems. Thank you for it."

"We have about two standard hours before they arrive at the drop point to pick us up."

"They're flying helos down that canyon? The sound will echo for miles."

"They'll fly on the outside of the ridge until they get closer, and then they'll come for us here. They'll be using the silent birds." He looked down at his comm where the coordinates blinked. "Not exactly here. We need to move back two clicks or so. Near that last set of pools we found."

"Silent birds really exist?" Wow, that was huge. She'd heard they had the technology, but the idea of a totally silent helo seemed too much like a fantasy. And she'd be flying one.

Even better, she saw from the look on his face that he understood just how thrilled she'd be.

"Let's get moving then." She held her hand out, and they got a move on to get back to the extraction point.

Piper was so far in love with Andrei she could barely put one foot in front of the other without tripping. The way he'd handled the situation with her anger and shock at Kenner's involvement had been utterly selfless. He could have argued with her, made her see reason. Now that she'd gotten some distance from the first telling and he'd given her more information as they walked, she'd come to understand the whys of it.

But for that moment when she'd heard, fear swallowed her. All the fear she'd been swimming against since they'd arrived and she'd had to helo-jump. She'd been drowning in it, and he simply stood back and let her process. Even when she knew she asked the impossible and to stop Kenner when he arrived, Andrei had said yes, risking losing his commission and being tossed in permanent lockup for refusing an order during wartime.

And he'd done it for her. Put her before all else. That's what had done it in the end. The slap in the face of just how much he loved her and just what he'd do to make her happy. What woman could resist such a man? He wasn't big with flowery words, but hadn't she told him she wanted deeds and not words anyway? Well, he'd given her exactly that.

No, as things stood, they were stretched for specialists. Julian was off dealing with Ceres; Vincenz was coming with two other operatives. This was purely a snatch, grab and destroy mission. Every man needed to contribute with whatever skills he had. Of course her brother would see an opportunity to help in a situation like this one and take it. It was who he was. Who Taryn had raised them to be.

Tired, sweaty and covered in dust, undergrowth and a few dead spiders, they arrived at the extraction point.

She needed to do something other than wait.

Checking that they had the time and seeing they did, she peeled her clothes off and jumped into the bottom-most pool. They'd tested the water when they'd passed by earlier that day and found it clean enough to bathe and even drink after he used the treatment drops in it.

The cool of it against her heated skin made her feel better immediately, and when he swam past, equally naked, dark hair wet and slicked back, she knew what else they could do to pass the time.

Diving, she swam across to him, surfacing and sliding her body up his. "I need you."

Treading water, he touched her, sliding the pad of his thumb over her cheekbones, tracing. "It seems I always need you. I touch you and the noise quiets, the calm descends and all I can see and feel is you. Everything else falls away."

Piper understood just then that she was his respite as equally as he was hers. She was his place of home, of calm and good things. And it made her proud. She'd never imagined that she'd feel honored to be loved by the right person. Gods knew that she'd have laughed if someone had told her how fulfilling it would be to be that to someone . . . *home*. That when he touched her and all his pain dropped away, all his guilt and fear gone because of her, it simply meant everything.

He swam backward as she rested against his chest, safe in his arms.

"Wait here a moment." He hopped out, and she watched as he rifled through the pack and brought out one of the sleeping bags and laid it down. "Now, come join me."

"You're so good to me." She moved to him, lying with him in the circle of his arms.

"I'm about to get better." He laid her on her back, kissing his way straight down to her pussy. Her breath gusted from her as he licked and sucked, tickling her clit, building her up. She had to bite her bottom lip to keep from making too much noise.

He touched her with ministering hands, each kiss and caress a shouted declaration. Even with his mouth on her cunt, there was something sweet about it, tender. Her emotions, still close to the surface, ran riot as tears tracked down her face.

She rolled, scrambling atop his body. "I need you inside me."

Reaching back, she grabbed his cock, angling it and sliding back, filling herself with him as he caressed her torso, tracing over the love bites, rolling and tugging her nipples as she rose and fell over him.

"I love you, Andrei."

"I can't imagine why, but I'm grateful for it nonetheless."

She bent to kiss lips that tasted of her body.

"You are everything," he said, and she swallowed his words, letting them fill her in a way as integral as his cock had.

"Not true. *We're* everything." She braced her hands on his ribs, loving the feel of him, solid and hard. He used his body over and over again to protect her. Because he loved her.

She swiveled down on him, fully enjoying the feel of him deep inside her.

"I'm so wet," she leaned down again, kissing his chin. "The things you do to me, Operative Solace."

"You mean my mouth on your pussy? My tongue sliding through every fold and dip? You taste so good I want to gorge and gorge on you."

She shivered as his words played between them.

"Mmm, your cunt just squeezed me. You like it when I say dirty things." His smile promised wicked things, and she couldn't wait.

She nodded. "Yes. Because I know you never show this side of yourself to anyone but me. It makes me feel special and beautiful to move you to speak like that."

"You devastate me. Your taste on my lips, your feel on my hands, my cock deep inside that molten heat. So tight that when I first slide in you it's all I can do not to blow right then."

"You're going to make me cry." She kissed him again and straightened.

"Those good tears?"

She laughed, leaning back, bracing her hands on his thighs. The change in angle was delightful, and she danced right on the very edge of coming.

He reared up, holding her down on him as he thrust up over and over, so hard her breasts swayed and she made a sound she hadn't intended to each time he slammed home.

This Andrei made her light-headed. His jaw was clenched, teeth bared as the muscles on his forearm corded where he held her down and those in his magnificent belly flexed as he moved.

"Come all over my cock, Piper."

A gasp tore from her lips as she considered denying it was possible, but she made herself a liar by exploding around him, coming hard and fast.

A snarl of her name, and he pushed up again, the jerk of his cock as he unloaded into her body. His fingers dug into the muscle of her thigh and ass.

She fell over with a limp sigh.

"I feel much better than I did back there on the ridge."

He chuckled. "They'll be here soon. Let's get cleaned up, and I'll go over the plans with you."

Chapter 19

The helo flew fast and low, Kenner at the controls. The breeze blew through Andrei's hair as he kept watch.

As he'd told Piper, the helo was silent when it landed.

There was only one.

Instead of two extra teams, it was just Kenner, Vincenz and Fen. Fen was a newer member of the teams. A munitions specialist.

"There was a problem with the other helo. We just have the one." Vincenz came to join them.

Kenner and Piper embraced, and when she broke away, she put her hands on her hips and they stood still to watch.

"Kenner Roundtree, what do you think you're doing?"

Kenner barked a laugh. "I'm serving my government, Piper. Just like you. Just like Andrei and the others."

"They have people for that. You're risking your life."

"I am people for that. This is war, don't you get that? There are troops all over the place. Attacks. Roman has ordered retaliatory attacks, and we've been seeing vid coverage of it all. They're stretched to get things done, and they needed me. What kind of man would I be if I just turned my back on them now? On us all?"

She heaved a sigh and whacked him upside his head. "Don't you dare get killed."

"I'll do my best. You, too."

The threat of bloodshed between siblings now over, Vincenz turned his attention back to Andrei. "What's the plan then?"

"I don't like the lack of the second helo. I don't like being out the contingency."

"I don't like it either, but that's reality." He lowered his voice. "Look, I know you're angry, and I don't blame you. But he's a damned good pilot. Smart, instinctive."

"And yet not bulletproof." Andrei shook it off. "All right, moving on. We need to blow the fucking building. We can't take the risk of leaving it operational for them at a later date. But that doesn't mean we won't take every last bit of the mineral and processed product we can find."

"We have a decent stock from the last shipment we stopped. But taking what they have will enable us to compare. Our own devices are nearly done, but we haven't tested them. A sample of what they have will help."

"We'll approach from the west and land on the roof. Once we've swept the area, we need to tap in the comm system to get the building plans. You hit the labs. Grab as much tech as you can. Fen will need to get those detonator packs in place. This needs to be surgical. We can't take prisoners."

They planned the approach as they went over the video they'd taken earlier. There was a nearly deserted looking helo-platform at the very top of the building. They'd land there and find a comm station to hack into for the building schematics and go from there.

"Let's move. Fen, you're on the pulse guns." Andrei tossed his and Piper's packs up into the helo. He didn't want to tell Piper she couldn't fly the helo, but as Kenner had flown it to them, he'd be better suited to it, and they needed every edge they could get.

"I know." She got into the back after whacking her brother on the back of the head again.

He took the other side with the plas-rockets.

"Move."

Kenner took off smoothly, pointing the helo toward the plant. Andrei went over and over the plan, working out contingencies and contingencies on top of those. They couldn't afford any mistakes now; too much was in the balance.

"Target in sight." Kenner was totally calm, made for this sort of thing. Andrei wouldn't say so to Piper just yet, knowing she was still angry Kenner was along at all, but he had more talent than Andrei had given him credit for.

Breathing out, Andrei cleared his mind and let his body do the work. Aiming and shooting, he and Fen cleared the platform in one clean sweep. Five Imperial soldiers down and the platform clear for landing.

They landed and Andrei got out, grabbing two empty packs for the samples and his pack with all his tools. Piper grabbed her own and another empty. He grinned at her momentarily.

"Kenner, you stay here and kill anything not us. Keep the engines online in case we come running out of there." Andrei had wanted Piper to stay as well, but there weren't enough people if that had been the case.

"Be careful."

Kenner nodded, giving two thumbs up.

Piper fell in beside him as they ran into the building.

Vincenz spoke over the comm. "No closed-circuit vid cameras on this level."

Which made things easier. At least for now. "We need to find an internal comm setup here so we can access the plans for the building." He led them down a hall, peeking into offices until they located what they needed.

"I've got it." She moved past him, making quick work of the keyboard and accessing the system.

"Vincenz, heads up for the building plans."

Andrei viewed the schematics, locating the foundation posts and the processing floor.

"All right, Vincenz, labs appear to be up one level. Fen, hit the four corners, and that will be more than enough. We're headed down."

They split up, Andrei and Piper heading down the interior stairwell. She checked the map on her comm, guiding them toward the first stop.

The building wasn't overly large. But there were more than those five soldiers they'd taken out on the flight platform. So where were the rest?

"Piper, I want you to extract the memory chips from every single comm we come across."

He noted movement, a shadow on a far wall, just around the corner, and held a hand up to stay her. She crouched as he'd showed her, her weapon at the ready.

Andrei crept forward, listening to all the cues telling him how many there were. Two. Taking a smoke break and totally focused on their talking, neither noticed until the first one had slumped to the ground with a broken neck.

The second one moved just a little too slowly and joined his friend in moments. Andrei dragged the bodies to a nearby office, dumped them in a closet and lifted their personal comms.

"I'll monitor their internal communication," Piper said as she zipped her pack up again.

He nodded, and they moved down the hall again toward the next set of stairs. The processing floor was only one more down, and they were in a big hurry, so they double-timed it as she kept him covered when he took each corner.

"There are three more down at the processing floor. One just asked when the evening meal break was. Another is laughing about how many people died here in Parron and how they'd be working a lot less hard if they just made the survivors slaves."

Andrei went very quiet inside as he looked through the safety glass and sighted the soldiers. The processing floor looked to be empty of human workers, instead using mechanized labor. He didn't have to kill a machine, so he moved past them as a threat and focused on the ones he did.

She waited for him, patiently and silently. He brought up the muzzle of his sniper blaster and aimed. Time melted away as he found the right place and moment and squeezed. The first fell, and while the other two were still shocked, he took out a second.

The survivor moved to hit a panic button as Piper worked quickly on her comm to try to route around their internal security.

"I don't know if I can get through this security," she muttered.

He had to move and move right then. Exposing himself to fire, he stepped from the stairwell and onto the processing floor.

The noise was deafening, but it helped him keep focus on the soldier.

A bullet tore through his calf, mainly hitting muscle, but it hurt like all seven hells as he used the forward motion to hit the ground and spring up on the other leg, aiming and catching the man in the head as the sirens began to sound all around.

"Get that turned off here at the source," he yelled to Piper.

"You're injured!"

He bent to tie it off just above the wound.

"I'm not dead, nor do I plan to be. Shut this off. I'm going to get some samples."

He moved past her, trying not to limp.

There wasn't a lot of the raw product left, he noted as he shoved the tubes of gel and the sheets of Liberiam into the empty packs.

Three levels up, Vincenz found his way into the main lab offices. He had the recorder located in the bill of his cap on to go back over later. The place was nearly deserted, so he didn't have to waste ammo. Instead he was able to snap necks, which he found far more satisfying after witnessing the destruction his father had rained down on Parron and her people.

He still reeled from it all. From the sense of shame he had that his own blood had been responsible for such horrible acts. He felt alone. Carina was off in Ravena, but he spoke to her often enough to know she felt the weight of what their father had done as deeply as he did. But she had Daniel and he . . . well he'd been alone a long time. A man without a 'Verse. First viewed as a traitor and then slowly earning trust.

And then this war. And then Marame. And then Julian. Gods,

how unexpected his attraction to Julian had been. There was a vul-
nerability in him that Vincenz found compelling, found it easy to
connect to.

Whatever it was, it was slow and fragile, but deep.

Vincenz didn't need to question it. Just feel it.

The main comm was in the center of the room and unlocked.
Vincenz downloaded it before uploading a virus into their system,
hoping the comms were connected back to Caelinus. Endless stations gleamed in the light. Most unused. But he hit every single
one. Methodically searching the drawers and grabbing the chips
from each station.

He grabbed hard copy notebooks on some desks and the testing
journals he found and stuffed them into his pack as he moved
through to the next set of rooms in the lab complex. Quiet in here.

The hair on the back of his neck rose. He wasn't alone. He spun,
his weapon out and ready, but saw no one.

Moments later, a muffled sound echoed through the room, and
he crouched, seeking the source until he got to the far wall.

A one-way glass and behind it a person.

A woman.

Crouched in a far corner, rocking and making a keening wail.
Her hair was unkempt, and he had no idea if she'd been alone in
there for very long.

He tried to harden his heart and walk away; he had no idea who
she was, and that should have been enough. She was not his mission. Getting the data out and blowing this building to eternity was.

But he couldn't leave. Not without a little more information at
least.

The gleam of the testing journal in the rack to the left of the
door caught his attention. He'd find answers in there, wouldn't he?

He read it, getting several pages in and skimming, turning and turning until he wanted to vomit with the knowledge. And then he wanted to break his father's neck with his own hands.

He unlocked the door, and she backed up into a corner, making herself very small. He decided clear and blunt would be the way to go.

"My name is Vincenz Cuomo, and I'm here to help you. I'm a Federation military officer, and we're about to blow this place up. Do you want to live?"

Green eyes filled with panic and a hint of madness met his. She gripped the bed and stood on shaky legs.

She licked her lips and tried to speak, but instead she nodded her head and took a step to him, faltering, and he moved to her, catching her against his body.

"I have to pick you up, all right?"

Another jerky nod, and he did, cradling her against his chest as he got the fuck out of there and headed to the roof.

"I'm a go and on my way back," Fen's voice sounded over the comm.

"We are as well," Piper answered, yanking the pack from Andrei's hand as she looked back at him, worried. "You're bleeding."

"We'll be blown to bits if we don't get moving. Step to it, Piper. Believe me when I tell you I've been hurt far worse than this. He used a bullet. I haven't been shot with an actual black powder bullet in years."

"So glad you can feel nostalgic about it." She showed him her teeth and kept moving.

He talked to her as they pounded up the stairwell to the landing pad on the roof. Probably keeping her mind off the fact that he'd left a trail of blood in his wake.

"I have a . . . victim. Found her in the labs." Vincenz's voice crackled over the comms as they burst from the stairwell out to the landing pad.

He stood there holding a woman close to screaming, if the look on her face was any indication of her emotional state. Bedraggled. Wild-eyed and white with fear.

Piper's heart ached for the woman and whatever she'd endured to give her that look.

"We can chat later. Let's get out of . . ."

Andrei's voice cut off, replaced by a sound she'd not heard for many years. It was the same sound he made when he came home to find his mother dead in their home and his brother gone, taken by the authorities.

She looked around, expecting to see him hurt more, or to see Fen or one of the others injured. Instead, she saw Kenner.

Slumped in the cockpit, a bloom of red where his beautiful face once sat.

"Get down!" Andrei shoved her to the pavement at her feet, and she lay there. Screams tore from her mouth, and she couldn't seem to remember how to stop.

Vincenz crawled to her, the woman in his arms now quiet as she watched Piper with wide, curious eyes.

"Shhh, honey, please." He tried to put the woman down, but she made a sound, clutching him tighter, so Vincenz dragged Piper toward the doorway and some sort of cover.

He wanted to help more, but the women nearly drowned him with their fear and grief.

The woman he held, well, she was his to take care of now. Once he'd opened that door and made the choice to save her, he'd made the commitment to see this through and get her out of there safely.

And none of that would help Piper. He held her with one arm, keeping her from rushing back to where Fen and Andrei were in the firefight.

The stench of weapon fire, of pulse cartridges discharging, and the noise of it—the humming of the helo, the humming of the weapons recharging, the ping of cartridges hitting the ground—was all a sick nightmare of an opera, and Vincenz had no choice but to keep where he was, holding the women in place as destruction rained down all around them.

"Die, you fucker!" Fen screamed as the last Imperialist soldier fell.

Bits of pavement broke as the bullets hit it. A few tore into her skin, and she didn't even feel it. Felt nothing but the yawning horror of her brother's dead body.

"Let's go." Andrei came back with Fen. "Detonator will be hitting any minute now, and I don't want to give them the satisfaction of killing any more of us."

Vincenz moved past with the woman still in his arms, her face buried in his neck, trembling.

Andrei moved to Piper and hauled her up, hustling her toward the helo. "I'm sorry. I'm so sorry."

She came back to herself a moment, and the screaming came again. He bent and tossed her over a shoulder and then into the helo.

Thank the Gods Fen had moved Kenner's body, covering him up. Andrei got into the cockpit and fired up the thrusters. Vincenz was in the back with the strange woman from the labs, and Piper, who'd stopped screaming, sat there blank-faced and pale.

Fen hit the nav seat and they lifted off as Andrei ignored the throb in his leg as he used it to control the helo and get it back toward the Portal.

They were nearly back when Fen turned to Andrei. "No. Head three clicks southeast." He loaded the coordinates into the nav comp.

Then the reality of it hit as he listened to comm traffic. Imperialist soldiers had surrounded the Portal.

"We're flying straight to the private portal. Get me clearance and a transport. We have priority one cargo." It would be gods damned close when they arrived. He only hoped there was a transport there and ready to go. Fen was on the comm with them, so Andrei turned his attention back to the other important task he had to take care of.

"Parron Governance Portal. *Get. Out. Now.* We have reason to believe the Imperialist soldiers have a device that will collapse the portal. Send everyone you can into the available transports and get off Parron before it's too late."

"Portal ahead," Fen said.

"Wish I was a better pilot," Andrei muttered and banked enough to get the helo aligned and landed with far less grace and accuracy than Piper or Kenner had shown.

"We're green." Fen grabbed all the packs, and Andrei scooped Piper up and ran toward the transport. The pilot held the doors open, and Vincenz cleared them with the woman, Andrei next with Piper and then Fen with Kenner over his shoulder.

He nodded his thanks at the other man and got out of the way, going in the direction they were pointed.

The doors slammed. The engines hummed. The clamps groaned as they were blown off in an emergency maneuver instead of manual uncoupling. And they were moving.

Chapter 20

"Citizens of the Federation Universes, Family members, Ministers, I speak to you tonight of terrible things."

Andrei stood, watching the screen in the media room. Watching Roman Lyons address not only the Full Council but every citizen as well.

"The Portal in Parron was collapsed earlier today by Imperialist forces who used our own portal against us. More died in the last stand at the Portal before we were able to use a device we've been developing for such a contingency.

"The Portal is open again, but it will take a considerable amount of time to get back to full power."

The floor of the chamber went wild with noise until Roman cut off the microphones and hit the klaxon to get order again.

"We have arrested Bas Thrater, the Stationmaster at the Waystation Portal. We also located and took Ang Thrater, his nephew, as he attempted to use a private portal to get out of Federation territory. Through the information we've extracted from them and from corroborating evidence from an accomplice, we have uncovered a vast network of bribes given for access through the Waystation and into our 'Verses. As well as for information they lifted from different transports moving through from one side to the other."

More chaos, and Roman let it go for a while longer.

Andrei's hands clenched into fists as he thought about what those three greedy bastards had done.

"Quiet." Roman held his hands out in entreaty. "We will move swiftly and with confidence in our goals. I have ordered strikes on Imperialist military targets. As of now, *we* control the Waystation. We have closed off all access from the Imperium into the Federation. But we can—we will—use it to enter their territory. I will not stop until Ciro Fardelle is on his knees."

"House Lyons, why risk more lives?" someone called out from the floor.

The chorus added, "Close all the Portals past Sanctu. Why not collapse them ourselves if we have that technology? That way none can enter."

"Yes! Give up the Edge. They're nothing to us in the larger scheme of things. This solves the problem forever, and we can get on with our lives. This sort of thing slows commerce."

"I will not give the Edge up. This matter has been resolved. Every single 'Verse within this Federation is part of the whole. I will not show my belly and abandon the Edge for expediency's sake. I will not hand them over to their fate, abandoned at the end of the world without any traffic, left to die without help."

"But you'll send our young men and women out there to die? For what?"

Andrei's gaze narrowed. How could that even be a serious question?

"Those young men and women come from every 'Verse. Just as a soldier from Asphodel—*three* soldiers from Asphodel, as it happens—were the ones who saved us all by getting the materials we needed to create our own device.

"I don't send them lightly. But with a heavy heart. A heart sure that every life in my 'Verses deserves protection. We are family, we are the Federation Universes and we will *not* act like the Imperium to get out of our duty. I am House Lyons. I do not run, I do not hide and I do not give in to the petty demands of cowards to save my own ass."

He paused, Andrei noted, totally understanding the impact of that quiet moment as Roman scanned the room and into each of the vid cameras.

"We are at war. And just as we did at Varhana, we will win the day. I will not stop until Ciro Fardelle and his empire are nothing but rubble. Citizens, I will call upon you to do your part when you can. Military units are being mobilized. Remember that all military personnel are not to have their homes or jobs confiscated while they are away on active assignment. Any rumors of profiteering on supplies that may be harder to get will be punished severely. This is the time for us to stick together, not fray at the edges and toss our compatriots to the gathering storm. We are the Federation Universes, and we will win the day."

He bowed his head.

"Thank you."

Daniel blew out a long breath. "Well, that's it then." He turned to face Andrei. "How's Piper?"

"Still out. I left her sleeping right before this came on. The medtech said she'd be coming out of this soon. I don't want to go anywhere until I know she's safe."

"You love her."

Andrei nodded. "Yes."

"You need to get papers. Marry her. She needs that security in times like these especially." He paused. "And so do you."

"I don't know. Not about marrying her. I want that. But it can wait."

"Why? Why should it? Things are uncertain. Give her some certainty, and damn it, Andrei, let yourself be happy with her. Claim your future. Do you remember when we were finally on our way back here with Carina? You gave me a talking to about being stupid for resisting claiming her as my own."

Andrei sighed. He remembered, and he got the point. "I'll be back as soon as I can. The window may still be open in the municipal office next door."

"I'll make a call to be sure of it. Go, soldier, double time."

Vincenz stood outside her room, watching her sleep.

Her name was Hannah Black, and she'd been a scientist. They didn't know a lot more just yet. What he could tell from the testing journal was that they'd taken her from wherever she'd worked and begun experimenting on her.

Extreme isolation.

No one spoke to her.

No one touched her.

All food was given through a slot in her door. When they

needed a blood draw or any other physical test, they gassed the room and did it while she was out.

Sometimes they hadn't fed her for a few days just to see her response.

This angered him more than he could say. And yet, she'd survived. Survived the kind of torture that broke men in his line of work.

Julian had come back from Ceres, the grief back in his features. He stood with Vincenz, an arm around his waist, his head on his shoulder as they both watched her rest. He'd spent several long meetings with Ellis debriefing over what he'd learned while Vincenz had used the workstation just outside Hannah's door for the last hours.

"Makes me want to hunt Fardelle down and shoot him in the face." The anger was there in Julian, deep, and sometimes Vincenz wondered if he'd ever fully exorcise it all.

Hannah had affected them both on a deep level. Vincenz didn't understand why, not for either of them beside the normal human concern for another who'd suffered.

But she did, and his heart ached for the way she'd clung to him. When he'd put her down and tried to move away, she followed. When they had to deal with meetings and were away from her for very long, he'd found her curled into a ball in the corner, her blankets around her body, eyes closed. At his soft use of her name, her eyes startled open, and she'd moved to him, nearly tripping over the bedding.

"Touch," Julian had said. "She needs it. Needs stimulus. Can you imagine what it must have been like for her?"

So Vincenz had laid on the bed, putting a blanket low to assure her it wasn't sexual. She burrowed into his body, and Julian had gotten on the other side as her blood pressure lowered and the doctor made noises and took notes, saying exactly what Julian had said.

She had been deprived of touch for so long, she craved it, would be a little crazy about it for a while. Maybe always. They didn't know at that stage.

She'd fallen into a deep, medicated sleep, and Vincenz and Julian had gotten up but had been unwilling to go too far. Vincenz had to keep looking in to reassure himself. Her, too, he supposed. He couldn't shake the feeling that Hannah would be important.

"I missed you," Julian murmured, bringing his thoughts back to the man standing with him. Vincenz turned to face him.

"Me, too. I know it was hard. Back on Ceres."

Julian shook his head. "It's over. We got a great deal of information, and I'm here with you now."

A soft kiss. The brush of lips and the scratch of beards. Kissing a man was not the same as kissing a woman. Julian's mouth was bigger, surer than Vincenz's female lovers had been. There was a gnash of teeth, the feral grunts and the slide of tongue against tongue. The body under his hands was hard and utterly male.

In Julian, Vincenz found a piece he'd been missing. A piece to fill part of the emptiness he'd been feeling as long as he could remember.

They had a depth of connection and companionship that had soothed Vincenz's gaping wounds. And, he liked to think, Julian's own wounds were healed a little as well.

They'd come together in an improbable way. But most things in Vincenz's life had been improbable, so he went with it. Accepted it.

* * *

*P*iper woke up with the telltale symptoms of having been tranqued. She sat up and realized they weren't on Parron anymore. They weren't on a transport of any kind either.

She remembered two things. Kenner, dead. She clutched her chest as the pain nearly felled her again. And Andrei shot. Panic ate at her insides.

"Andrei?" she called out, getting from the bed.

The room smelled like him, and she realized wherever they were, he'd been with her not too very long ago. Her panic subsided a little by the time she reached the door.

On the other side she heard voices, his was one and Taryn's was the other. She moved toward them, calling out for Andrei.

They were in a communal space of some sort. Probably a military installation. Where, she didn't know.

He jogged toward her, and she held her hand out to stay him so she could look at his leg.

"Your leg?"

"I told you it wasn't a big deal. Tore through some muscles, shot clean through. I'm fine. Not even limping. Are you all right?" He sighed, shaking his head, impatience on his face. "I'm sorry, stupid question."

Taryn moved past Andrei to hug her. "You're awake. We were worried for a while."

Tears hit again as she simply flopped down on a nearby couch. The sadness made her so cold. As if she were made of ice. Just numb and it felt better than the rage. Better than the hollow grief.

Taryn sat on the couch next to her and Andrei fell to his knees before her, his head in her lap. "I'm sorry. I'm so terribly sorry." Emotion tore at his voice.

"Did you kill the one who did that to him? Destroyed his face and left him to die alone?"

Her voice was flat, and Andrei lifted his head.

"Yes."

"Did the processing plant blow?"

"Yes."

"I wish I could go back there and kill them all twice."

Andrei said nothing, simply remaining at her feet.

"I shouldn't have agreed to his coming."

"Do you think you could have stopped him, Piper? Really?" Andrei's gaze on hers was gentle and full of emotion. She took his hand in hers, joining her fingers with his.

"It was too dangerous. He wasn't trained for that sort of thing. He wouldn't have been there if I hadn't been."

"Neither of you would if I hadn't put you there. I'm sorry. So, so sorry."

She saw it clearly then, the way he'd expected her to blame him for Kenner's death. He blamed himself for it, so why shouldn't she?

She took his face in her palms, tipping it so he faced her fully. She shook her head. "No. Oh, baby, I'm sorry. You can't possibly blame yourself."

"I could have fought harder to keep him away."

"Bullshit."

Piper looked up, startled to find the man she'd only seen on a vid screen.

Daniel Haws paced over to where they sat. "Fought harder? How so, Andrei? You argued yourself very nearly into the brig on this."

Piper looked back and forth between them. "What?" She'd

known he'd protested, and she really wasn't surprised he'd gone that far for her, but he hadn't even hinted at that sort of trouble. She'd yelled at him about Kenner coming, and he'd never tried to defend himself.

Heart overflowing with love to counter the sharp sting of grief, she turned to Daniel.

"Stop it. Now's not the time." Andrei glared at Daniel.

"Again, that is bullshit. You told Wilhelm Ellis you'd quit your commission if he sent Kenner." Daniel looked back to Piper. "And Ellis reminded him you were out there and how could he get you back safely if he just quit. And he threatened to send him to permanent lockup and you'd be out, unprotected, all because he refused an order from his superior."

Piper shook her head sadly, with a sigh. "He wanted to be there. Kenner, I mean."

Taryn snorted. "Gods, yes. Piper, you couldn't have stopped him. He begged to go, especially after the attack on Ceres and Julian was called away. I was there. He made a strong argument. Appealed to Ellis's sense of honor and duty."

Daniel scrubbed his hands over his face. "Ellis gave him his word, which is why he pushed Andrei back so hard."

"He wanted to be there." Piper accepted it as she said it. Let the blame go.

Well, not entirely. She had a bill she expected the Imperialists to pay.

"It's not your fault, Andrei. Or mine. It was the fault of an enemy soldier on our land. The Imperium is responsible."

Andrei nodded. "The Portal . . . in Parron." He paused. "They collapsed it. We used the device, but it took half a day to get it there. They're trying to figure out the extent of the damage. More dead, obviously. But we know there's some time lag before the Portal is totally destroyed."

"That's something." Her lips were still numb.

"Yes, and small bits of good news are better than none. Troops have been mobilized, and we've closed the border with the Imperium. Roman ordered strikes on Imperialist targets using portals he's been hoarding for years and years."

"Sneaky bastard."

Piper looked up, surprised to hear Wilhelm's voice and even more surprised to see Roman Lyons standing next to him.

Ellis got to one knee as Andrei had moved to stand when the leader of the Federation Territories had entered the room.

Wilhelm bowed his head. "Please accept my deepest condolences. It was my decision to send your brother to the field." He looked up to Andrei briefly before he turned his attention back to Piper. "Against my third-in-command's very strident protest. Kenner wanted to do something. I gave him my word to allow him to serve his government. I am truly sorry he paid with his life. But he gave it with honor and a sense of duty I found myself deeply humbled by. Your brother was a true hero, Ms. Roundtree."

She nodded, unknotting a little more. "Yes, he was. Thank you."

"If there is anything I can do to help you and your family in this difficult time, please let me know." Roman Lyons bowed deeply over her hand.

"There is something you can do. Since you offered and all."

She tipped her chin up, daring him to back out.

"Ask it."

"I would like to be made a permanent member of Phantom Corps. *As* Andrei's partner. I want him to be my primary trainer. I expect to be his backup on every operation."

Roman stood, clearly surprised.

"Well, every operation it is appropriate I accompany him on. I can give that much."

Daniel murmured something to Andrei about never introducing her to Carina or there'd be more trouble than the men could handle.

It was Comandante Wilhelm Ellis who answered.

"Done. But being in Phantom Corps is not easy. Do you think they came to me polished and trained? Hells no! Andrei got into fights at training camp all the time for the first year. Daniel couldn't use a knife to save his damned life. And now look at them. I will train you until you are broken down and remade into a stronger, better, brighter human being. You will understand your worth by the time I am through with you. If you truly want this, you need to understand I expect a total commitment from you. This isn't a favor so Andrei can get tail while he's on an op. You want in, you earn it. Do we have an understanding?"

She stood, moving next to Andrei. "Yes sir, we do. And thank you."

Ellis snorted. "You joined the military during wartime, young lady. Don't thank me for your foolhardy sense of loyalty to yon lunkhead there." He indicated Andrei, who sighed heavily.

She sat back down, pinning Andrei with a glare. "Sit down! You have a wounded leg." She couldn't resist sending Wilhelm a glare over that.

Andrei sent her a look from the corner of his eye.

"She's right, Andrei. Sit."

"Where are we? I don't remember a lot. The roof. There was shooting." Piper slid a palm up her forearm, remembering the sharp bits of pavement. She found the skin patch just below her elbow.

"Ravena. This is Corps HQ." Andrei adjusted as she curled into his side.

"Andrei's leg needed treatment, so everyone was brought here. He insisted you be seen by the medtech as well," Daniel explained.

She sat up, remembering more. "Vincenz had a woman with him." Piper paused, remembering the way the woman had clung to him, as if her life depended on it.

"Her name is Hannah. We're working on more, but she's . . . having a rough time of it." Daniel began to pace.

"They'd been experimenting on her. We know that much. Vincenz is working on the test journals to figure out what exactly they did to her." Exhaustion threaded Andrei's voice.

"I want to go home."

Andrei froze and then took a deep breath. "All right. It'll take a while to get you and Taryn a transport. But I'll make it happen."

She turned to him, the sound of his voice catching her, jagged and sad. "No." She snorted. "Your flat. I just had to pledge my ass to Comandante Ellis there. Do you think I'd run after I did that?"

"Oh." A small word, filled with emotion.

"There'll be a briefing in four hours. If you're feeling up to it, your presence is required." Ellis checked his comm. "Conveyance outside to take you to your flat."

"If it's all right with you two, I'm going to stay here for a while." Taryn shoved his hands in his pockets.

"Why?"

"I ended up speaking with one of the Federation scientists on your transport from Parron. I might be able to give some help with the work they're doing to create weather-hearty grain."

She realized she wasn't the only one who'd been limiting her options by remaining out on the Edge running cargo.

It was Andrei who spoke next. "My flat has an extra room, and you're welcome to it for as long as you need it. The address is in your personal comm. Come when you're ready."

He took Piper's arm, and they got out of there before another disaster struck. As it was, he knew there'd be a fast turnaround before they were rotated back into the field.

The ride to his flat was quiet as she stared out the windows. It was full day, and the streets teemed with people on their way somewhere to do all manner of something. He saw it through her eyes. Remembering what it had been like the first time he'd made this trip through the city.

Miraculous to have landed here after Asphodel. So big and bright. Clean. Organized. It wasn't until he had gone farther out, into the other circles of Ravena, that he discovered poverty and hunger were not just a product of places like Asphodel.

"It's massive."

He rolled the windscreen down so she could get a better look. The breeze was warm as it lifted his hair. The warm season. In other years people would be talking about their trips to the lake district or other outings to forests and other 'Verses for holiday.

This year they talked of war.

"Are you mad at me?" she asked still looking up at the spires as they reached into the clouds.

"For what? What could I be angry over? It's you who should be angry with me." The guilt at losing Kenner burned in his belly.

"It's not your fault, Andrei. I know that, and you should, too. I mean, I barged into your life and then made your boss hire me. You're stuck with me, so I hope that if you are angry, you get over it fast."

"That was a ballsy move." He smiled, remembering the surprise on Roman's face and the pleasure on Wilhelm's. "He admires that. Not that he'd tolerate it on a regular basis, so keep that in mind."

"So neither of us is angry at the other. Why are we being so careful?"

Leave it to Piper to simply say it out loud.

"Because this is the next step."

The conveyance stopped. "We're here." He passed some credits to the driver and they got out.

His building was on the edge of the Second Circle of the capital city. The neighborhood was noisy and colorful. A riot of shops and restaurants.

"I like it here. Is there always music in the air?"

"Down here at street level, yes. There's a music school just down that side street there." He pointed. "And a social club on the other side of the tram just at the end of that block. They have music and dancing most every weekend."

He let her look her fill, her hand in his. He nearly forgot they were at war until a tank moved into place near the tram stop.

"Even here?" She tipped her chin toward the tank.

"Especially here. If they attacked here, it would be a huge blow to Roman's power base."

She nodded. "Show me the flat, and let's talk about this next step stuff."

She tried not to gape as Andrei opened the door. It was spare. Not a lot of decoration or even a lot of furniture.

What it did have, she noted as she wandered around ignoring the way he watched her reactions, was a lot of books. From the floor to the ceiling on row after row of shelving. "I'm . . . totally overwhelmed. Andrei, this is amazing." Those books told her more than pictures on the walls ever could.

He walked past, fingers tracing the spines of the books with the same sensuality he used on her. "I pick them up here and there. So many worlds and ideas. I like them here in my house."

"Have you read them all?"

"Not all of them. Some of them are in languages I don't speak, but for one reason or another I liked the book or the cover. Most of them I have. Yes."

This was the secret part of him. She realized as she stood there in his flat he probably only rarely brought people to this place. His private place. "I like this place."

"I'll move to Asphodel." He blurted it, startling her. Touching her.

"Why do you say that? To work or to . . . ?"

"To be with you. I don't want to pull you away from your family. I can work from there."

"As easily as here?" She toed her boots off, lining them up near the front door and headed back into the main room where he still stood.

"No. But that doesn't matter. You have people there. A life. I can't ask you to toss it all away."

But it did matter, she knew. And that he'd do it anyway meant more to her than she could ever say. Instead, she went to him, making herself at home in his arms when they encircled her body.

"It does matter. And . . . I think I could do something here. I think I can do something with you. I like working with you, and now I can. With Kenner gone and me on this path, it's high time Taryn got to make his own choices. To start living instead of just making it through every day."

"And those in your compound?"

"Eiriq could easily take over the runs if he chose. They all know

him and trust him." She shrugged. "I used to fool myself into believing I was the key to why it all worked. That I had to stay there to
make everything work. But I wonder, now that I've got some distance from it, if it wasn't the other way around. I feel selfish about
that. Maybe they all stayed for me."

"You built something important there. They're part of it. Maybe
you all stayed there for each other. Don't feel that you have to leave
it to be with me. I'm telling you, you don't."

"I know that's what you're saying. And, well, it means a great
deal to me. But I've lived the same way for all these years. My
whole life it's been that way. And now I find myself confronted with
options for the first time in a long time."

She sighed and moved to look out the windows at all of Ravena
spreading out in every direction as far as the eye could see. He didn't
interrupt her, merely sitting down in a worn, comfortable looking
chair nearby. He probably read in that chair in his free time.

"They can make it without me. I can send back credits from
time to time, like you did. Visit when we can. After all this is over.
And it will be, because I have you, and I'm not going to let Fardelle
mess my future up."

Turning from the view, she found him, and everything inside
her clicked into place.

"There are other things to worry about just now. This war. All
this death and destruction. The fact that we'll be meeting Roman
Lyons in a little while. We have other things to do, and I'll be there
with you every step. But after, when all is said and done and it's just
Piper and Andrei, I want to embrace that future fully. I want to do
more than make it through each day. I want to live and build a life
with you. Here. I've never lived in a city before. This is staggeringly
massive. I want to explore every bit."

"That'll take a few years. We can work on it when this is all over. I have so many things to show you."

"What changed your mind?" she asked.

"About what?"

"Being with me."

He laughed and shrugged. "There was no mind changing. We were together before we went into that processing plant."

"I know that. I mean, this is that next step, I suppose." She smiled.

"I knew what I was doing when I chose your camp over any other. I knew what I was in for when I saw you again and everything rushed back. And more. I wanted you the moment I saw you, and I want you still. I shouldn't. You'd have a far better life without me and what I do in it. But you're stubborn and cranky when you don't get your way."

He had no idea what he did to her. She shook her head, coming to where he sat and kneeling, resting her head on his lap. A mirror of what he'd done only an hour before.

Gentle hands kneaded her shoulders and neck, leaving her totally relaxed.

"One more thing."

"Hmm?"

"I have marital papers in my pocket."

She jumped up and into his lap, wrapping herself around him.

"You're going to marry me?"

"What kind of man do you think I am? Do you think I would go all the way to Asphodel to bring you back to just fuck you and say, hey, let's take it day by day?"

She frowned, properly abashed.

"I don't have a ring for you. I . . . haven't had the opportunity. I only left you long enough to go to the municipal complex next door to the Corps Headquarters to get the papers. We can do that soon."

"All right. I don't need a ring anyway. I just need you."

He kissed her. A gentle brush of lips, and she sighed.

"I know it's too soon. I don't want to pressure you." He spoke as he kissed her temple and stroked his hands up and down her back.

"It's not that. I need you. I need to feel alive after . . . Parron." So much death. So much needless destruction.

"Let's go to the bedroom then. I'll run a bath. I should clean up before I settle in to ravish you."

She scrambled off, knowing if she hadn't, he'd have tried to carry her on his messed up leg.

Andrei ran the bath, anxious that she like his flat. Their flat. Whatever. He wanted her so fiercely his hands shook. So much had happened over the last few days. So much devastation. It seemed to have ramped up the need he had to reconnect with her.

She'd endured more than anyone should have to, and he wished with all his might that he could change things for her. He'd been terrified when they'd had to tranq her. She wouldn't calm, and she kept waking up crying.

On the transport and then back to Corps HQ, he'd watched her. Anxious that she be all right. Hurting for her. He expected her to blame him. And it would have been all right, he would have borne that weight, because he'd held himself responsible anyway.

And then she hadn't. Which had, he admitted, done something to him. Losing Kenner had been like losing a brother. But it did not compare to what Taryn and Piper had to go through. And neither had blamed him.

What a truly humbling experience that had been.

Daniel had come right away once they'd arrived back in Ravena. It was Daniel who'd encouraged him to go and get the papers. Daniel who'd told Andrei she wouldn't blame him. Daniel who'd urged Andrei in no uncertain terms to marry and be the man Piper needed and deserved.

Daniel, newly married himself, had been right. Andrei owed him an ale now.

"I can't believe what a secret hedonist you are." She wandered in, naked, snagging his attention.

"How so? And does this mean you plan to walk around naked all the time to fulfill all my filthy urges?"

"I'm available for filthy urge fulfillment any time." She stepped into the bath and sighed as she settled in. "This bathing suite is not at all what I expected."

He pulled his clothes off, nearly preening when her gaze caught on him and she simply stared.

"I like a big tub." He slipped in behind her, and she leaned back, her head on his chest, their fingers joined. His injured leg he propped up on the side of the tub.

"I do, too, apparently. I've never been in anything like this before."

He wanted to shower her with experiences. With things she never had on Asphodel.

"It's a good thing the tub and shower stall here are so big. We do seem to combine water and sex. Lots of room in here to get that done. How nice of you to think ahead."

He poured the soap into his hands and began to wash her.

She turned to face him, on her knees. "No. You took care of me the last time we did this. Let me." She took the soap. "Lean back and close your eyes."

"If I close my eyes, I won't see how pretty your nipples are as they play peekaboo at the waterline."

He caressed her thigh, walking his fingers up toward her pussy.

"First things first." She said it primly, but the next moment, her grin broke through and spoiled the attempt. "You're always taking care of people. Let me take care of you for a change."

To underline her point, she gripped his cock in a slippery fist. "Now, you see, you have this protective thing about you." She pumped her fist up and down slowly. "It's one of your finest qualities. By the way, when were you planning on telling me you paid all the debts we had at the compound?"

He growled when her pace changed, teasing him.

"Oh, a growl. Well, you do know what that does to me. I can't be responsible for my own actions now."

Gods, he loved her. It filled him up from head to toe. A sense of belonging to someone. Of being part of something bigger than himself in a wholly new way.

She accepted him. All of him.

"I know. It has to be difficult for you." She leaned in to kiss him. "So gruff. Everywhere we go people scurry out of the way. Scary." She kissed him again and then another time for good measure.

"You're not afraid of me at all."

She laughed, moving to sit astride him and press herself to his chest. "No. Because I know you, and I know you'd sooner do yourself harm before harming me. As we can see by the new scars you'll have since I came back into your life."

One of his brows rose, and she kissed it and the other one, too. She wanted to spoil him with love. Wanted him to know with every bit of himself that she adored him.

"I love you." She kissed over his cheek, across the bridge of his nose and over to his ear.

He hummed his pleasure, and she snuggled closer.

"You keep squirming around up there, and I'll give you something else to love."

"Promise?"

She moved to her knees and slid herself against him.

"I do." He paused and then forged ahead. "I love you, Piper."

Her eyes widened, and she actually made a squeal of delight. Her reaction was perfect, and he knew it had been right to say it.

"You said it!"

"I must be insane."

"You are. Which is why we fit together so well. Now that you've said the big, bad three words, let's get to fucking."

"Fucking in water isn't comfortable. However, eating your pussy when it's warm from the bath? I bet that's just fine." He lifted her, placing her on the ledge, her feet still in the tub.

"No. It's my turn to make you feel good." But when she looked down at him, she felt a little faint at the image of her man on his knees between her spread thighs. It made her heart skip a beat or two.

She'd tell him to stop again in a moment.

He nuzzled the space just behind her knee, and she went all gooey. "Stop that. You're a rogue."

"I am." His tongue trailed up her inner thigh. "I have a little problem with being told what to do."

"And so you join the military because no one ever bosses anyone around there."

He grinned against the place on her thigh where he'd paused long enough to nibble. "I've been told I'm a man of contradictions."

"Good gods, you're charming. I'm utterly defenseless against you, you know that, yes?"

He rolled his eyes up, deliberately taking a long lick through her pussy.

"I suppose"—he paused and licked his lips, making her shift to get closer to him—"I'd best use my powers for good."

He moved back to her pussy, and she watched down the line of her body at his mouth on her. The water steamed around him as he got to work with the talent of a true genius.

Taking care of her. This was more than the sex. He touched her in every possible way. He made her safe and loved and happy, even on the saddest day of her life.

She'd take care of him after this. "Lovely," she murmured, sifting her fingers through his hair.

Lick after lick, he gave her pleasure. Her muscles were loose and warm, primed to receive as she leaned against the wall at her back, widening her thighs. He suckled her clit until little whimpers she couldn't remember making came from her lips.

When she came, it was on a gasp, a rush of pleasure she didn't know would hit so hard and so fast.

He continued to lick and nuzzle until she pulled him away.

"Come on. I don't want your leg in the water any longer than it's already been." She scrambled out, and he followed.

And then he blocked her way. "Hands on the counter. I want you bent so I can fuck you from behind and watch in the mirror."

Yes, he was indeed using his power for good.

"I'm not sure how this is me serving you though."

He met her eyes in the mirror as he widened her stance, teasing her gate with the head of his cock. "Your obedience is serving me."

Oh. My.

He thrust in one movement, his cock slicing through her pussy, slick and swollen for him.

She couldn't tear her gaze away from their reflection in the mirror before her. From the picture they made as he fucked into her body. His features fierce with concentration.

He wrapped her braids around his fist and pulled, arching her until he paused with a satisfied grunt. All while he continued to stroke deep and hard.

When he was this way, she lost herself in him, gave over and let him control everything.

He looked down, first into her face and then lower, between them. "I'm watching my cock come from you, dark and juicy. Never in my life have I seen a more beautiful sight." His head tipped slightly back as he licked his lips. "Your inner walls squeeze me tight when you hear things you like."

The smile he gave her shot straight to her clit, so filled with wicked promises.

His hands on her rough and sometimes dark and harsh. But never to harm. Every touch from him was a poem, a declaration of his love.

This man, this man who from the outside seemed cold and remote, never touched her with anything less than reverence.

"I want this to last forever," he murmured, dipping down to kiss her shoulder and then the side of her neck. She arched back, baring more, craving the sharp sting of the way he bit and sucked, marking her as his.

"I try. To make it last and last, but you feel so good. The moment I dip the head of my cock into you, it's a struggle between the part of me who wants to fuck you silly and come hard and fast, and the part of me who wants to prolong the exquisite torture of your pussy for hours and hours."

Her eyes went half-lidded as she dived into the way he made her feel.

"It's a battle I wage every single time."

"I want you to take me however you want to."

He snarled a low curse and began to speed his thrusts.

"Not alone, my bronze beauty." He slid his free hand down her belly as she watched in the mirror. Down to her pussy where he circled her clit with the tip of his middle finger.

She exploded almost embarrassingly fast, a second and third wave hitting when he marked her shoulder.

"Gods above and below, you are written into my soul, Piper," he said softly as he pulled out.

Overcome, she turned and hugged him tight.

"We can do this."

He nodded. "Sometimes it won't be easy. We will lose others. That's the way of it. I want you to be prepared for it."

She nodded as he cleaned up and they got dressed.

"And I want you to know I will die before I let that tragedy be you. You will not argue your way out of it. You will not. Not on this point. I will protect you, and since you put yourself right in the line of fire, I'm in charge. I am your man and your superior officer. Oh, and your trainer. So your ass is mine in every way. Do not get it hurt, or I will toss you in the brig until the war is over."

She cupped his cheek. "I'm going to agree, and you're not going to believe me."

"Because you're stubborn."

"Ha! I'm *tenacious*."

Chapter 21

The room was full when they arrived. Andrei inclined his head toward Ellis as he and Piper found a seat near Daniel and Vincenz. He'd read the briefing update as they made their way back and had commed with Daniel to firm up their understanding so they were all on the same page.

"As you all know, we are at war. Our job is different than that of the great majority of those in the military corps. We are the special teams. We will coordinate with the other branches and continue to keep up our operations."

Daniel stood. "We have intel that the Imperium had only one device ready, and we now have it. Foolishly, their troops left it behind when we used our own device to stop the damage and reopen the Portal. We have reason to believe the Imperialists have set up a lab to attempt to clone the materials they have been stealing from us."

Ellis took over again. "Julian has been running the interrogations of those prisoners we've taken on Ceres. As expected, we were able to beat them back within hours. Our troops will stay on the Edge. A buildup is necessary, and we will meet any aggression with a bounty of pain and retribution."

"For the time being, Andrei Solace will work from Ravena. All intel you gather goes through him, and he'll take it to me or the Comandante when he deems it necessary. *Nothing* is insignificant. We found the processing plant because Piper Roundtree, our newest operative, refused to let go of a feeling she had about Parron. That gut feeling, backed by a very persuasive argument, may have sped the end to this war."

Andrei barely resisted a look in her direction. He needed to keep his work face, but he'd tell her how proud of her he was when they were alone.

He stood. "Each of you will find your roster updated. Be ready to leave at a moment's notice. I'd also urge everyone to be in some sort of physical training every day. You'll need to be at your absolute best. The Skorpios Fardelle uses are pumped full of stims and narcotics to keep them ready to kill. We need to be better."

And he did not want to have any more memorial services.

Everyone filed out, leaving him there with Ellis and Daniel. Piper squeezed his hand. "I'm going to find Taryn and give him the good news."

She sauntered off and he didn't even try not to watch.

Roman walked past her into the room and sent a raised brow his way. "Are you objectifying one of your charges?"

He blushed, and Daniel burst out laughing.

"I filed marital papers. She and I are going to have a small ceremony in a few days. You're all invited, of course. Daniel, I'd be honored if you'd stand for me."

"Of course. You just did me the same honor. Carina has been at me to bring Piper around. Of course I admit I'm concerned that my lovely wife will think she should be able to be an operative now."

"Congratulations, Andrei. I quite like your Piper. She's a good match for you. And permit me to offer our gardens as a place for the ceremony. I feel as if there has been so much negative, so much pain, a little celebration would be a good thing."

"I appreciate that more than you know." Not having any blood family he was in contact with, the others in the Phantom Corps were his family in every way that counted. This outpouring of well wishes was important to him. "But you have a baby due any time and a war to manage. Really, I don't want to add to your list of concerns."

Roman laughed. "The best thing about being the boss of everything is how many people I have working for me who handle these details. Please let us do this for you. You've done this government a great honor, risking your life over and over. Abbie and I respect you and enjoy your company a great deal. Especially Abbie, because you so rarely speak and she can talk and talk without being interrupted."

"All right. Thank you. We appreciate it." He inclined his head. "And your wife is lovely. I trust she's well? The babe?"

"Annoyed that she's hot all the time. But the boys dote on her, Mercy spoils her rotten and of course, I do my best."

Andrei snorted a laugh, knowing just how much Roman Lyons spoiled his wife.

"Go to her. I can see you're antsy." Ellis nodded his head toward the door. "We'll have twice daily briefings. The first is an all-corps meeting with all branches represented. The second is all special teams."

Ellis walked out with Andrei, pausing when they'd gotten far enough away from everyone. "I wanted to apologize to you for putting you in the position I did by sending Piper's brother on the op. I should have shared the promise I made with you, but the comm exchange had several other people online, and I didn't want any of them to doubt his ability."

"I understood it when you spoke of it with Piper. For what it's worth, you did the right thing. Even if it turned out badly."

"We're facing times filled with all sorts of decisions that will be made that we won't agree with. I want you to know I have every confidence you will continue to excel at your job."

Andrei walked toward Piper, who turned to him, a smile of greeting on her face. Things were indeed dark, but the woman he'd joined his life with would continue to be his light and his heart.